GLASTONBURY
TALES

Fool Me Twice

JL MERROW

RIPTIDE
PUBLISHING

Riptide Publishing
PO Box 1537
Burnsville, NC 28714
www.riptidepublishing.com

Fool Me Twice
Copyright © 2025 by JL Merrow

Cover art: Cora Graphics, coragraphics.it
Editor: Grace Stack
Layout: L.C. Chase, lcchase.com

ISBN: 978-1-963773-28-6

First edition
February, 2025

Also available in ebook:
ISBN: 978-1-963773-27-9

GLASTONBURY
TALES

Fool Me Twice

JL MERROW

RIPTIDE
PUBLISHING

Table of Contents

Chapter One
Zig

A ni was behind the bar of the Cock & Bull as Zig turned up, whistling, for work. He flashed her a smile, cos she was one of the decent ones. "All right, Ans?"

Dark, troubled eyes met his. "Eh. Surviving. There's been a bloke looking for you."

"What can I say? I'm in demand." Zig winked. "What kind of bloke? The sort I'd want to find me?"

Her expression didn't lift. "Doubt it. He said you owe him. You been messing with loan sharks or something?"

"What? No." Unease sent icy fingers along Zig's ribs. He darted a glance around the pub, but all he could see was the usual sort of drinkers. "When was he here?"

"Couple of hours ago. Are you in trouble?"

Maybe. "Did this bloke give a name? What did he look like?"

Ani shook her head. "No name. He wasn't anyone you might've hooked up with, put it that way. Maybe their dad. His hair was grey, 'cept he'd shaved it so it was just stubble. Tall like you, but broader. More muscley. Had a gold tooth next to a chipped one, I remember that—I mean, if you can afford the gold, why not get the other one seen to?"

Zig's whole body went cold. *Shit.*

He should have known it would happen—should have made plans—but he'd told himself Dad would leave him alone. He'd told himself Dad couldn't know what he'd done. *Idiot.* "What did he say? Exactly?" Zig's mouth was dry, and it came out as a rasp.

Ani's brow furrowed. "Like I said. He asked when you might be in. Said you owe him. I told him you weren't working till tomorrow."

Thank God for that, but he needed to get out of town, and do it now.

"Cheers, Ans." Zig's face felt weird when he spoke, like his smile had frozen stiff. "Gotta go. I'll see you, yeah?"

He legged it out of the pub to the sound of her calling him a *stupid arse* and, as he slipped out the door, yelling at him to *take care, okay?*

Yeah, she was one of the decent ones. Zig didn't like leaving her in the lurch. But weeknights weren't the busiest at the Cock & Bull, and face it, it was just as well he was getting out of her life.

He darted his gaze all around as he hurried down the street. Just in case Dad hadn't believed Ani, who wasn't exactly the world's greatest liar. No sign of him, thank God. Or of Trent, thank all the bloody gods and the devil too.

Jesus, where the hell was he gonna go? He couldn't stay in south London, that was for sure. If they'd found him here, they'd find him anywhere. But Zig had spent his whole life here, only leaving it for trips up west for clubbing and that. Well, apart from the years he'd been away.

He'd have to go a lot farther west than Soho to slip off the radar.

A memory stole into his head—Si, too many bloody years ago to count, his thick country accent warm. "The West End? You call *that* going up west? That's like saying you're going abroad when you take a day trip to the Isle of Wight."

The pain the memory brought was familiar, almost comforting. Si had been the one that got away. Probably always would be. Zig hadn't understood, when it'd ended between them. Well, in his defence, he'd been all of eighteen, give or take a week or two.

Si had been decent, through and through. If he'd seen an old man get his head bashed in, he wouldn't have just set off an alarm and trusted the emergency services to get there in time. He'd have stayed with the bloke. Done first aid. He'd have *helped*. The Si Zig had known would have helped anyone, and he didn't reckon that would've changed over the years.

A crazy burst of hope crashed through his chest. *Anyone?* Even a shitty ex-boyfriend on the lam?

Maybe.

Course, Zig would have to find him first. Zig laughed despairingly, then glared at a passing couple who looked at him funny. *Think*. Si had gone back to Glastonbury, but had he stayed there? It'd been five years, nearly six. He could be anywhere by now, and how the hell was Zig gonna find out?

He could start by asking around, maybe. Stick his head in the Dog and Duck in Peckham, see if Si's mate Adam still drank there. He'd know where Si was, for sure. Adam had plenty of reason not to piss on Zig if he was on fire . . . but then, if he'd known the truth, the police would've been knocking on Zig's door years ago, wouldn't they?

Zig had been walking blind, desperate to get some distance between him and the Cock & Bull, but now he realised he wasn't far from the Peckham bus route. Only a couple more streets and he'd be there. Right. Positive action. That had to be better than running around like a headless bloody chicken. He'd look for a lead on Si, and if it didn't pan out . . . He'd just have to think of something, that was all.

Hanging around at the bus stop gave Zig time to feel bad about leaving Ani short-staffed with no explanation and no apology, so he gave her a call.

"Are you all right?" she asked, without bothering with *hello*. "Where the hell are you?"

"Right now? Waiting for a bus to Peckham. Sorry about the shift, but call Tim, yeah? He's always up for some extra work."

"Already done. He's on his way." He could picture her eye roll as she said it.

At least that was one less thing to feel bad about. "Listen, I'm gonna be leaving town for a while. Family emergency," Zig added with grim humour. "That bloke? He was, uh, joking about me owing him."

"Are you all right?" she asked again. The worry in her voice made his chest go tight.

"Yeah. I mean, I will be." *If* he managed to find out where Si was. "You know me. Always bounce back."

"Right." She didn't sound convinced. "So do you want me to say anything to the boss?"

Zig was tempted to hedge his bets, say no. But who was he kidding? He'd be moving on no matter what happened tonight. "You can tell him I've quit. I'm owed three nights pay, so he can take that as notice." He could have done with the money, but he couldn't afford to let it slow him down.

"Okay. Stay in touch, yeah? And I hope it all works out all right. With your family." The doubt was clear in her voice.

"Yeah. Me too. Cheers, Ans, you're a mate." They hung up, Zig feeling a bit off-balance at the concern she'd shown and how much it had affected him.

Then he shook himself. The bus was here, and it was time to get down to business.

Peckham had smartened itself up a bit since the last time Zig had been here. He passed several businesses that'd been turned into hipster hangouts on his way to the Dog and Duck, and hoped to God Si and his mates' old local hadn't met the same fate. What were the chances a bunch of brickies would still be patronising a pub if it now served organic microbrews and boasted entertainment by arts students?

Luckily, the Dog and Duck sat, unchanged, on its side street, its mock-Tudor front looming over the paved beer garden at the front. It even still had the same old red telephone box standing outside it, and you didn't get many of them to the pound these days. Now, Zig saw, it housed a defibrillator. He pitied any poor sod who had a heart attack and then had to deal with a pub-full of drunkards gamely trying to resuscitate him.

Zig had a sudden flash of memory: a summer evening sitting outside the pub with a rum and coke as the sun went down, listening to Si have a heated debate with himself about the best companions in *Doctor Who*. Zig smiled. He'd been so bloody enthusiastic, Zig hadn't had the heart to tell him he'd never seen the show. When he'd finally admitted it—later on, when they'd sneaked into Si's room at his mate Adam's dad's house for some privacy—Si had been mortified. And very, very keen to make up for "boring" him.

Jesus, that seemed so bloody long ago. Was he crazy thinking Si would have any time for him now, after all the years that'd gone by?

Ah, sod it. He was here now. Might as well go in and see if there was anyone he recognised. Zig crossed the road, strolled across the paved area—dark and empty now, with a chill wind blowing through it—and pushed open the heavy front door.

Inside was exactly as he remembered it: Browner than an old man's trousers. There was the wood panelling and bare wood floor of a proper old boozer, the crowd inside proving it hadn't totally gone out of style with the creeping gentrification. Zig couldn't see Adam Merchant's dark head among the drinkers, but—his heart gave a jolt—there were a couple of other blokes he recognised from all them years ago.

He'd always been good at faces, and the kind of blokes who worked on building sites didn't tend to change much. Guys Zig knew from the clubs, yeah. They'd switch up their hair colour and style every other week—their gender presentation too, some of them—but brickies? Most of them gave into the macho peer pressure and stuck with what nature had given them. There was a ginge there, red-faced from the sun even in December, who he'd have known anywhere.

Zig strolled up to the bar and ordered a pint, then leant back with an easy stance, sipping it for a while. God, it tasted shite. What he wouldn't give for a rum and coke.

Not to mention, someone he cared about to drink it with.

Having drunk half of his pint and established his manliness credentials, Zig ambled over to the group he'd clocked earlier.

"All right, lads?"

None of them answered, and the ginge sent Zig an unimpressed look. Then he frowned. "I know you, don't I? Ain't you that lad who used to hang around the boss's son?"

Boss's son's mate, actually, but who cares?

Zig smiled. "Knew you'd remember me." It'd been a fair bet; the eyes were a dead giveaway. "How's it going?"

"All right. If you're looking for Adam, he's buggered off back west."

Shit. "Back to Glastonbury?"

The ginge huffed. "Gonna be a tattooist. All that money his old man spent sending him to uni, and he's pissing it away drawing bloody flowers on people."

The bearded bloke next to him—who had plenty of ink on his bare forearms—scowled. "Fuck off, Letch. It's art, innit? He's good at it."

"Don't need a bloody degree to do it, though, do you?"

"Got an address for him?" Zig asked, trying to get them back on topic.

"Why? Does he owe you money?" Ginge wasn't so friendly now.

Zig took a step back. "I fancied getting back in touch, that's all."

Beardy stood up—and Jesus, fucking *up*. "I don't remember you ever being that matey with Adam. What *I* remember is him getting pissed off about you sniffing around that mate of his all the time."

Well, this was a fucking bust. No point asking any more questions here. Zig gave a big, face-splitting smile. "Lovely to see you too. Looking well, mate. That nasty rash clear up okay?"

Then he legged it, because stupid, he was not.

Sitting on the bus home, his head aching from a bunch of rowdy teens crammed into the back seat who shrieked every time they rounded a corner—Christ, was he getting old?—Zig tried not to let his spirits sink. So plan A hadn't worked out. He just needed to work on plan B.

Think, you useless wanker.

The bus lurched to a halt, and with a chorus of profanity, one of the teens fell off the seat. Zig smirked.

Adam had gone to Glasto—did they call it Glasto?—to be a tattooist. That meant a studio, and how many of those could there be in a town out in the West Country sticks? He had to be findable. Risky to rely on Adam, though, cos his mates were right: he'd always had that face on him like he was sniffing a dog turd every time Zig turned up with Si. Trying to get Si's address out of him had to be a last resort.

Shame you haven't got a fucking first resort, though, innit?

No, wait. Si's parents must be old, right? So chances were they had a landline. Maybe their number was even listed, and how many Grecziks could there be in Glastonbury? Zig could call them up, spin them a yarn about wanting to reconnect with an old mate—for fuck's sake, it was actually *true*—and get Si's address out of them.

And his number, but hanging up a call was easy. Si might not answer an unknown number. Too risky, and Zig needed to get out of town anyhow.

No, go see him face-to-face, and with that big, soft heart of his he wouldn't turn Zig away.

Probably.

Well, if he did, Zig could always keep going. He wouldn't need a passport for Wales, would he? Zig wasn't sure about Ireland, but anyway, there'd be time to worry about that later. He pulled out his phone and searched *the phone book*. He remembered his gran, back when he was little, telling him the phone book used to be, like, an actual book, and they'd sent one round to every house each year. Jesus, how many trees had died for that? And how fucking big were those books?

There was only one result for *Greczik, Glastonbury*. Zig clicked on it, his heart beating hard. *Robert Greczik*. That could be Si's dad. And Jesus fuck, it gave the number *and* a street address. Even a handy distance in miles from the centre of town. Who the hell ever thought that was a good idea? What about security? Data protection?

Right. So Zig could turn up on their doorstep. Yeah, that was a plan. If Si had moved away, chances were he'd be able to blag a bed for the night.

Plan B was ready to go.

A strong whiff of alcohol reached him. The teens must be passing around a bottle—cheap rum, maybe? Whatever it was, Zig didn't need to be here when the bus driver caught on and chucked the lot of them off. Or when one of them threw up, whichever happened first. He glanced out of the window. Yep, they'd reached Lewisham. Close enough to where he lived that he could walk the rest of the way, easy. He pressed the button for the next stop.

When he got to his street, he checked all around, but he couldn't see anyone waiting in the shadows. He got out his keys, jogged to the front door of his shared house, and opened up.

Then he ran up the stairs to his tiny, mildew-pocked room, and got packing.

Chapter Two
Zig

The train glided to a halt at the final station. Bristol Temple Meads. Zig heaved his rucksack onto his shoulder and stepped off the train, not looking back. He strolled confidently down the platform into the main part of the station, then ducked behind a convenient brick pillar. He'd made sure to leave the train by the front carriage, so everyone who got off here had to file past him.

He bounced on the toes of his Converse as he watched them, but there was no one he recognised. No one who sent alarm bells ringing in his mind. Good. He probably needed to work on this paranoia he'd developed. Then again, better he jumped at shadows than got jumped himself.

Zig let out a long breath that steamed in the chill air, then headed towards the main station entrance. It was gone five, and dark had fallen while he'd been on the train. He'd meant to get away earlier, but he'd slept badly and got up late. Most of his housemates had been out at work, but Lena, who worked evenings like him, had slouched into the kitchen while he'd been raiding the cupboards for breakfast and portable snacks.

On the plus side, it'd saved him sticking a note on the fridge to say he'd moved out and wouldn't be back. On the minus side, he'd had to endure an earful of abuse for leaving the rest of them in the lurch with the rent. The fact he'd already paid up for the month, and wouldn't be getting his deposit back either, hadn't seemed to register with her.

Well. He was here now. And he hadn't told Lena where he was going, so she couldn't grass him up to anyone who might come calling.

There was a line of black cabs outside the station—funny, he'd thought they only had those in London—but he walked past them. Too expensive, and cab drivers remembered people. *Google, don't fail me now*, he prayed, as he searched for a bus going to Glastonbury.

Bloody hell. Sixty-three stops? At that rate, he might as well have got the National Express from London, instead of forking out for the train. For a moment, Zig seriously considered staying in Bristol.

Right. Where there's no one with any reason to help you.

At least there was a bus leaving within a quarter of an hour. Zig shifted his rucksack on his shoulder, and made his way to the stop.

The bus ride was boring as hell. There was probably all kinds of scenery going on out there, but with it being black as pitch, all Zig could see was the reflection of his own face. He was getting sick of the sight of it.

For a bit of variety, he glanced around the bus. Big mistake. An old bloke across the aisle with a long, grey ponytail met his gaze and immediately leaned over towards him. "Cold night, tonight," he said, his accent a lot like Zig remembered Si's being.

"Yeah," Zig said shortly, too on edge to think of anything else to say. If they ever finally got to Glastonbury, which Zig was beginning to doubt, would Si be happy to see him?

"You look troubled," the old man persisted. "Something on your mind?"

Zig dredged up a smile. "Nah, I'm good, ta."

The man glanced at Zig's backpack. "Not sure of your reception?"

Ouch. That was so on the nose it physically hurt. "Maybe." Zig sighed. "It's someone I ain't seen for a while, that's all."

"Parted on bad terms?" The tone was sympathetic.

"No— Ah, I dunno. Difference of opinion, maybe? Nothing that couldn't have been smoothed over."

Si hadn't even known the whole of it. Zig rubbed his hands on his jeans legs cos yeah, he felt pretty guilty about that. But that was all in the past, back when Zig had been a total fucking moron who'd believed all the shit his dad spouted.

"But it never was?"

Again, he sounded sympathetic, and understanding, and somehow it all came spilling out. "I thought we were gonna be okay, you know? Then out of the blue, I get 'Sorry, mate, being a brickie ain't working out for me,' and he gives me a kiss and buggers off back to Somerset."

The old bloke didn't seem fazed by Zig outing himself. "That must have hurt."

"I was fine," Zig protested automatically. Okay, so maybe *fine* wasn't the word. Maybe it'd been like a knife twisting in his gut, but that was cos Zig had had the wrong idea about him and Si. Same as he'd had the wrong idea about a shedload of things back then. See: total fucking moron. Si, on the other hand, wasn't stupid. He'd sussed out that Zig wasn't the sort to get mushy feelings about. That was why he'd found it so easy to leave him.

The old man was nodding. "And that was a while ago, now?"

"Half a decade ago." Zig laughed bitterly. "Just hope he still remembers who I am."

"You don't seem the sort that anyone forgets. Not with those eyes, and that hair. Very striking."

Zig was starting to wonder if the bloke was hitting on him. "The hair was different back then. Bright red." He'd dyed it black with blue ends last night. Maybe that had been a mistake?

The old guy laughed. "I suppose you change your eye colour any time you feel like it too."

"These? They're real, not contacts." He wasn't the first person to assume that, but Zig's mismatched pair—one blue, one brown—were what he'd been born with.

Cobbled together out of old parts they found on the scrap heap, weren't you? his dad's voice sneered in his head.

Fuck off, Dad, Zig thought tiredly.

Maybe he ought to actually get some contacts? It'd been years since he'd last tried them, back before he'd been away, and they had to have got better. There was a chance they wouldn't scratch his eyeballs raw now.

"Ah well. I'm sure your young man will be happy to see you. And you'll fit right in, here in Glastonbury."

Zig shrugged, a little more jerkily than he'd intended. "We'll see." At least he could be fairly confident on the second part. He'd watched some YouTube vids last night while he was failing to get to sleep, and

Glastonbury was full of people who dressed weird, looked weird, and fuck him if some of them didn't act pretty weird too. Mismatched eyes probably didn't rate a mention.

"Good luck," the man said, and pulled himself to his feet as the bus lurched to a stop. Glastonbury Town Hall. Huh. They were there. Zig grabbed his rucksack and followed the trickle of passengers off the bus.

Jesus, the wind was cold. Zig hunched his shoulders as he tapped at his phone, wishing for a moment that he'd chosen his jacket for warmth and not for how cool he looked in it. Si had always liked him in leather, though.

Fuck, this was crazy. Despite what the old guy had said. Why the hell would Si help him out after so many years? *Because he's a decent bloke, that's why.* Zig couldn't imagine Si had changed much. Maybe he'd got himself a significant other and settled down, though? Shit. That'd be a right spanner in the works. No S.O. was likely to be happy with Si's ex turning up unannounced and wanting to stay.

Could Zig lean on Adam if Si let him down? He ought to be easy enough to find. How many tattoo studios could there be in this town? *Then again, like that beardy bloke down the pub said, Adam never really liked you, did he?* Zig shivered, shoved his hands into his pockets, and picked up his pace.

Si. He was the one who'd always taken Zig's part, despite . . . Anyway, he'd help, even if it was only for old times' sake. Even if he was all loved-up these days with some West Country lad with an accent as thick as Si's. Si would see him right.

Right?

Got to get to him first, though, haven't you? Zig peered at the map Google was showing him, and tried to work out which way was which. Okay. Si's parents' house was that way. And seriously, only twenty minutes' walk away? *Result.* Zig hadn't taken on board how bloody *small* Glastonbury was. Like, seriously small. He should have twigged when he found out it didn't have its own railway station, but for fuck's sake, they held the UK's biggest music festival here every year. How was he to know that probably increased the population by a factor of, like, a million?

He set off briskly down the road.

Si's parents' house was at one end of a red-brick terrace. There was a small front garden with a tiny lawn and a tree strung round haphazardly with fairy lights, but no off-road parking. A security light flashed on when he approached the front door, nearly blinding him.

Zig rapped on the door and got his face ready to smile.

The bloke who answered was middle-aged and a lot shorter than Zig was expecting. Si was, like, six foot and then some, but this guy was shorter than Zig's five ten (*Five nine if you're lucky, Sunshine*, his dad's sneering voice told him).

The bloke was frowning. "Evening?" He sounded doubtful.

"You'd be Mr. Greczik, right?" Zig said cheerily. "Si's dad?"

A blink. "Yeah, that's right. Have we met?"

"Nah, I'm just up from London. Me and Si was mates when he was working there, a few years back? I was hoping to look him up while I'm in the area."

Mr. Greczik's face cleared. "Right! Come on in, then, no need to stand out in the cold. Di, love?" he yelled over his shoulder. "It's one of Simon's old friends. Put the kettle on."

Thank God. Zig eyed the line of shoes in the hall and kicked off his Converse, then followed Si's dad into a small living room. There were photos everywhere of a little girl— *Shit, that must be Si's sister.* Zig hadn't seen a photo of her before, but he'd never forgotten Si, a few pints in, crying as he told him how she'd died when he was small. There were no pictures of Si himself that Zig recognised.

"He still lives round here, right?" he asked.

"Oh, no." Something must've shown in Zig's face, as Mr. Greczik's eyes went wide. "I mean, not *here*, here. He's got a flat in town. Wanted his independence, but that's young lads for you."

"Kettle's on," a female voice said from behind Zig. "Would that be a tea or a coffee?"

Zig turned. "Blimey, I can see where Si got his height from," came out of his mouth with no assistance from his brain whatsoever. But seriously, Mrs. G must have been six-foot tall, easy. She was a looker, too, even at, what, fifty or so? Dark hair, still thick and lush, and big dark eyes like her son. "Did you used to be a model?"

She grinned. "And who says I'm not still one? No, my lover. I've always worked in admin. Pay's not so good, mind, but you can eat what you want. Oh, that reminds me, are you hungry? I can do you some eggs and bacon in a jiffy."

Even as his stomach rumbled, something about her whole-hearted welcome made Zig feel exposed and raw, and he had to clear his throat. "Yeah, that'd be great. Cheers. Decent of you."

"Oh, it's no trouble. And I know what young men are like. I swear, the weekly shop doesn't cost half as much since Simon moved out. You'll be wanting his address, I expect." She spoke over her shoulder as she headed out of the living room, presumably to the kitchen.

Zig could have cheered, although he wasn't sure whether to follow her or not.

"Let me write it down for you," Mr. G said, deciding for him. "It's right in the centre of town. He's got a flat over a shop—you know the sort we get round here."

Not as such, no. "What, like groceries?"

Mr. G rolled his eyes with a chuckle. "Nothing so useful. Incense and magic tricks. She knows her stuff, mind."

Zig was rapidly losing the plot. "She?"

"Esme. Simon's landlady. She owns the shop. You watch *Dragon's Den*?"

"Uh . . ." Zig was a bit out of touch with what was on the telly. "Is that the one where small business owners try to blag money out of people who've made it big?"

"That's the one. She'd fit right in on there." He didn't specify which side she'd be on. "Now come on, you sit yourself down. Oh, and I'm Bob, by the way."

"Zig." He took a seat on the squashy sofa, having to shift a couple of tapestry cat cushions to find room.

Bob settled into what Zig had already pegged as his armchair—the one with the TV remote on the arm. "Zig. That'd be the eyes, right? For Ziggy Stardust?"

"Yeah."

"Bit before your time, I'd have thought." He laughed. "Before mine, come to that. I was never much into Bowie, but my sister used to have his posters all over her walls. How long are you in Glastonbury for?"

"Not sure. Kinda thinking of moving out of London permanent-like?" Zig smiled encouragingly.

"Well, you wouldn't catch me living there. Got to think about jobs, mind. What line are you in? No, don't tell me, let me guess." Bob peered intently at Zig, then nodded. "Car salesman. Am I right?"

Zig laughed. "Got it in one." *Not even close, thank God.* He didn't reckon *career criminal* would get him that address.

And anyway, it wasn't true, was it? Not anymore. He could be a salesman. He could be anything, so long as whoever was hiring wasn't too picky. "So, uh, Si's address?"

Bob rolled his eyes. "Forget me own head next. Now, paper and pen, paper and pen . . ." He looked around distractedly as if they were going to leap into existence on demand.

"Tell you what," Zig said hastily. "You tell me the address, and I'll put it in my phone, okay?"

Bob reeled off the street name and number. "And the shop's called Sage & Seer. That's double-*e*, not *e-r-e*. Simon's door is on the left of the shop."

Sere was a word? Zig was still tapping it all into his phone when Mrs. G came back in with a plateful of food. "Here you go, my lover. You eat up. You're all skin and bones. Doesn't your mum feed you?"

Zig's chest hurt, and Jesus, what was *wrong* with him these days? "No, uh, she, uh . . ." *Fuck, get a grip. Like they want you whining on about how she left you when you were a nipper?* "I'm big enough to feed myself these days."

He bent his head and set into the bacon, eggs, fried bread, and beans, balancing the plate on his lap, although his appetite had buggered off and left him. This wasn't what he'd signed up for. He'd simply wanted to get Si's address and go.

Fuck it, though, he should have known. Where had he thought Si had learned to be such a decent, honest-to-God *good* man? Not in a family like Zig's, that was for sure.

"Nice time to come here, with all the shops done up for Christmas," Mrs. G said.

Bob rolled his eyes. "He's from London, love. They'll be way fancier over there, with Selfridges and Hamleys and what have you."

"Ooh, and don't they have ice rinks and Christmas fairs these days, like in Germany? I bet they're lovely. Where do they have those?" Mrs. G asked.

Zig swallowed his mouthful of bacon. "Hyde Park? I don't get up that way much."

"Always the way, isn't it, love?" Bob said to his wife. "When was the last time we were up the tor, eh?"

"You speak for yourself. Me and Rina took our lunch up there only last week, that day we had the sunshine. Bloomin' freezing, it was. Lovely view, though." Mrs. G turned to Zig. "You make sure Simon takes you up the tor on a clear day. No point going when you can't see your hand in front of your face."

Zig smiled and nodded, which seemed to be all that was called for, seeing as Mrs. G was now telling her husband all about her mate Rina's car troubles. He managed to wolf down the last of his meal while they argued about timing belts, and stood up. "Cheers, Mrs. G. That was great. Really hit the spot. Kitchen that way?" He gestured with his plate.

Mrs. G promptly took it from his hands. "It's Di. And don't you worry about that. Bob'll wash up."

"Oh, will he, now?" Bob said good-naturedly. "It's domestic abuse, this is."

No, it really fucking isn't. Zig controlled his expression. "Well, cheers again. I'd better be on my way, but it's been great meeting you."

They walked him to the door, and Bob shook his hand with a smile. "Hope we'll be seeing you around some more. You go careful now, Zig!"

Zig grinned back at him. "Course I will." Then he saw Mrs. G's face.

She was staring at him wide-eyed, no trace of a smile. "Zig?"

Was he still smiling? His face felt frozen. "Yeah, that's right. Cheers for everything, Mrs. G. Appreciate it. Be seeing you, yeah?"

Then he turned on his heel and headed out the door, sharpish.

Not quick enough, though, to avoid hearing Mrs. G's tense whisper, "You never said it was that boy—"

Zig rounded the corner, heart thumping. Some girl coming down the street on her own looked at him like she was about to call 999, and he forced his pace to slow. So maybe Si had told his mum a few things about Zig. So what? He had that address now. He'd be okay.

Google told Zig it was a twenty-minute walk from Si's parents' house to his flat. Plenty of time for his mum to ring him. Zig jammed his hands into his pockets. It was bloody bitter out here now; the sun had been down for hours. What had Si told her? Did she know they'd messed around, back in the day?

Fuck, did she and Bob even know Si was into blokes? Maybe she knew and wasn't happy about it? Did she reckon Zig had led her darling boy astray, all them years ago?

Or was it the other thing?

Chapter Three
Zig

The shop Si lived over was up the far end of the high street, next to some kind of clothing boutique—vintage, maybe? Like most of the shops he'd passed on the way here, Sage & Seer had its window display done up for Christmas, only not like Zig would've expected.

The streetlamps threw enough light for him to make out white tinsel and stars hanging around a tableau of figurines. There were owls, deer with big antlers, and in the centre, a woman with one tit out. Zig wasn't sure what all that had to do with Christmas—except maybe the deer—but were witches allowed to celebrate Christmas anyway? Maybe they called it something else, like Midwinter, or Yule.

Zig hadn't believed in the baby Jesus, or Santa for that matter, since Christmas holidays halfway through primary school. His dad had taken him on his first break-in and then clouted him for setting off the alarm after squeezing through a window, like he was supposed to be some kind of expert on house-breaking at age eight.

At least he hadn't left him behind, like Zig had been terrified of at the time. Course, that would have been a one-way ticket to jail for his dad and the care system for Zig.

Would he have been better off that way? Never know, now, would he? He stood there a mo, finding more details in the dimly lit display the longer he looked. There were flowers, and holly, and something with wings that wasn't an owl. And was that figure at the back a woman or a rabbit, or some weird mix of the two?

It was strange, though—while he couldn't work out what it all was, it was clear that it meant something. But nothing Zig could understand. It was a world away from the shops back home, done up with fake snowmen and Santas made in China.

It was also fucking freezing out here, so why the hell wasn't he knocking on Si's door? Zig clenched his fists tight, then relaxed his hands and pulled them out of his pockets. Door on the left, Si's dad had said. Right. He could do this. *Ring the bell, you twat*, he told himself, and did.

There was a long enough silence that Zig was about to go find the nearest pub and get plastered, but then the thump of footsteps down stairs held him frozen to the spot, his breath caught and his heart beating way too wildly and *Jesus, get a fucking grip—*

The door opened.

Zig had been prepared for some changes in Si's appearance since they'd last seen each other. He wouldn't be so fresh-faced, and he'd probably have filled out a bit. Even *Zig* had filled out a bit, although no one would have known it from the way Mrs. G had been talking earlier. But Si . . .

Fuck me, he's gone all biker. With a side order of lumberjack. Si had never been skinny like Zig, back in their teens, but now? Now he was fucking *built*. Shoulders that could hold up a bloody marquee, and thick muscle everywhere, with a hint of softness on top. He had a full, dark beard now, and was wearing a faded black hoodie with a print of a skeletal hand making the horns gesture. He was a great big metalhead bear of a man, and Zig had never been so conscious of the year or so between them. Had never felt *young* next to Si before.

Behind that beard, though, Si's face had paled. "Zig?"

Zig pasted on the cocky smile he should have been wearing from the start. "All right, mate? I've come for a visit. Catch up with me teenage sweetheart. How you been?"

Si's eyes widened. Then he stepped forward.

Zig froze—and relaxed again as, instead of decking him, Si enveloped him in a huge bear hug.

Jesus, that felt good. Si's hoodie was the softest thing he'd felt in a long time, and his chest was warm and inviting. Zig could've stayed in that embrace for the rest of his *life*, except the hot air from inside the flat was making his eyes prickle. He stepped back, making sure his smile was firmly in place. "Reckon you can find room on your sofa for me?"

"Course I can." Si's voice was deeper than Zig remembered too. Growlier. It did stuff to Zig's insides. "Come on in."

Chapter Four
Si

Si's head whirled. Seeing Zig on his doorstep, it was like he was nineteen again and on his first trip to a gay club. Zig didn't look exactly the same, of course. He'd always changed his hair colour as often as he changed his socks. His face wasn't so soft around the edges, and his frame seemed more solid, less witchy-thin than he'd been as a teenager. But that crooked smile was the same, and bloody hell, them eyes were even more dazzling than Si had remembered.

It hadn't been a conscious decision to hug him. It had just been so *bloody* good to see the bloke alive and well. Bit painful, too, he wasn't gonna lie. But Zig had fit into his arms perfectly. Solid. Real.

Over the years, Si had wondered how Zig had been since they'd parted. Hadn't been able to stop himself, despite knowing it wasn't helping him move on one bit. Would Zig still be breezing through life, or would he have come a cropper, due to the company he kept? Had Si done the wrong thing, leaving him? Should he have stayed? Tried harder to overcome all them other influences in Zig's life? Could he have made a difference? Would Zig have wanted him to?

Now here he was. In Si's flat, with his black-and-blue hair and trendy clothes, acting like it'd been no time at all since they'd last seen each other.

Or maybe not quite like that. Zig had seemed hesitant at first, when they'd hugged. Like he thought it was weird, and maybe it was at that. But *gods*.

Si took a deep breath. *Get a grip.* "You hungry, mate?" he called over his shoulder as he led Zig down the narrow hallway into the living room. "Can rustle you up something on toast, or there's plenty of takeaways if you'd rather."

"Nah, cheers, mate. I've eaten." Zig paused in the doorway, glancing around the room.

Bugger. There were bike mags and Doctor Who crap all over the place. Si should have tidied up, but who ever came round but his mates?

"Actually, your mum fed me," Zig went on before Si could muster an apology for the mess. "Thought she might've called to let you know I was on me way?"

Si blinked. "No, haven't heard from her. You were round my mum and dad's?" Back when they'd been going out, Si hadn't even *thought* of introducing Zig to his parents, and now he'd been round for dinner?

"Well, yeah. Didn't have your current address, did I?"

"S'pose you didn't." What would Zig have done if he'd gone to the old address and found nobody home—or if Mum and Dad had moved? Asking the question seemed a bit personal, somehow, so he didn't. Weird, though, to think of Zig in the house Si had grown up in. He couldn't remember giving Zig the address, but he must have, he guessed. And Zig had kept it all this time? Si's chest tightened.

"What did you tell 'em about me?" Zig asked. There was a strange tension in the way he was holding himself, and he wasn't looking Si in the face.

Si frowned. "Not much, I don't think. Bit hard to remember, after all these years."

"Yeah? Your mum seemed to recognise my name, that's all."

"Oh—" *Shit.* Si smiled awkwardly as the memories came flooding back. "Yeah, that's right. Must've mentioned you a few times."

Sobbed my bloody heart out over you, more like. Told her I'd finally met someone I wanted to be with and he'd turned out to be a wrong'un. And he didn't even feel the same about me, neither.

Si's heart clenched. "Just gonna put the kettle on." He went into the kitchen, where he'd left his phone on charge. On silent, too, as it turned out. Two missed calls from Mum. He ought to ring her back, but what was he gonna say? *Yeah, he's here now. No, I don't know why, after all this time.*

Yes, I think I still care about him.

Chapter Five
Si

Six years ago

They'd met not long after Si had gone down to London to work for Adam's dad. It'd been wicked, being with Adam again. They'd kept in touch, course they had, but it wasn't the same being best mates from a distance.

Funny, though. Adam's phone calls had been all about the clubs in London, but after Si moved there, they seemed to spend every Saturday night down the local pub. Which was a laugh, but Si had been expecting something more. Something different. Something that'd help him work out who he really was. Who he wanted to be with.

So the next time it seemed like they were headed for the same old, same old, Si cleared his throat. "Listen, I was thinking . . . maybe not go to the pub tonight?"

There was a beat, then Adam said, "Sure. We can stay home, watch a bit of telly. If that's what you want."

"No—I wanna go out. But maybe somewhere different, like? A club? One of them ones you told me about before I came down here."

"Yeah? You sure about that?" Adam was frowning.

Si bristled. "Why not? You worried I'll show you up or something?"

Adam laughed. "What? No, course not. I didn't reckon you'd wanna come, that's all."

"Why wouldn't I?"

"Cos, well, it's gay clubs I go to, yeah? Didn't think you'd fancy blokes hitting on you all night."

"That what happens when you go out, is it?" He supposed it probably did. Good-looking, Adam was. Sorta foxy, if that was a thing? For blokes, like. All angles, accentuated by the shadows.

Si maybe fancied him a bit.

But only a bit, mind. Adam was Si's best mate, and he wasn't gonna screw that up. 'Sides, it'd be weird. Like snogging your brother. And with them both living at Adam's dad's house, and Si working in Adam's dad's business . . . Nope. Not gonna touch that one. Not with a flippin' bargepole, whatever one of they things was. Barges, now, he'd seen plenty of them, down on the river. Poles, though—

"Oi, where you gone, mate?" Adam was waving a hand in front of Si's face. "Anyhow, I didn't think there'd be much in it for you."

Si frowned. "What if I want to meet a bloke?"

Adam stopped dead, and his eyes widened. "Do you? I always thought you were straight. Didn't you have that thing with Lucy Mansfield in fifth year?"

"She 'ad a thing with me, maybe." It'd been weird. One day she'd just started hanging around. It'd been sorta nice, flattering, like, 'cept she'd wanted to snog all the time, and once when they were in the cinema, she'd tried to put her hand down his jeans. "And who says I can't like both?"

"Do you?"

Si shrugged. "Maybe? Bit hard to tell when I never meet no one, ain't it?"

"You've met loads of blokes since you moved down here. What about all the lads who work for Dad?"

"All straight, ain't they?"

"*All* of them? Doubt it."

"Can't you tell? What about that gaydar?"

"Well, of course they all *act* straight when they're at work . . . Huh. See what you mean. S'pose even if there was one who was into you, and you were into him, you'd get the shit ripped out of you if the others found out."

"That why you never gone out with any of 'em?" Si asked.

Adam shrugged. "Be a bit awkward anyway, with Dad being their boss."

Si nodded. "So are we going clubbing or what?"

Him and Adam got the Tube into central London, getting off at Leicester Square. Si had been here before—his mum and dad had brung him down to see a show one birthday. Dad had driven up to Bristol and they'd got the train from there. Flippin' long journey, it'd been. They'd had to stay the night, after, in the poshest hotel Si'd ever been in. Mum must have got some kind of deal. Si didn't remember much about the show they'd seen, but he remembered this place. Heaving with people, it'd been, and it was now and all. Si stood for a mo, disorientated, as groups of young men and women strode past in all directions.

Adam seemed to know where he was going, though. He grabbed Si's arm, pulling him in the direction of the square. Neon lights were blinding, making the darkness even more impenetrable. "Scratch?" Si turned at the sound of his old school nickname to see Adam pointing. "It's this way."

"Right." Si tried to make himself as small as possible so as not to terminally elbow anyone as they squeezed through the crowds milling around. "And it's Si while we're in London, right? I don't wanna spend half my life explaining my nickname."

"Si. Yeah. Sorry." Adam sent him a grin that was almost too broad for his face.

Best not to focus too hard on that smile, or he'd be getting confused again. And there was plenty else to get distracted by. People dressed different in London. Sharper. Not so colourful. Same boatloads of tourists, mind, some in big groups and some in families. There was a tiny Japanese kid in white socks and Hello Kitty backpack out past her bedtime, waiting patiently while her parents argued over directions—

Si startled as Adam yanked on his arm.

"Jesus, mate, watch where you're going! You nearly ran into those girls."

Si blinked at a group of brightly dressed women in platform shoes, and blushed when they laughed.

"You can run into me anytime, darling!" the one in the gold heels yelled back at him as they tottered on their way.

Adam nudged him. "Sounds like you could have been well in there."

"Bollocks. They was only teasing." Si knew what he looked like, and it was like what you'd get if you tried to build a skeleton out of coat hangers—all his limbs too long, and his frame too large.

"Nah, seriously," Adam went on, the London accent he'd picked up in the last couple of years coming out strong. "They was well into you. Working for Dad's been good for you. Made you fill out a bit." He gave Si a quick look up and down as he hustled him into a side street.

Huh. Did Adam maybe fancy *him* a bit too?

"Would you be into it if they were?"

"What, them girls?" Si shrugged. "Dunno. Don't know 'em, do I?"

"You don't have to know someone to know if you fancy them." Adam hesitated. "Or have you decided it's just blokes for you, like me?"

Si was still trying to work out how to answer that when they turned a corner and walked under a giant red-and-black gateway covered in oriental symbols. Sweet and spicy aromas filled the air. "Hang about, this is Chinatown, innit? You sure this is the way?"

"It's *a* way, all right? Don't carry a map in my head, do I?"

"You got a phone."

"More fun this way. You get to see all the sights." Adam led the way down Gerrard Street, and turned right. They passed under a string of red paper lanterns—'cept they couldn't be paper, could they? What if it rained?—and crossed a busy road. The farther they got, the fewer Chinese restaurants and shops there were. Plenty of other restaurants, though—how did they all survive?—and bars too. The streets were darker here.

And there seemed to be a lot more young blokes walking around in twos. Some of them were holding hands. Si's heart beat a little faster as he tried not to stare. "We there, then?"

"Nearly." Adam took another right turn and led him down Old Compton Street. "Ta-da!"

Si took a deep breath as he gazed at the big, silver letters spelling out G-A-Y. "Right, then."

This . . . this could be the start of something.

Course, once he'd been in the club for half an hour, Si wasn't so sure about it. Adam had bought him some mystery drink he said Si would love and then buggered off to dance with a bloke he'd met here before. It left Si propping up the end of the bar on his own. Adam probably thought he'd be enjoying the scenery, with all them topless blokes around, but to be honest, it was all a bit much.

Si took a gulp of his drink and made a face. Some sickly sweet alcopop shite. "No, Adam, I bloody well will *not* love this," he muttered under his breath.

"Mm, could take it off your hands if you want," a smooth voice purred in his ear.

Si looked round, and his breath caught. The man—boy?—person?—in front of him was like someone off of a music video. Or who'd hopped a boat out of Lothlórien and gone shopping in Wardour Street. He had a pointed chin, sharply cut straight hair that was dark at the roots and flame red at the ends, and full, wide lips that curled in a mocking smile. Not to mention the most mesmerising eyes Si had ever seen: one blue, one brown.

He looked like he was expecting a snappy comeback. "Uh?" was all Si managed.

The bloke who'd now definitely be featuring in Si's fantasies laughed, showing straight, white teeth—perfect except for one crooked one at the side that lent him a reassuring touch of humanity. "Your drink, love. Unless it's the place in general you were complaining about?" Those unusual, mismatched eyes flashed. "Or maybe your present company?"

"Nothing wrong with the company!" Si almost spilled his drink thrusting it into the bloke's hands. "Yours, if you want it."

"Are you? Bit forward." The stranger's Adam's apple bobbed as he took a deep swallow of Si's drink. "Gonna have to buy me more than one drink first. I'll have another of these. I'm Zig."

"Si."

"That a name, or are you narrating yourself?"

Si blanked.

Zig laughed again and put a warm hand on Si's shoulder. "You know. *Sigh*?" He leaned in close and breathed a long, heavy sigh right in Si's ear.

Bloody hell, Si was probably redder than them Chinatown lanterns right now. "It's a name," he croaked out, and cleared his throat. "I'll get the drinks."

He pulled out his wallet and waved to the barman, half expecting Zig to disappear as soon as his back was turned, cos seriously, what the hell was a bloke like Zig doing with someone like him? A warm arm slid around his waist, and he almost jumped out of his skin.

"I'll have a pint of lager, and a . . ." Si floundered.

"Smirnoff Ice," Zig provided.

The barman, who looked old enough to be Si's dad—no way was he a day under thirty—gave Zig a weird look, not too friendly. "Got ID?"

"Uh, yeah, mate. Hang about." Si fossicked in his wallet for his driving licence.

"Not you. Him."

Zig smiled, all teeth, and gave Si a squeeze. "Not buying, am I?" Zig put Si's empty glass down on the bar with a clunk, like it was punctuation.

The barman frowned but handed over their drinks and took Si's money.

"Haven't seen you around here before," Zig said, taking his drink with a brush of fingers over Si's hand.

"No—I only been here a couple of months. Got a job with me mate's dad. Brickie." *Gods, Si, stop talking about your boring self.* "Uh, what do you do?"

Zig shrugged. "This and that. C'mon. Let's get out of the crush. We'll have our drinks and then you can show me what moves you've got."

"You mean, like, dancing?"

Zig grinned. "That as well if you like."

Si's heart was beating louder than the bass from the speakers.

After they'd finished their drinks, they danced—Si horribly conscious of every single one of his limbs, none of which seemed to be moving in time with the music. And they'd had more drinks, and then they'd kissed, and it had been nothing like kissing Lucy Mansfield, nothing at all. It'd been like someone was setting fireworks off in Si's head—and in other parts of him too. He'd wanted to punch the air, yell out *Yes* and *Get in there* and other stuff he'd only ever heard people say before.

He hadn't cared about Adam finding other blokes to dance with, to drink with. And when the place had closed, and they'd had to leave, Zig came with him, pushed him up against a wall, and kissed him until he didn't know which way was up.

(Except he did, cos, well, part of him was pointing that way pretty emphatically.)

And then Zig said, "Better let you go. Your mate's getting well impatient. Maybe I'll see you again, yeah?"

Si didn't want to let him go. "Next—next Saturday? You'll be here?" He couldn't keep the pleading out of his voice.

Zig grinned. "You take care," he said, and left.

Chapter Six
Zig

Six years ago

Zig strutted down the dimly lit streets of Soho, heading for home. He could have got on the Tube, but he'd fancied a walk. Just him and his thoughts.

Fuck, that lad from Somerset was cute. So wet behind the ears you'd probably find a diving board and a pair of Speedos if you looked hard enough. And that accent . . . After kissing him, Zig was surprised he wasn't picking half a haystack out of his teeth. God knew why he was so hung up on the bloke. He wasn't Zig's usual type at all.

Zig whispered his name into the shadows of the alley in a drawn-out, mocking breath. "*Siiiii* . . ." Then he laughed out loud. He'd had plenty of cocky London lads, all tight jeans and swagger. Maybe it was time for a change. It was refreshing, meeting someone who wasn't all front. Someone honest.

Zig had played it cool, after their snog-session outside the club—fuck, he was getting hard thinking about it—but yeah, he'd be there next weekend. Maybe then he'd finally get to find out what Si kept in those painfully unfashionable jeans of his.

His route took him to Fleet Street, where he hopped on the bus. It was too far to walk all the way from Soho to his dad's house in Barking. Anyone who tried would have to be, heh, barking. Zig had timed it well and got the direct bus, but it was still an hour's ride. He dozed off en route, his internal alarm clock waking him up in time for his stop.

It was only a ten-minute walk from the bus stop to Dad's house. Zig turned the key in the lock with care and slipped through the front door. Then the bastard thing wouldn't close behind him, so he had to slam it. Bugger.

Sure enough, there was a shout from the living room. "Oi! Where the fuck have you been?"

"Anywhere but here," Zig muttered, heading for his room.

Too slow. A hand grabbed him by the shoulder and jerked him back. His dad's unshaven face glared at him, eyes bloodshot. "What the fuck did you say?"

"I said . . ." Zig's mind went into overdrive. "Uh, not anywhere you'd want to hear about."

Well, bollocks. That wasn't a lot better, was it?

Dad's face darkened. "Pissing about with a load of pansies again, were you? Jesus, where the fuck did you come from? You bloody didn't get that from me. Are you drunk?"

Not as drunk as you. "No. I only had a couple."

"Good. You're going out with Trent tonight. Scrap merchants."

"What? I'm tired." Zig made as if to walk off.

The hand on his shoulder tightened. "If you want to live here, you'll damn well earn your keep. He'll be here in half an hour. Now go and put on something fucking suitable. You look like a bloody rentboy. Smell like one too." Dad gave one last, painful squeeze, and let him go.

Zig slouched his way down the hall to his room. He didn't roll his shoulder until he was inside with the door shut. No sense letting the old bastard know he'd hurt him.

Si must have got home ages ago. Peckham might be south of the river, but it was way closer to the centre than bloody Barking. Maybe he was already in bed, asleep? Or lying there thinking of Zig? He smiled briefly at the thought. Either way, Si's day was over, whereas Zig's wouldn't end for hours yet. An odd twinge hit him in the chest as he wondered what Si would think if he knew how Zig and his dad earned their money.

Ah, what the hell. What he didn't know couldn't hurt him.

Chapter Seven
Si

Present day

When Si got back to the living room, mugs of tea in hand, Zig was relaxing on the sofa in that easy, familiar sprawl that made him look all legs.

"Cheers, mate," Zig said as Si handed him his tea.

Si perched on the other end of the sofa. "So what have you been up to, then, for the last . . . Blimey, has it been five years? Six?" He rubbed his nose. *Five years, eleven months, but you're the only bugger who's been counting. Zig was never in as deep. Gotta remember that.*

"Oh, this and that," Zig said easily enough, exactly like he always used to, 'cept his eyes slid away to the side. Course, maybe they'd done that way back when and all, but Si had been too bloody naïve—*and horny, don't forget that*—to see it. "Six, anyway."

Si blinked. "You what?"

"Six years, near as. You left right after New Year. Couple of weeks after me eighteenth." This time, Zig's gaze met Si's, and it was Si who looked away.

Those eyes of Zig's hadn't got any less intense, had they? "Right. Right. Long time ago, now. We've all passed a lot of water since then, as the saying goes." It didn't mean anything. Si had to remember that. Just cos Zig had kept track . . .

Zig laughed. "Can see you've been spending some time in the gym. Or did you give up hauling bricks around so you could get into the lumberjack business?" He looked at Si appreciatively.

Thank all the gods that blushes don't show through beards. "I'm a locksmith, these days. Got me certification and everything. There's jobs where a bit of muscle comes in handy. You working at the mo?" Si did his best, but he couldn't help it coming out like a challenge.

"Been doing bar work." Zig's face turned serious. "Me and my dad had a bust-up. Haven't been working for him for years now."

That was a relief. That was a bloody relief and a half. While it made his heart do weird flips in his chest to see Zig again, Si hadn't been able to stop the little voice in his head whispering that where Zig went, trouble followed.

"Sorry you and your old man are on the outs," he said awkwardly, seeing as it was a lie.

Zig barked a laugh. "No, you ain't. And I'm not, either, so you don't need to pretend. So this locksmithing, what made you go for that? Always fancied learning how to crack a safe, did you?"

Si shrugged. "Oi, you, no taking the piss. Like doing stuff with me hands, don't I? And if there's one thing you learn *hauling bricks around*, it's that you don't get nowhere without a proper trade and qualifications and that."

"Yeah, you got that right." Zig's smile was crooked.

Ah, shit. "But bar work, that's steady," Si said quickly. "Folks are always gonna want a drink."

"You ain't wrong there." Zig's face darkened. "Nah, I know it's going nowhere. Missed me chance, though, ain't I? Who wants a twenty-five-year-old apprentice?" He grinned, suddenly. "Anyhow, forget all that depressing bollocks. What do you do for fun around here?"

Same old Zig. "If it's nightlife you're after, well, mostly it's just pubs." Si racked his brains. What the hell was there in Glastonbury that Zig would call fun? The teenaged Zig he'd known back in London wouldn't have been impressed by anything Si could think of. "The Prince of Wales has got an open mic night tomorrow. And a band on Friday. If, you know, you're planning to be around that long."

Si's heart clenched. How long *was* Zig planning to stay? How long would it take him to change his mind when he found out how quiet Glastonbury was in the middle of winter, especially compared to London?

"Sounds good. Hey, reckon they'd be hiring?"

Si blinked. That sounded like . . . Nope. Best not read too much into it. "We can always ask. You, uh, you wanna head on down there tonight?"

"Nah. I'm beat. Come all the way from London, ain't I? It's getting late, anyway, and I'm guessing you've got work tomorrow. Quiet night in, that'll do me." Zig gave that smile that'd always melted Si's insides like a blowtorch to the heart.

Si coughed. "Right. I'll, uh, I'll look out the spare duvet, then. You'll be all right on the sofa?" Heat rose in his face. Should he have offered Zig the bed? Except, if he'd done that, what if Zig insisted it was big enough to share? If there was one thing Si couldn't handle, it was sleeping next to the bloke he'd lost his heart to. Knowing Zig—if Si still did know him, that was—it wouldn't end at sleeping, neither.

Or would it? *Just cos he fancied you six years ago don't mean he does now.* And why did that thought hurt so much?

"Cheers, mate. Sofa's cool." Zig patted a cushion. "I wasn't expecting you to roll out the red carpet when I turn up out of nowhere after all this time."

Si couldn't let that stand. Even if it was sorta true. Why the hells *had* Zig turned up? Why here? Why now? Seemed kind of rude to ask. Like he didn't want Zig here. "You know it's good to see you, don't you?" he said awkwardly. "Looking so well, and all."

Zig gazed at him, the intensity a bit more than Si could handle. "You too, mate. You too."

Gods, that tone, and those eyes . . . Si had to look away. *It don't mean anything. You know that.* "I'll, uh, I'll get you sorted, then." He hurried away.

Si turfed out his summer-weight duvet from the under-bed storage, gave it a shake to evict any dust bunnies that might've burrowed in, and wrestled it into a clean duvet cover. Then he added a couple of blankets so Zig wouldn't freeze when the heating went off overnight.

He took a mo to steady himself, then carried the bundle into the living room. "This all right for you?"

Zig was crouching by the telly, eyeing up Si's DVD collection. "See you got into antiques." He held up a *Doctor Who* boxset starring Jon Pertwee.

"Oi, that's a classic, that is."

"Did I say it ain't? Have you got more recent ones too? The ones with Jodie Whatsherface? I didn't get to see them." Zig's tone was weirdly bitter.

Maybe he'd been with a bloke who hadn't liked the show?

Come to think of it, since when had *Zig* liked the show? He'd used to laugh at Si being so into it, seeing as it was supposed to be a kids' show. Si stroked his beard. "Yeah, I got 'em all. Over on the right there. Didn't think you was into sci-fi."

Zig straightened and shrugged. "Eh. People change, don't they? You used to go on about it so much, I thought I'd give it a go."

Despite himself, warmth spread through Si's chest. "Wanna watch the first Jodie episode, then? She proper cracked it."

Zig threw himself onto the sofa and leaned back, his long legs stretched out in front of him. He looked relaxed, and happy, and not at all like he belonged there. "Line it up, mate."

Si grabbed the remote and switched on BBC iPlayer.

Who'd have ever thought he'd be doing this with Zig, back when they were teenagers in London?

Chapter Eight
Si

Six years ago

Si lay on his bed in Adam's dad's house in Peckham, his muscles aching from work and his belly full of hearty, plain food, thinking about Zig. They'd met up three more times since that first night in Soho. They'd danced together, they'd snogged, and last night—Si's knees went weak thinking about it—Zig had given him his first blowjob, in a back alley in Soho that reeked of rotting garbage and piss.

It'd been bloody *epic*. Si couldn't wait to return the favour. He was nervous about it, mind, cos he didn't want to make an utter balls-up of it, but he still couldn't wait.

And now he was getting a stiffy, so it was a bloody good thing he'd come up to his room.

They hadn't actually *said*, but Si reckoned him and Zig were a thing now. Boyfriends. That was what Adam called Zig anyway: *Seeing your boyfriend tonight?* Or when that sharp-dressed, older lad Zig hung around with sometimes turned up at the pub: *your boyfriend's mate's here again*. It gave him a good feeling, hearing that word. Warmth spread through him.

Mind, he had no clue how his mum and dad would react if he told them he had a boyfriend. Would they be disappointed? Si didn't like to think of that. It'd never come up while he'd been living at home. He'd never had a proper boyfriend or girlfriend while he was at school. Lucy Mansfield hadn't hung around long enough to count, and he still wasn't sure how he'd felt about her. It'd been too confusing, he'd told Adam one night, cos he liked boys and girls.

"Yeah, but who do you wanna shag?" Adam had asked.

"No one," Si had answered, because he didn't feel that way about any of his mates and why would he want to shag someone he didn't know all that well? 'Cept that hadn't been the right answer, cos after that Adam thought he wasn't into sex at all.

To be fair, for a while *Si* had thought he wasn't into sex at all. But then he'd come down here and met Zig, and Si was absolutely, one hundred percent into having sex with Zig.

Zig was the one thing that made being here worthwhile. Well, him and being with Adam again. But Adam would be going off to uni soon, and if it wasn't for Zig, Si would be packing his bags to leave too. Being a brickie wasn't all it was cracked up to be, 'specially when your best mate was planning to bugger off and get an education. Si didn't really feel like he fit in, somehow, with the work crowd. Most of the others were older, and they talked about their wives and kids and mortgages. The ones who were younger mostly bragged on about all the alcohol they'd drunk and the girls they'd shagged. Every time he met one of the girls down the pub, Si was tempted to tell her how her bloke talked about her when she wasn't there. He didn't, though. He didn't much fancy getting an "accidental" two-by-four in the face from said bloke once they were back on-site.

Adam didn't exactly fit in, either, but then, he was the boss's son and was on his way to uni and some artsy-fartsy career in design. This was it for Si.

Unless he got his head out of his arse and worked out what he really wanted to do. But that'd probably mean going back home to Glastonbury, and well . . .

Zig was in London.

Chapter Nine
Zig

Present day

Zig and Si spent the rest of the evening in front of the telly, cos nobody stopped watching after one episode of a series anymore, did they? Si had been right: Jodie Whittaker had proper cracked it. The "fam" were okay too. The older man reminded Zig a bit of his gran's fella, Ray, whom he hadn't thought of in years. But that made him think of another old man, which led him down roads he didn't wanna tread right now, not while he was cosied up with Si. Anyway, Jodie was the one who stole the show.

Si's phone rang once while they were watching, and he frowned at it, rejected the call, then texted furiously for half a minute. After that, he switched his phone off.

What the hell was that all about? Zig reckoned it'd be better not to pry. Course, it might not be Si's mum telling her son to kick him out on the streets, but best not to get into it, just in case. He didn't want to ruin the mood.

He stretched out on the sofa, more relaxed than he'd been in fuck knew how long. Zig hadn't spent a lot of time with his housemates in Lewisham, mostly because they were wankers. And his box of a room hadn't felt like home. Si's place, though, felt lived in. The sort of place you could put your feet up on the table and not worry if you had a hole in your socks. It was warm, and cosy, and there wasn't any mould on the walls or the ceiling. Not even in the bathroom. Si's furniture was like the man himself: solid, comfortable, and totally unpretentious.

Jesus, Zig could get used to being here. *Too* bloody used to it.

After the third episode, the Rosa Parks one, Si hit Pause. "Sorry. You probably don't wanna spend the rest of your life watching *Doctor Who*."

Zig laughed. "There's worse ways to spend it, believe me. But yeah, we could take a break. Catch up a bit. You, uh, you seeing anyone right now?"

"What, me?" Si's eyes widened, as if Zig had asked him whether he'd done a lot of interplanetary time-travelling lately. "No. You?"

Was there something hopeful in his tone? Or was that simply Zig hearing what he wanted to? "No. Not for a while." Where he'd been, for most of the time since he'd last seen Si, wasn't the sort of place he'd have gone looking for a long-term partner. And after that, Zig had been too busy trying to build a life on the straight and narrow to worry about finding someone for more than a hookup.

Si coughed. "So, you been here before? Glastonbury, I mean?"

"Me? Never." Zig flashed him a grin. "I'd have looked you up if I'd been here, wouldn't I?"

"S'pose."

"Go on, then, tell me about the place. I know it's got a festival, but that's all." Zig shuffled closer to Si on the sofa.

Si seemed to stiffen, and not in a good way. "Well, the famous thing is the tor. Glastonbury Tor."

"Yeah, I think I've heard of that. Dunno what it is, though."

"*Tor*'s a word for a hill, innit? In Old English or summat. You'll have seen it on your way into town. Got a tower on top."

"Right, that thing. Yeah, I saw it." Pretty hard to miss, seeing as it was taller than anything else for miles around.

"Course, in German, see, a tor is a gate. I learned that off a tourist. Which is fitting, like, cos the tor's s'posed to be a sort of gateway to the spirit realm if you ask the New Agers. Then again, in your old Norse, *gate* means street, and that's why you get streets called Stonegate or Swinegate and all that bollocks in some Northern towns that were under the Danelaw, way back when." Si paused for breath.

Zig laughed. "You nervous or something?"

". . . No? Just thought you might be interested, like?" Si reddened, or at least the small amount of his face that wasn't covered in hair did.

Zig slung an arm around Si's shoulders. Fuck him, they were broad these days. "I'm interested, okay? Tell me more. Seduce me with your sexy dead languages."

Si pulled away from him, eyes narrowed. "No one's seducing anyone round here, you got that?"

It was like a stab to the gut. Zig forced a smile. "Not even for old times' sake?"

"Not even."

Fuck. "Well, you're no fun these days."

"Don't s'pose I ever was," Si muttered to his socks.

That twisted the knife. "Who says that? I never said that. You're plenty fun, all right? Go on, tell me more about archaic *tongues*." Zig licked his lips and quirked an eyebrow.

Si rolled his eyes, but he was smiling again. "Fine. But this is your last one. Torpenhow Hill, up north somewhere."

"Hill-pen-how-hill?" Zig guessed.

"Nope. Better than that. It's in three different languages—Old English, Norse, and Welsh, I reckon? So it's *hill-hill-hill-hill*."

Zig laughed, and even to him, the sound was brighter than it usually was. Cleaner. More honest. God, he'd missed this guy. Why had they ever broken up?

Because he saw you for what you were, and he knew you didn't deserve him, a harsh voice said in his mind. Thank fuck he'd learned years ago how to ignore it.

"Got time for one more beer before bed?" he asked with a grin. He was prepared for Si to say no. It was well late now for someone who worked nine to five or whatever hours locksmiths did.

"Just the one, then," Si said.

Internally, Zig cheered. Maybe Si had missed him too.

Maybe.

Chapter Ten
Si

Si got out another couple of beers from the fridge. Drinking with Zig probably wasn't the best idea right now, or ever, come to that. But Si was buggered if he was gonna do this stone-cold sober. Whatever *this* was.

He wasn't daft. Well, not all the time, anyhow. He could tell Zig was coming on to him. And it was working, because, well, *Zig*. It was just so bloody good to see him again. All them thoughts he'd had about Zig over the years . . . They hadn't been happy thoughts. Si wouldn't have been at all surprised to hear Zig had ended up in prison—or worse. Truth be told, it was a relief and then some to see him looking so well, and smiling that smile of his. Si would simply have to remember it didn't mean nothing, not to Zig.

But why was he here? Now? It had to be trouble, had to be. There was no way Zig had spent the last six years pining over his teenage sweetheart. Nobody was daft enough to do that. Present company excepted, of course.

Si laughed bitterly under his breath as he reached for the bottle opener. Thing was, Zig had always been able to make him feel like he was the centre of the bloody world. Like it was only the two of them, and no one and nothing else mattered.

Except they did, didn't they? Family mattered. Friends mattered. And when he'd found out what Zig had been up to when Si wasn't with him . . .

Didn't feel so good then, did you?

Si shook his head, cracked open the beers, and headed back to his sofa. And Zig.

Chapter Eleven
Si

Six years ago

Si could remember the night it'd all come out. Adam had come back from uni for the Christmas holidays, and it'd been great to catch up with him, but it'd been different, somehow. All his stories were about people Si didn't know and places he'd never been. Adam was always on his phone, in touch with someone or other.

Si could've understood if it'd been a boyfriend. He knew he'd been crap company when he'd first got together with Zig. But Adam said they were only mates. *Better mates than me?* he wanted to ask, but he didn't.

That night, Adam's dad had been in a right mood over supper. Stuff had gone missing from the site again, and he was worried it had been an inside job. The thieves had known exactly where to look and what for, he reckoned. Someone must have tipped them off.

He sent Si a sharp glance at that point, and Si's stomach lurched.

Adam put down his fork with a clatter. "Oi, you'd better not be suggesting Si had anything to do with it."

Si's heart warmed.

Mr. Merchant's face softened. "Of course not. Christ, I hate the thought that one of the lads who work for me could be dishonest, though."

Si swallowed his mouthful of potato. It didn't go down easily. "Maybe someone was talking, like in the pub, say, and let it slip by accident? Didn't mean no harm by it?"

"Maybe." That sharp look was back in Mr. Merchant's gaze for a mo. "If that's the case, I hope whoever it was will think a bit more carefully about who they talk to in the pub, next time."

Si nodded and forced another forkful of supper down his throat. Normally, he'd stick around downstairs after they'd finished. He'd watch telly with Adam while his dad frowned at the VAT receipts—or maybe the list of stuff that got nicked, tonight. Instead, Si sloped off to his room.

It didn't work. Adam was at his door in five minutes flat. "Si? I'm coming in," he said in a low voice.

Si thought about yelling back, "I'm busy!" which was their usual code for *having a crafty wank*, but to be honest, the five minutes of alone time he'd had hadn't been much fun. Too many thoughts going round his head. "Come on, then," he said dully.

Adam slipped in, like he was trying to be furtive, and closed the door quietly. "*Do* you know anything about those thefts?"

Bloody marvellous. "No, go on, say what you *really* think."

Rolling his eyes, Adam flopped onto the bed next to Si. "I don't think you had anything to do with it, obviously. Just— Look, I know you like Zig, and I'm not saying it was him neither, but that Trent bloke he's matey with is well sus. He'd shaft you soon as look at you. And not in a good way." He smiled weakly.

At least this was a safe subject. Ish. "Yeah, he's a right bastard. Don't like the way he looks at Zig, neither." All smug like, as if he could make him do anything he wanted.

Adam was silent a moment. "So, you know, be careful what you say around him, yeah? Cos I hate the thought of Dad getting ripped off. He's been great to me, he really has. He doesn't deserve it."

"He's been good to me and all." Si managed to get it out without his voice cracking.

Adam stretched and flung himself off the bed. "Right. TV's shite tonight, so I'm gonna get the Xbox out. You coming?"

"Yeah, all right." Si followed him downstairs. A bit of *Tomb Raider* would take his mind off his worries.

Trouble was, once he was lying in bed that night with the light turned off, it all came back, along with the sick feeling in his stomach.

He hadn't thought anything of it that night at the pub when he'd had a few too many. Mostly cos Trent had turned up like a dodgy twenty-pound note with a pocketful of cash, and if there was one way to dull the disappointment of seeing that bastard at Zig's side, it was by letting him buy the drinks.

Trent and Zig seemed to spend a lot of time together—with Trent working for Zig's dad—and while it was daft to be jealous, Trent was older than them, around twenty-five, and he had broad shoulders and proper muscles, not skinny, gangling limbs like Si. Trent's light brown hair was always perfectly gelled in place, and even Si could tell he dressed sharp. It was hard not to feel a bit inadequate, next to him.

Well, until the bloke opened his mouth and reminded the world what a knob he was.

He'd been having a dig that night, Trent had, saying it was bollocks how builders walked away with hundreds of thousands for, basically, a heap of bricks piled on top of each other. Like any toddler could do it if they had the muscle.

Of course, Si had jumped in to say, hang about, there's more to it than that. And yeah, he'd made a point of listing all the skilled labour that went into building a house, but he'd also gone on about the cost of materials. The copper piping, the tools, the fittings.

He'd had a fair few pints by then, so it was all hazy in his memory, but hadn't Trent asked outright what they had on-site right now? Right *then*, rather, seeing as it wasn't there no more. And hadn't he waited until Zig had gone to get a round in to ask about it?

Si could believe Trent had ripped off Adam's dad— Shit, was that where he'd got the cash for all them drinks he'd been buying? Some other poor bastard he'd done over? Si felt sick.

Oh gods. He was gonna have to tell Zig. Tell him he reckoned his mate might be a criminal. And what about Zig's dad? Was he involved too? The things Zig said about his dad, off-hand comments made with a laugh or dark mutterings after he'd been drinking, they'd all made him sound like someone Si wouldn't want to meet.

Sometimes he wondered if Zig was scared of his dad, but that couldn't be right, could it? Scared of his own dad? And yeah, Si knew some dads were bastards, but not anyone related to people he *knew*, right? And definitely not someone like Zig. Half the time Zig talked about his dad like he actually admired him, and anyone *Zig* admired had to be someone pretty special, right?

Nah, all the negative stuff was just cos Zig's dad didn't like him being gay. Had to be. And it wasn't like that was unusual, was it? Dads were often funny about that.

Chapter Twelve
Si

Six years ago

Si waited to drop the bombshell until the next time he saw Zig. It wasn't the sort of thing you could put in a text, was it? *Btw, ur mates a wrongun. :-)* They'd arranged to go down the pub on Saturday night. Si had told Zig he wouldn't be around to go clubbing, with Adam home, and Zig had seemed happy enough to join them in Peckham, rather than go anywhere more exciting.

Si's stomach fizzed with nerves as he and Adam strolled down the street to the Dog and Duck. He'd have to get Zig on his own somehow, and tell him his suspicions about Trent. The first bit shouldn't be hard, at least. Adam was a good mate about giving them couple time.

Guilt churned. Should Si have said something about it to Adam? To his dad? 'Fessed up, that his were the loose lips that'd sunk all them ships? The police hadn't come up with any leads on the theft from the site.

No. He didn't *know* anything, did he? Just had a hazy memory of running his mouth off in the pub, that was all. But Zig deserved to know about it, so he could be on his guard, in case Trent tried to drag him into anything dodgy.

They made their way into the bar and grabbed a couple of pints and a table.

It wasn't long after that Zig came through the door, looking fucking gorgeous in his leather jacket, the red tips of his dark hair falling softly on the collar. Si's heart jolted and then plummeted. Trent was right behind him, a smirk on his lips and his hair gelled to rigid perfection.

Si reckoned Adam would be well pissed off, but he wore an odd smile as he greeted them. "All right, Zig? Trent? What are you drinking?"

There was a flicker of some emotion Si couldn't identify on Zig's face—just for a moment—and then he smiled. "Nah, I'll get 'em. Usual?" He glanced down at Adam and Si's half-empty pint glasses.

"We're good, ta," Adam said curtly, his eyes still on Trent.

Trent pulled out a chair and sat down. "All right, Si?" he asked, pointedly ignoring Adam.

"Yeah, I'm good." Si paused awkwardly. "Uh, you?"

"Peachy."

"Been busy lately?" Adam put in.

Trent looked at him sharply. "I'm always busy. Some of us have a living to earn."

"My dad had a break-in at the site. Maybe you heard about it?"

"No." Trent's tone was bland, conversational. "Lose much?"

Adam snorted. "Like you don't know."

The look got sharper. "Meaning?"

"I think you know what I mean."

Si put down his pint. "Lads . . ." Accusing Trent directly hadn't been part of the plan.

Trent leaned forward. "I think you'd better explain yourself, Adam Merchant. So's I don't get the wrong idea. Wouldn't want that, would you?"

Si didn't want *any* of this. "Adam, mate, you can't—"

Adam cut him off and spat at Trent, "Funny how Dad never had any trouble until *you* showed up on the scene."

"Scene? What fucking scene? Not like I'm one of your dad's bloody grunts, is it? What, am I not allowed to come out for a pint with my mate and his bloke?" He leaned back as Zig plonked a shot glass on the table in front of him.

"Got you a double, Trent. Cos I'm generous like that," Zig said, sliding into the seat next to Si.

"Cheers." Trent raised the glass and took a hefty swallow. "Hope you said hi to Ems for me."

Zig grinned. "Course I—"

"We hadn't finished talking," Adam cut in.

Si's heart sank. "Don't you think—"

"Hadn't we?" Trent's face hardened. "I ain't got nothing more to say about it."

"No? I reckon you could tell us plenty more."

At Si's side, Zig had stiffened. "Hey, Adam—"

It was like neither Si nor Zig was there, as Trent put his glass down. "You might want to rethink that. A bloke could get into trouble throwing around wild accusations."

Zig laughed nervously. "Oi, nobody's accusing nobody of nothing." Which was rich, seeing as he hadn't been there for most of the conversation, and Adam very definitely *was* accusing Trent of stuff, not that he actually had any evidence. So, what the hell was he hoping to achieve? Si felt sick.

Zig's hand crept into his, and he clutched it like a lifeline.

Adam's face had gone a harsh, blotchy red. "Are you threatening me?"

Trent sneered. "Just saying it how it is."

Adam picked up his pint glass, paused, then slammed it back down onto the table. A small puddle of beer sloshed out. He stood. "I'm not staying here. Si, you coming?"

Zig's grip on Si's hand tightened.

"I . . ." Torn between his best mate and the bloke he loved, Si gestured helplessly.

"Fine. I'll see you back home." Adam turned and strode away.

"Go on, run home to daddy," Trent shot derisively at Adam's retreating back. "Fuck it. I'm off too."

Zig's hand shot out and grabbed him by the arm. "Oi. He's Si's mate."

"Did I say I was going after him? Jesus. Just gonna have a word with Ems at the bar, then I'm heading up west."

Si tried to fight down the feeling of nausea that mingled uneasily with the relief he felt on seeing Trent head to the bar and not the door. Had Zig really thought Trent might, what, go after Adam and beat him up? Si opened his mouth, but Zig beat him to it.

"What the hell was that all about? What's Adam got against Trent?" Zig's tone was abrupt.

Si darted a wary glance to where Trent was leaning on the bar, trying yet again to chat up Emma the barmaid, judging by the smirks he was giving her and the pissed-off looks he was getting back. "He's got this idea Trent might have had something to do with the site thefts."

Mismatched eyes narrowed. "Oh? Why's he think that?"

Was that guilt? Si's gut twisted. "I dunno. Thinks he's dodgy."

Zig laughed. "He's that, all right."

Si couldn't tell if that was disapproval or admiration. The pain in his gut got worse. "And, well, he did get me talking about the site and that the other night. When you was off getting the drinks in."

"He did, did he?" Zig wasn't laughing now.

"Why do you hang around with him?" Si blurted out. "If he was my mate, I'd tell him to piss off."

"He's not a bloke you want to get on the wrong side of. You might wanna tell Adam that. And I've gotta work with him, haven't I?"

Si frowned. "Thought you were working in that shop?"

"Yeah. I am. But sometimes I have to do stuff for my dad. And Trent works for him. So I've gotta keep him sweet." He flashed a smile.

"Not too sweet, I hope," Si muttered, the jealousy he'd tried to drown resurfacing briefly.

"Course not." Zig slung his arm around Si's waist. "Come on, let's leave this shithole and I'll keep you sweet as you want."

As they left the pub, Si couldn't help asking, "So what is it you and Trent do for your dad? You've never said."

Zig kissed him on the neck. "This and that. Come on, I'm horny."

It wasn't easy, but Si disengaged himself. "You always say *this and that*. What does that mean?"

Zig stood there, looking at him, his arms folded. "You want to do this now? Fine. He buys and sells stuff. Well, sells it, anyhow." He grinned cheekily.

Si's blood ran cold. "Stuff that don't belong to him? Like they copper pipes and all from the site? What was stole from Adam's dad?"

"Jesus, your accent sometimes. Oi, don't look at me like that. I never said it was Adam's dad's stuff. Dad and Trent, they don't tell me everything they get up to. Anyway, so what if it was? He'll claim it on the insurance, get his money back, and then everyone's happy."

Si didn't reckon Mr. Merchant was ever gonna be happy about having his stuff nicked. And anyway— "What about the insurance company?"

"Who gives a fuck about them? They're minted. Stick it to the man, love."

Si was pretty sure that wasn't how insurance companies worked. If people made claims, they put up premiums, didn't they? So stealing stuff was sticking it to *everyone*. His heart plummeting, he tried to explain that to Zig.

Zig got hacked off with him. "You telling me that boss of yours ain't loaded anyway? He can stand to lose a few grand."

"But it's theft."

"Jesus, Si, grow up. Everyone's on the make. You telling me your boss don't fiddle his VAT? What goes around comes around."

Si couldn't believe it. Did Zig really think stealing was okay? No. No, he couldn't mean that, and he hadn't had nothing to do with whoever had ripped Adam's dad off.

He couldn't have.

But if he can't see there's anything wrong in stealing . . . What else did he think was okay? Gods, what else had Si been blind to, dazzled by good looks and a flirty smile?

Zig had his hands in his pockets, and his voice was strange—strained, almost—when he spoke again. "So, we good?"

They weren't, were they? They weren't good, and Adam wasn't living here no more, and Si had gone and ballsed everything up for Adam's dad by running his mouth off.

He could feel his heart tearing itself apart as he forced himself to say, like it didn't matter, "Uh, yeah. Fine. Know what though, I reckon I'll be heading back to Glastonbury soon. This being a brickie lark, it ain't me. Gonna go to college, get a trade. Might as well go home and save on rent, like."

Zig's face froze for a mo, then he gave his usual blinding smile. "Yeah, no worries. See you around if you're ever back this way again. It's been fun."

Then he strolled off into the night, leaving Si alone in the cold with his heart in pieces.

Chapter Thirteen
Zig

Present day

Sitting on Si's sofa—the man himself a solid, comforting presence beside him—Zig had been more than half planning to sneak out of the living room in the night and into Si's bed. The thought of those arms around him, that big body pressed against his, chasing away all the fears that'd followed him here from London . . . Well, Zig was only human, wasn't he? And it was just so *bloody* good to see Si again. Smiling at him, too. Hugging him, even. It was like the last six years and all the shit they'd brought him hadn't happened. Having a night or two—or maybe more—with Si wouldn't be the worst thing in the world, would it? Not so long as he kept his head. Kept reminding himself it wasn't gonna last.

But after Si went off to get those last beers, the mood had seemed to change, somehow. Had his mum been texting him again? No, he hadn't taken his phone into the kitchen. But *something* had made him avoid Zig's eyes after that, though.

It was like . . . It was like something had happened to make Si see Zig differently.

Like the night they'd broken up, six years ago.

Zig had been actively avoiding thinking about that night. He'd had enough pain to deal with in the present, since then. But now . . . now the memories were flooding back regardless of whether he wanted them to.

Shame twisted his gut in knots. Looking back, the blinkers finally off, it was no wonder Si hadn't wanted to be with him anymore. Zig could hardly believe the bloke had let him in the door when he'd turned up out of the blue, let alone allowed him to stay.

So, they'd sat in front of a *Taskmaster* rerun, drunk their beers—Si ended up leaving half of his—and said goodnight.

Zig spent the night on the sofa, cuddling a bloody cushion instead of Si's solid form. Fuck it. At least this way Zig didn't risk getting hurt when it inevitably went tits up, and Si deserved better than him, anyway. Maybe he'd leave in the morning. Carry on going west until he . . . What? Landed in the sea?

He fell asleep at last, and dreamt weird, watery dreams.

Si seemed in a better mood after he'd slept, which made one of them. "Mornin'," he called out cheerfully, plonking a mug on the table by Zig's head. "Still take your coffee black?"

"Perfect." Zig stretched, sat up, and reached for the mug. He'd been drinking it with milk lately, but life had taught him not to be fussy. He took a sip, and the rich texture and spicy aroma filled his mouth. "Oh, fuck me, that's good." Maybe it wasn't such a shitty morning, after all.

Si's grin was broad enough to shine through all the hair. "Proper stuff, that. From the Eden project in Cornwall. Mum and Dad brought some back from their holidays."

"Cornwall. That's even farther west than this place, right?"

"Almost as far west as you can get without getting your feet wet. Why? You planning on moving on?"

The grin was gone. He was disappointed. Zig was almost certain of it. His spirits rose with his caffeine levels. "Nah, thought I'd stick around here for a bit."

Si nodded, which, what the hell did that mean? Zig couldn't tell if he was pleased or pissed off by the news. "Crackin'. So, I gotta get off to work, but you can stay here, or you know, do what you want? Esme—that's me landlady—she'll let you in the flat if I'm not around."

That was fair enough. Zig wouldn't have trusted himself with a spare key, either. "Yeah, I'll have a wander. See what's what."

"Twenty minutes okay to get ready?"

"Plenty, long as I can use your shower?"

"Course you can. I'll grab you a towel." Si looked shy, somehow. "I'll introduce you to Esme on the way out. She owns the shop downstairs."

"Witchy stuff, right?"

"That's right. But don't go asking her about naked sabbats, or you'll end up with a bunch of incense sticks shoved where the sun don't shine."

Esme-the-landlady didn't look much like a witch to Zig. For a start, her hair wasn't long or dyed. It was neatly cut in a natural-looking blonde bob. Okay, yeah, she was wearing a black dress, but it was knee-length and figure-hugging—and she had plenty of figure to hug. With her smart heels, statement necklace, and subtle makeup, she looked like she'd be more at home in a boardroom than on a broomstick.

"Es? This is Zig. He's an old mate. From London."

Zig pushed down the stupid pang of hurt at *mate*, smiled, and stepped forward, putting out a hand. "Nice to meet you."

She left him hanging and raised an eyebrow. "Likewise, I'm sure. How long are you staying for?"

Cheers for the effusive welcome, missus. "Not sure. Never been round this way before. Gotta see all the sights and that."

"Oh, you're here for the *sights*, are you?"

Zig's smile didn't waver. He made sure of that. "And to look up my old mate, Si." *See? I can use the m-word too.*

"Si?" She cocked her head, her brow faintly furrowed.

Beside him, Si, well, sighed. "It's me name, innit? Short for Simon." He turned to Zig. "Course, she knows me as—"

"Mr. Greczik," Esme interrupted him with a knowing look. "We're very formal here. So what should I call you, Mr. . .?"

"Call me Zig." He wasn't gonna play this game. What did she need his surname for, except to stalk him online?

"Oh, really?" She folded her arms and placed a finger on her chin. "You know, it's been a long time since I met a Zigmund. Quite an unusual name around here."

Si snorted. "It ain't short for Zigmund. It's a nickname, Es. Or should I say, *Ms. Vile.*"

Zig narrowed his eyes. Was Si taking the piss? Was she? "Talk about your unusual names. *Vile?*"

"There were over two hundred of us in the county in the 1881 census. Almost common." She said it smugly.

Right. "Course, could be worse. I used to know a bloke whose surname was Smelly. Everyone called him Fartface. You get any bad nicknames at school?"

"No, I can't recall that I did." Zig had to hand it to her: she had the best poker face he'd seen in a long time. "And I'm not surprised your friend decided to lose touch."

Not a friend. If Zig saw Fartface again, he'd cross the street to avoid him, and not only because the bloke had developed a vicious temper and a fondness for knives. "His loss." He smirked.

Si burst out laughing. "I can find some old boxing gloves if you two really wanna have a go at it. Es, give him a break."

Esme's smile made her look like a different woman. A much less scary one. "Oh, you know how I like to tease. Zig, welcome to our humble abode. I hope you'll enjoy your stay. And if you trash the place, remember, I *am* a witch."

"Uh, thanks? No worries. You won't know I'm here."

"Oh? That'll be a shame. It's always nice to have something pretty to look at."

Zig gave her his best smile, and a knowing look. "Could say the same."

She raised one perfectly groomed eyebrow. "Really? Does your mother know you flirt with her contemporaries?"

Si was making frantic *stop* gestures.

"No," Zig said. It came out a bit harsher than he meant it to.

"No," Si agreed firmly, giving Esme a meaningful look.

Oh. He'd told Si his mum was dead, hadn't he? It'd felt true enough, at the time.

Esme clearly had a degree in reading expressions, cos her face fell, then softened. "We all have our sorrows. Glastonbury can be very healing, you know."

"I'm fine," Zig said, because he *was*. Why would he worry about a mum who'd walked out when he was four and who hadn't cared enough to keep in touch?

Maybe she was dead, at that. It wasn't like he'd know.

"I'm glad to hear it," she said warmly. "Now, I know Scr— Mr. Greczik has to go to work, so if there's anything I can do for you?"

Si shuffled his feet. "Yeah, I'd better be off, but I could meet you for lunch? Oh— Hang about. I said I'd see Adam and Sash, and Corin'll probably be there too."

"Sounds a bit crowded to me," Zig said quickly. He wasn't that keen on seeing Adam again. He was pretty sure the bloke had never liked him, and, well, these days he felt kind of guilty about what he'd done, back in the day.

Fucking moral compass.

"I'll see you back here tonight." Zig smiled brightly and strode out of the shop.

Right. Eight hours to kill in the freezing bloody cold.

He could do that.

Chapter Fourteen
Si

Rather than going out on jobs, Si was working in the shop today, which was good. Kept him busy dealing with customers. Stopped him thinking too much about Zig.

He cut a key for a customer and she left with a smile, a chill gust of wind sweeping into the shop in her wake. There was a right nip in the air today. Was Zig hanging out in a café somewhere, keeping warm? Or was he out and about on the tourist trail? Si wouldn't have reckoned he'd give a monkey's about Glastonbury's mystical sites—then again, he wouldn't have reckoned Zig would want to watch *Doctor Who*, either. Perhaps he had changed.

Still seemed the same old Zig, though. A bit rougher around the edges, maybe. A bit more . . . not *cynical*, cos he'd had that in spades as long as Si had known him, but *knowing*, if that was the right term? When they'd been together, Si would've pissed himself laughing if anyone had called Zig naïve, but looking back, yeah, it'd been there, in that blinkered world-view he'd had, and that unquestioning obedience to his dad. He'd grown out of that, or life had knocked it out of him.

Was that why he'd had that—what had he called it?—that bust-up with his dad? Si couldn't be sorry about that. Maybe he was too ready to find excuses for Zig, but he'd wished more than a few times, over the years, that Zig hadn't been stuck in the sole care of a bloke who didn't have two morals to rub together.

And he'd been so young, back then. *Si* had been so young too—barely twenty—which was still two years older than Zig had been.

Everyone made mistakes when they were young, didn't they?

It made Si's heart beat faster to think about Zig—which just proved how bloody daft his heart was, cos hadn't it ended up in shreds the last time he'd got involved with Zig?

The *only* time. Not the *last* time, because there wasn't gonna be a next time. Or a this time. Whatever. Si was older now. Wiser. There were some blokes who breezed through life, never let nothing or no one touch them where it hurt, and that was fine. Si wasn't one of 'em, that was all.

And Zig *was*—Si could still remember his carefree smile as they'd split up, and Si's numpty of a heart twinged at the thought. So, they were just gonna be mates this time around.

Now his conscience socked him in the gut. Could he really forgive and forget the past? Mind, he didn't *know* Zig had done anything wrong. Not absolutely one hundred percent. Granted, it'd been pretty clear Zig's morals back then had been a bit, well, skewed . . . More like totally bent out of shape, if he was honest, but people changed, didn't they? Got older and wiser and all that bollocks.

Buggrit. So much for not thinking about Zig. Then again, maybe he *ought* to be thinking about Zig. Wondering what had brought him here, after six years of silence. A bad breakup, maybe? From some bastard who'd left him thinking fondly of his younger days with Si? Or was it something worse than that? Something that'd end up coming back to bite them both—

The bell on the door jangled, and Si found himself looking straight into his mum's face. She wasn't smiling.

Si's stomach sank. "Ullo, Mum." He tried to muster a smile.

"Don't you *Hello* me, young man. Don't think I haven't noticed you've been ignoring me."

"Mu-um. I'm at work. Thought you would be too."

She folded her arms. "Then you should answer your phone in the evening, shouldn't you?"

Si cringed inside at the thought that she'd taken time off because of him. "I was busy."

"Busy. With *That Boy.*" Si could hear the capitals. He hoped to gods none of the lads would come back from a job in time to see him getting his ear bashed.

"He's a grown man now, Mum. So am I, in case you ain't noticed."

"*Haven't.* And that changes nothing. Do you remember the year after you came back from London? Because I do. Thought you'd never smile again."

"I was a kid, weren't I? Things hit you hard at that age. It's fine now. Water under the bridge and all that."

"Why's he here?"

Si shrugged, not sure himself. "Passing through, thought he'd look me up." The bell jangled again, and a middle-aged bloke walked in.

Mum didn't seem to notice. "Passing through? So, he'll be moving on soon?"

"'Spect so. Mum, there's a customer waiting behind you."

Mum turned, probably with one of her patented death glares on her face, seeing as the customer took a step back. "You're not in a hurry, are— Oh, Peter, I didn't realise it was you. How are you?"

"Fine, fine." Whoever Peter was, his face and his voice were calling him a liar. "And no, no hurry."

Mum smiled in a way that had Si's heart plummeting to his boots. "No, you go ahead. Simon, I'll speak to you *later.*"

Her tone made it clear that turning off his phone again wouldn't be an option. Not unless he fancied repercussions on a scale that'd make him long for the days when he only had to worry about Mum embarrassing him at work.

After his harrowing morning courtesy of his nearest and dearest, Si half considered begging off his lunch with Sasha and the others. He could nip back home instead. See if Zig was there. And then Si wouldn't have to say anything about him to Adam and Sash and risk more disapproval.

Right. Cos avoiding them for however long Zig was staying, that'd make perfect sense and in no way cause them to wonder if he'd lost his flippin' mind. Or go absolutely ballistic on him—and probably Zig—when they found out the truth.

Si dithered so long that he was the last one to get to Sasha's tattoo studio: Furious Ink. Then again, seeing as how Adam worked there too, it was only Si and Corin who had to travel—

"Scratch? You in there, mate?" Adam waved a hand in front of Si's face.

Si reared back like a startled sheep. "Oi, where else would I be?"

"Off with the fairies, by the looks of you," Sasha said, arching both of her ink-dot eyebrows. "Everything all right?"

"Fine. Smashin'. Why wouldn't it be? You all good?"

"Yeah, we're good." That was Adam. Corin, his bloke, who was sitting on the little sofa in the window with his mouth wrapped around a doorstep sandwich, waved.

Sasha gave Si a pointed look. Then she sighed. "What happened to that bacon butty you promised me? Cos if it's in your pocket, it's gonna be squished."

"Bollocks." He had promised, hadn't he? "I'll get it now. Sorry." It wasn't like he'd remembered his own lunch, neither. "You want anything, Adam? Corin?"

"Not for me, ta." Adam was frowning.

Bollocks.

Corin swallowed audibly. "I may not be here when you get back—Got a meeting scheduled. I just dropped in to say hi. We'll have to catch up another time." He smiled like all them undercurrents were washing right over his head.

Bollocks, bollocks, bollocks. Now Si was gonna be left with a suspicious Sasha and Adam, and no one to distract them from him.

"Right, I'll be back in a jiff," he said, and fled.

On the way down the street to the Breezy Moon Café, Si thought furiously. Maybe he could make up his own urgent appointment? Drop the goods and run?

Nah, if he played it cool, he'd be *fine*. They'd have forgotten all about it by the time he got back.

If they didn't spend the entire time he was gone talking about him, that was. Shit. Si quickened his pace.

Twenty minutes later, he breezed back into Furious Ink with his arms full of food. "All right, my lovers? Sasha, my sweet, I got you a bacon butty and one of them chocolate whirl things you like, to say sorry for forgettin'. Adam, I got you and Corin some spekulatius, cos they're doing 'em special for Christmas."

Sash and Adam looked up. Was it just Si, or did their smiles look a bit forced? True to his word, Corin had disappeared.

"Cheers, mate," Adam said easily enough. "I'll take them round to Corin's tonight."

"Yeah, thanks, Scratch." Sasha grabbed her butty hungrily.

Si perched on the desk and opened up his own bag to take a bite from his jumbo sausage roll.

Then he thought of all the Freudian whatsits of *that* particular choice, and put it down again. "Enough brown sauce for you, Sash?"

Mouth full, she gave him a thumbs-up.

Adam had finished eating, which unfortunately meant he had his mouth free for talking. "Listen, about earlier . . . Me and Sash couldn't help noticing something's up."

Bollocks.

"Are your mum and dad okay?"

Guilt stabbed Si right where his jumbo sausage would have been if he hadn't lost his appetite. "They're fine. Sorry. It's nothing to worry about. Honest. Just had a visit from someone we used to know, that's all." *Shit.* He'd meant to say *I* used to know.

Adam cocked his head. "Yeah? Who's that, then? Not one of the lads from London, is it?" He smiled.

"Uh . . . kinda? 'S Zig," Si muttered, giving up.

Adam's face went stonier than the abbey ruins. "Zig," he said flatly. "What's he doing here?"

"Told you. Come for a visit." Si stared at his sausage roll. It was nice of Adam to get concerned, course it was, but Si really wished he'd drop it.

Sasha put down her bacon butty, a smear of sauce on her chin. "He's the one you told me about, isn't he? The one who—" She darted a glance at Adam and fell silent.

Si's heart was beating double-time. He'd told her *everything*, when he'd come back to Glastonbury, and they'd become friends. Way before she'd met Adam.

"The one who hurt him so bad he hasn't been out with anyone since," Adam told her angrily, turning to Si. "That's what you told me: you left your heart in London."

And that was all Adam knew, wasn't it? Si hadn't been able to bring himself to tell Adam the rest. All he'd said was that they'd split up, and he'd let Adam assume Zig had dumped him for someone better.

"Why didn't you tell him to piss off?" Adam demanded.

Si shrugged. Tried to make his tone sound light. "It's been years, ain't it? Gotta forgive and forget."

"Bugger that," Sasha said harshly.

Adam sent her a startled glance. "You know him too?"

"Only what Scratch told me about him. Which was plenty." She narrowed her eyes at Si. Then she hurried over to hug him. "Babe, we don't want you to get hurt again."

Si wondered what she'd seen in his expression. And if she realised she'd wiped sauce on his Abbey Locksmiths shirt. He forced a smile. "I'll be fine. Big boy, ain't I? Now, are we all on for Friday night at the Prince of Wales?"

Adam gave him a dark look. "Is Zig going?"

"Dunno." Si shrugged, hoping it looked natural. "Dunno if he's staying that long."

Adam grunted, which as an answer wasn't all that helpful.

"I'll be there," Sasha said. "If he's still around, I wouldn't mind having a word with your Zig."

Si winced internally. "Yeah, reckon he'd love to meet you and all." He coughed, forcing himself to sound more cheerful as he went on. "Hey, Sash, you heard anything about the band they got playing this week?"

She smiled sweetly. "Only what you told me last Friday."

Bugger. He had, hadn't he? "Right, right. Forgot it was gonna be them." He took a big bite of his sausage and got out his phone, cos he had no interest in seeing whatever significant looks Sash and Adam were exchanging right now.

It wasn't until Adam nipped out back to the loo that Si got to talk to Sasha alone.

He leaned in close and kept his voice low. "Sash, that stuff I told you about Zig. About what I reckon he done for his dad, back in the day. You can't tell Adam. He'd hit the flippin' roof."

"People who can't do the time shouldn't do the crime."

"I don't know for certain if he did, all right? And he was a kid back then. Doing what his dad told him to. He's a different bloke now."

"Is he?"

Uncertainty stabbed Si in the chest. Because Zig was . . . Well, he was Zig, wasn't he? A little older, maybe, but . . . "He says he don't work for his dad no more. Gone legit, like." Okay, so Zig hadn't exactly said that, but then he'd never actually admitted to anything criminal neither, so it balanced out, right?

"And you believe him?" Sasha sighed. "You want to believe him." She said it flatly. "Babe, have you got any reason to think he's not gonna hurt you again? What's he here for, after all this time?"

Si screwed up his face. "I think . . . I think something's happened. Something that shook him up. Dunno what, though."

"He's in trouble?"

"I didn't say that. Could be that bust-up with his dad." Except Zig had said it'd been years, hadn't he? "Or, I dunno, he had a bad breakup?"

"So you're gonna let him rebound onto you?"

"No! It's not like that. Not this time. We're just friends. Catching up. I'm not daft, Sash," he added. "I broke up with *him*, remember?"

"Yeah, but not until he did something really shit. Gonna wait for that this time too?"

"I told you, I don't reckon he had nothing to do with robbing Adam's dad." Shit. Why did he have to go and tell her his suspicions about Zig?

"Ripped off plenty of other people though, most like." Sasha's face softened, and she grabbed him by both arms. "I don't want you getting hurt," she said in that little-girl voice he almost never heard from her.

Yeah. That was why. "You don't have to worry. I'm on me guard. I'm not gonna let things go too far."

She frowned. "How far have they got already?"

"They haven't!" Si blurted, then cast a worried glance towards the back of the studio. Adam hadn't emerged yet, for reasons Si didn't want to speculate about. "Told you, I'm being a mate. Letting him stay for a while. That's all."

"Right." Her tone said she wasn't sure she believed him. "You see that it stays that way."

Chapter Fifteen
Zig

Zig wandered down what passed for a high street in Glastonbury, although it was missing all the usual chain stores. Instead, there were more of the witchy-type shops he'd seen last night, all done up for the season. The vintage clothing store was all right—reminded Zig of Camden—but who the hell bought the crystals and dreamcatchers and other mystic stuff? Was that what the locals were into, or was it all for the tourists? And did anyone actually buy incense, when they could walk through town and get a lungful of the stuff for free?

On the corner, there was a bloke with feathers in his top hat selling stuff out of a handcart. Zig strolled closer. Wands. He was selling wands. Zig gave a half-despairing laugh. Jesus, what he wouldn't give for a way to magic all his problems away. Still, he should be safe here, shouldn't he? No reason for anyone back in London to guess he'd come here.

A couple of women bustled past, one of them wearing long skirts and an honest-to-God cloak, like she'd stepped out of *Lord of the Rings*. Zig turned to watch her, and noticed nobody else did, although one or two looked at *him* funny. Like he was the weirdo, for staring.

Huh. She was probably a lot warmer than he was in his jeans and leather jacket. Maybe he ought to get himself one of them cloak things. If anywhere had shops that sold 'em, it'd be here. Zig shoved his hands into his pockets and wandered on, smiling at a Yorkshire terrier that scurried over to sniff at his ankles. "All right, mate?"

"Merlin!" The dog's owner, a middle-aged woman in wellies, pulled him in firmly by his lead. "Sorry about him."

"Hey, no worries." He flashed her a grin, and she blushed and hurried on.

Glastonbury, Zig realised a moment later, was full of dogs. Every second pedestrian seemed to have a dog on a lead, and half the shops had their own doggy sales assistants keeping the humans company from a basket by the till. Dogs of all shapes and sizes trotted briskly along the streets, breath steaming in the chill air. Zig was amazed the streets weren't knee-deep in dog shit, but it seemed people were a bit more diligent about picking up after their pets than in his neck of the woods.

His *old* neck of the woods. Zig's throat was tight. Would he ever go back to south London? Could he?

He'd spent his whole life there— Well, give or take a few years of involuntary banishment. And now he'd cut himself off from the place for God knew how long. Would it have been better to stay and face what was coming, instead of running away? When he'd packed a bag and hopped on that train, he hadn't thought about what it would mean long-term.

Then again, staying might have had long-term consequences too. Zig didn't know how much his dad knew, or guessed, about who'd landed him inside, but he'd told Ani that Zig owed him. Maybe it was simply a *You ungrateful child* sort of thing, but would Dad be bothering to track him down if that was the case? Zig shivered. It wasn't like Dad had ever been violent, exactly. He'd never been the sort to lash out for no reason. But when there *was* reason ... well, that was a different matter.

As for Trent, if *he* knew what Zig had done, God help him.

Fuck it. Sod the long term; Zig would be happy if he survived the short term with both kneecaps intact. He looked around and saw he'd strayed into a residential area. *Great.* He hadn't been paying attention to where he was going, and now he'd run out of town without realising it.

There was a brown tourist sign pointing the way to the tor, though, so Zig followed it out of a mix of one part mild curiosity to nine parts wanting to have the certainty of a destination in mind. The path led up steeply through a sort of country version of an alley, with trees and bushes on either side that at least cut off the wind. Round a corner, and he could finally see where he was going: the tor and its stone tower, not on the top like he'd thought but set off to one side, were visible beyond a big wooden gate. Zig pushed through it.

There was a homeless person settled in on the other side of the gate. They were bundled up against the cold in a sleeping bag and most likely several layers of clothing underneath, cos the face that poked out the top of all that bulk was thin, with delicate features topped by a riot of loose curls. They had white skin, like most people round here seemed to. Zig had heard most places were pretty un-diverse compared to London but it still felt weird and somehow old-fashioned, like a TV show from the last century.

"Spare any change?" the homeless person intoned, like the words had lost all meaning cos they'd said them so often.

Zig chucked them a few quid he probably couldn't spare, as a vicious gust of wind blew icicles down his neck. He hunched his shoulders, wishing again that he'd worn something warmer. The countryside had really opened up, this side of the gate, and there were no cosy cafés to duck into. "Shit, mate, you gotta find a better place to sleep. You'll freeze your bollocks off up here. Or tits, whatever," he added, cos it wasn't obvious whether or not they were of the bollock-owning persuasion.

They shrugged. "Don't sleep here in winter. I go down the town."

"Hostel?"

"Nah. There's places round the backs of shops. It's sheltered, but you're not in everyone's face, so the feds don't care. You from London?"

Zig froze. "What's it to you?"

They drew back, eyes wary. "Nothing. Just, you don't dress like you're from round here. And you talk like you're auditioning for *EastEnders.*"

Sod it. Way to fucking go, Zig. Frighten the homeless person half your size. "Sorry. Didn't mean to come over all heavy. I'm here for a fresh start, you know? Don't wanna think about where I came from."

The tension went out of their bundled-up frame, and they nodded. "I get that. I'm Kai. Same."

Zig hesitated, but Jesus, it wasn't like he was going around giving a false name to anyone else who asked, was it? "Zig. So, you been here long, then?"

"Since the summer. Came for the festival, then I thought I'd see what the town was like. Never left." They paused, then spoke in a rush. "You got somewhere to sleep? Cos there's a shelter—"

"I'm good, cheers. Staying with a mate. For now. When he gets fed up with me kipping on his sofa I guess I'll have to get me own place. Need a job for that, though." Zig's mouth rattled on while his brain listened in faint shock. Was that really what he was planning? To make a life here, in this tiny, tiny town? There weren't even any decent shops, just a load of hippie stuff and blokes selling wands on the street. Christ knew what the nightlife was like, if there was any.

Would Si get fed up with him? Zig snorted. *Course he fucking will.*

Shit. Yesterday, Zig had been totally focused on how Si might react when a years-ago ex turned up like a runny turd on his doorstep. He hadn't stopped to consider how long any undeserved welcome might actually last.

No wonder Si hadn't responded to his come-ons last night. Hah, maybe he was at the flat now, changing the locks . . . Except he didn't need to do that, did he? He hadn't given Zig a key.

"You all right?" Kai's voice broke into his reverie of despair. "I got a sandwich someone gave me if you're hungry."

Zig shook himself. "Nah, I'm good. Cheers, though. Things on me mind, that's all. Right. This tor's not gonna climb itself, eh? You keep warm." He flashed a smile and headed on up the path.

You wanker. Kai was probably gonna be down in town later warning all their mates about this mentally vulnerable bloke they'd met on the tor. *Comes off as a bit of an arse but he's probably harmless. Still, best to steer clear.*

There were sheep in the field, looking fluffy and weirdly clean for animals that slept outside. Thank God it wasn't cows. Zig had seen cows close up on a school trip to a farm once, and they were big bastards. One of his mates had told him they trampled people to death given half a chance. Which, fair dues, if *he'd* been kept in a field and had half his family slaughtered for meat, Zig would probably want to kill a few people too.

The sheep didn't look like they cared much, though, cos they kept chomping down grass as he carried on up the path. All except one bugger that stood and watched him all the way to the next gate, like it reckoned he had a butcher's knife stashed in his jeans.

Zig shuddered as a familiar image flashed through his head: the old bloke from that last job. *Chill, mate. No knives on me.* Ever.

On the other side of the next gate was a tree, its branches bare except that the lower ones were strung with ribbons. Was that for Christmas? Zig trod closer, careful not to get his Converse covered in mud. The ribbons were all colours of the rainbow, some of them faded and well tattered, like they'd been up for months. So, not for Christmas. What then?

There weren't any handy notice boards to tell him, so he shrugged and carried on up the path. It'd got even steeper, with steps cut into it. He was on the tor proper now, and he'd have said the end was in sight except the tower had disappeared somehow, so there was probably a fair way to climb yet.

Zig rounded a corner and stopped for a breather at a rough wooden bench. The wind had picked up with a vengeance, and his hair whipped into his face with stinging force. The air smelt damp and earthy, no trace here of the sweet incense that suffused the town.

He could literally see for miles. The red roofs of Glastonbury lay below him, huddling together as though they were as cold as he was. Then there were green fields, big as the town itself, with other towns visible beyond. It was like looking at Google Earth. It felt weird, knowing that the bloke with the wands and the girl with the cloak were down there somewhere. Si, too, doing his locksmithing. Fixing people's stuff, or driving around between jobs, or whatever.

He took a last look at the view, his eyes starting to water from the wind, and hurried on up the path. The tower had come back into sight, and with it, a few other idiots who'd come up the tor on such a bollock-freezing day. Course, they had big coats and hats and scarves on. Lucky bastards.

Zig sped up his pace, and the exertion made him at least a little warmer by the time he reached the tower. It was a lonely thing—old as fuck, around three or four storeys high—and he could see right through the arched doorways in front and back. He guessed there had been a church or something it'd been attached to, back in the mists of time, but no trace of that remained. People in the Middle Ages or whatever must have been really desperate for building materials to trek up here and carry the stones all the way down. Zig stepped through the doorway, trailing his fingers along the rough surface of the arch, feeling the rasp against his skin.

Inside the tower, a bearded guy in a woollen hat with a long, trailing pom-pom leant against the wall, a guitar in his hands. A young woman, her hands shoved deep into the pockets of a bright, shapeless orange coat, stood beside him as he struck up a few chords. Zig halted. Was he intruding?

The man glanced over at him and smiled. "Hope we're not disturbing you."

Zig blinked. "Nah, carry on, mate. Although I gotta say, you ain't gonna earn much busking up here."

Both of them laughed. "We're not here for money. It's about connecting with the energies of the tor."

Was this guy some kind of time traveller from the 1960s?

Saving Zig from having to find a reply, the guitarist launched into a tune. It sounded folksy—the sort of thing that would have got him laughed out of the pubs Zig knew in London. If the hat hadn't done that already. Up here, though, there was nothing ridiculous about it. It sounded fitting, somehow. The woman began to sing along, her voice high and lilting, with lyrics Zig couldn't quite understand. Something about a woman and her son, maybe, and . . . shapeshifters? It felt like the retelling of a tale all the listeners were supposed to know already, only Zig didn't.

Maybe there were books on that kind of thing in town?

When the song finished, Zig wasn't sure if he was supposed to applaud or not. Before he could make up his mind, a couple of people strode up to the couple and clapped them on the back. The newcomers were bundled up in scruffy padded jackets and hand-knitted hats. Zig hadn't noticed them come into the tower.

"Classic, mate," one of them said in an accent more like Zig's than anything local.

The guitarist grinned in response. "Good to see you. How's it going? Will you be coming up here for the solstice celebrations?"

"Course. Not gonna miss a chance to get me bodhrán out, now am I?"

Zig didn't like to speculate what the bloke's . . . boughron? . . . might be, or why he was so keen to whip it out on the top of the tor. He turned to go but felt a hand on his arm.

It was the singer. Close up, he could see she was older than he'd first thought, with fine lines around her mouth and eyes. "You should come too, if you're around. Lots of music. It's a great celebration of life and the cycles of nature."

"Uh, thanks?"

"We'll be up here to greet the rising sun. There's a real sense of community."

"Maybe I'll give it a go." Zig's tone was uncertain, but she still gave him a blinding smile before turning back to her friends.

He wasn't sure why she'd singled him out, as there were others around who'd presumably stood listening to the song. Still, solstice celebrations sounded cool, despite having to get up before sunrise. Better than Christmas, which was only about shops getting people to spend money they couldn't afford. And solstice was earlier than Christmas, right? He had a vague memory of reading something about it somewhere, and got out his phone to check with numbed fingers. Right. Twenty-first December. Much better date, if you asked him.

Maybe he'd see if Si was free that day and fancied a pre-dawn trek up the tor. If not, he could always come on his own. Or with Kai, if they were interested. Feeling a strange mix of excitement and nerves, Zig stood for a moment outside the tor, taking in the view, and then started out on the path back down.

Chapter Sixteen
Zig

Zig hadn't noticed it on the way up the tor—he'd had his back to it—but someone had stuck large, hand-drawn letters on the fence of the sheep field reading *GO WITH LOVE*. Like, not even advertising something. Simply wishing love to random strangers. Zig's stomach felt funny, looking at it.

He shook his head. *Get a grip.* It was probably hunger making him feel weird. It had to be lunchtime by now.

As if to prove it, Kai was eating their sandwich when he got down to the gate, and gave Zig a wave. Zig strolled over to them. "Not bad up there, innit? Got free entertainment and everything."

"Yeah, I saw Max and Leah going up. They're good, aren't they?" Kai smiled.

Zig nodded. "They were talking about the solstice. Thought I might come along to that."

"You should," Kai said enthusiastically. Then they frowned. "Better wrap up warmer, though."

"Too bloody right." Zig shivered. "I'm heading into town to warm up a bit. You gonna be okay here?"

Kai held up a takeaway cup from a coffee shop. "I'm good, ta."

"See you around, then." Hand on the latch of the gate, Zig paused and turned back. "You got a phone, mate?"

He got a wary look in return.

"Shit. Sorry. This ain't a come-on, and I ain't trying to shake you down. Just wanna give you my number. In case you need, I dunno, someone to talk to?" Zig cringed inside. Yep, Kai was definitely going to be having words with their mates about him. Something along the lines of, *Watch out for the sad lonely bastard.*

Kai brightened, though. "You can tell me it. I'll remember. Got a memory thing."

They were probably saying that to get rid of him, but Zig rattled off his number anyhow, then headed back down the path to town. He found a café on the high street, grabbed himself a bacon sandwich and a latte, and made them last, before checking his phone to see if anyone was trying to reach him.

No one was. It was equal parts a relief and really sodding sad.

After meandering round the town a bit more, Zig remembered he wanted a book of folktales and headed for the library. He liked libraries; they were warm, and nobody cared if you sat there for ages reading a book. Unlike bookshops, which understandably preferred you to buy the thing and bugger off home with it.

He found the library on a road off the high street, not far from a church with largish grounds in the centre of town. It was a modern, brick-built, flat-roofed building, with trendy round windows, and called itself a "hub," but the staff seemed welcoming enough.

Disappointingly, he couldn't find any books of local folktales. Maybe all the copies were out on loan, or had been stolen. Although, stealing would probably be bad karma or whatever people who were into that stuff believed in.

Course, technically speaking, *Zig* was into that stuff, and he didn't have a clue what he believed in.

Anyway, libraries always had plenty of classics. Since it was nearly Christmas, he probably ought to check out a Dickens to get in the mood, but fuck it, he was a rebel. Zig had a browse through the Thomas Hardies, ignoring *Tess* and *Jude*, cos who needed that depressing shit? He picked out *Under the Greenwood Tree*, another Christmassy book, and settled down for a reread.

"I'm sorry, but we're closing now, my lover." The soft voice jolted him out of the rural world of the Mellstock Quire and back into shitty reality.

"Uh, right. Sorry. I'll be on me way." Belatedly, Zig grinned cheekily to the middle-aged woman in a cardi.

She went pink, which was rich for someone who'd called him her *lover* with no sign of embarrassment. "Did you want to take the book home?"

"Uh, thanks, but I ain't got a card. Just visiting. Went to the tor today," he added, cos apparently he was a total saddo who was desperate for someone to talk to.

She brightened. "Oh? It's lovely up there, isn't it? Like you can see the whole world. Have you been to the Chalice Well? They do it up so nicely at this time of year."

"Next on me list," he promised, wondering what the hell a Chalice Well was. Si would know, he thought, and felt himself go pink as well. *Serves you bloody right.* "Well, cheers. You have a nice night, yeah?"

"And you." She sounded a little breathless.

Zig checked his phone as he sauntered out of the library and into the dark streets. Five o'clock. Would Si be finished with work yet? He searched *Glastonbury locksmith*, but it turned out there were way more than one and, like an idiot, he hadn't asked Si the name of the place he worked for.

And yeah, he could go back to Si's and get Esme to let him in, but . . . Fuck it, he was a coward. He didn't wanna face her without Si as a buffer.

He decided to go for a drink, ask if there were any jobs going, and turn up at Si's later. There was a pub a short way down the road, its lights warm and inviting, so he ducked inside. The place was pretty dead, so they probably weren't hiring, but he asked anyhow.

"Sorry, my lover," the girl behind the bar said with a look of genuine regret. "We're fully staffed."

Yep. He'd called it. Funny how the confirmation didn't make him feel any better.

"Have you asked at the Prince of Wales?" the barmaid went on. "I heard from my friend Immi they were looking for staff."

Zig's mood perked right up. "Yeah? Guess I'll head on over there. Cheers. You have a good night."

She beamed. "And you. Tell Ange that Chrissie sent you."

He quickly googled the Prince of Wales. It was the other end of town but, heh, there wasn't a right lot of town; it was only minutes away on foot.

Zig's phone took him down a side street, and there the Prince of Wales was, its white-painted front lit up yellow by a couple of carriage lamps and an old-fashioned streetlight. Inside, it wasn't exactly plush, with half the floor bare wood, but there was more of a buzz than there had been in the last place. Not bad, for early Thursday evening. Zig cast an eye around, then sauntered up to the bar.

The barmaid was middle-aged, with a fondness for henna and animal print, like she wanted to leave people with no doubt as to her profession. She certainly made Zig feel right at home, and he flashed her a smile.

She raised a cynical eyebrow, which made him feel even more at home. "What can I get you?"

"I'm looking for a lady called Ange."

The barmaid folded her arms. "Because?"

"Lovely young lady called Chrissie at the Isle of Avalon said you might be looking for staff."

"Got experience, have you?"

Well, he couldn't let that one go. "Oh, I got plenty. What kind of experience are you looking for?"

She snorted. "You're full of yourself, and no mistake."

"Everyone always tells me I'm full of something." Zig leaned on the bar and gave her his best grin.

She laughed aloud. "No argument there. I'm Ange."

"Zig."

"You working right now?"

"Nah. New in town."

"What brings a Londoner like you out west, then?"

"It's the accents. Can't get enough of people calling me *moi loverrr*." Zig laid it on thick, then hoped he hadn't overdone it.

She snorted. "Don't you go expecting that from me. Can you do weekends? That's Fridays as well."

"I'm easy."

"I've no doubt. Be here at five tomorrow, and we'll see how we go. It's minimum wage, mind, till you've been here three months, then an extra five percent if we keep you on. That okay with you?"

"Peachy," Zig said, and meant it. Fuck, was it really this easy? "How about a drink to seal the deal? Vodka and ice, and one for yourself?"

"Long as you're paying. And there's no drinking on the job."

"No problem." Zig laid a twenty on the bar with a smile.

She took it, filled his order, and gave him what looked like too much change for two drinks, but Zig didn't call her on it. He reckoned she knew what she was doing. He saluted quickly, and she nodded, turning to the next punter.

Zig eased his arse onto the last free barstool and savoured his vodka—the bite of the alcohol and the almost painful chill of the ice. *Fuck me, I've got a job.* He spent the time keeping an eye on the bar staff. There were two of them, both nearer his age than Ange's, and they were friendly and efficient. They wore Prince of Wales polo shirts, which meant he'd have to as well, but at least they were black with a discreet logo, not some cheap chest print that'd have him wincing at mirrors. Yeah. He could do this.

Chapter Seventeen
Zig

It was getting on for seven when Zig got back to Si's and rang the bell. The door opened sooner than he'd expected, like maybe Si had run down the stairs to get it.

"Zig!" Was that relief on Si's face? Hard to tell, behind the beard. "Was wondering where you'd got to. I'm making pasta for tea, that all right?"

"Course it is." He followed Si up the stairs. "Wasn't sure what time you'd be home, so I hit the pub on the way back."

"Yeah? Where'd you go?"

"Prince of Wales. You know it?"

Si's face split into a grin. "Course I do. Kind of me local, that place is. Go there most Friday nights."

"Yeah? Guess I'll be serving you drinks." At least there'd be one friendly face, then. And probably a few unfriendly ones right next to it.

"You— You gonna be working there?" Si's eyes were wide.

"Yep, unless I balls it up. Ange told me to turn up tomorrow."

"That's great!" Si's face did complicated things Zig couldn't interpret. "So . . . you're staying here, then?"

Well, shit. Zig was a bloody idiot for not realising how that had to look. "Yeah, but not *here*, here, right? I mean, I don't expect you to put me up long-term. Soon as I'm earning, I'll get meself a room somewhere."

Si blinked a few times. "You don't have to. You can stay here long as you want." Then he clammed up, like maybe he regretted what he'd said.

Which would be fair enough. "I'm not gonna take the piss. Hey, maybe you could ask around for me? See if there's anyone with a room going spare?"

"Maybe." Si frowned. "Think Adam's old place . . . but no, you don't wanna live there. Bunch of arseholes, them lot."

"Sounds like I'd fit right in." *Especially if you ask Adam.*

"No, you can do better than that. And like I said, no hurry, all right?"

"Well, cheers, mate." It made Zig feel weird. Like, warm inside, but also like he wanted to walk straight out the door again. Get away from this buff, older version of Si who was somehow still the same properly *good* bloke in his heart.

He wouldn't have said that if he knew what you'd done. Zig jumped as he realised Si had been talking again. "Sorry, mate, come again?"

"I asked what hours you're gonna be working?"

Zig shrugged, making an effort to appear normal. "Weekend evenings. Not sure about the rest. I'll find out tomorrow."

"That's band night, Friday. You'll be flat out, just to warn you."

"Eh, a little hard work never hurt anyone." At least being busy would stop him thinking too much.

Si smiled, and tension dropped out of his frame that Zig hadn't realised was there. "In that case, wanna chop some veg while I put the pasta on?"

"No problem. Got mad knife skillz, me."

"You can do the garlic, then. I hate them fiddly little buggers."

Zig didn't get the garlic chopped in record time, and it wasn't his neatest either, but to be fair, Si's vegetable knife hadn't just seen better days, it'd been bashed on the blade by them a few zillion times. "Babe, you gotta get some decent knives," he muttered, blinking as he diced the onion. "Did this one fall out of a Christmas cracker?"

"It was me gran's." Si's voice had a frown in it, and Zig looked up. Shit, had he hurt Si's feelings? "She got this fancy knife block and didn't want it no more. Blimey, I thought you was joking about them mad skills. You done kitchen work?"

"A bit, yeah. Didn't like the vibes, though, you know? Everyone acting like if the food don't go out perfect we're all gonna get strung up by our balls."

"Worked for Gordon Ramsay, did you?"

Zig laughed. "Christ, no. The wanker definitely saw him as a role model, though. Right, what else needs doing?"

It was good, cooking together. Fun. Zig hadn't often had that. Too often he'd been cooking for himself alone, bumping into annoying housemates all the time. There had been a girl he'd got on with at one houseshare, Ginny, and their schedules had matched enough to eat together half the time. But she'd moved up north with her bloke, and he hadn't seen her since.

Huh. He could have looked her up, maybe, when he was getting out of London. He hadn't thought of that. *Guess I know where I'll be heading if Glasto turns out to be a bust.* It should have been a relief, realising he had options.

It wasn't.

"You all right?" Si asked, looking up from the pan. "It's like you're miles away."

Zig grinned hastily. "I'm right here. Body and soul. Hey, any idea where I could get a book of local folktales? Library was fresh out of 'em."

"Yeah? Which one did you go to?" He ground some pepper into the pan, which smelled wicked, like an Italian restaurant.

Zig's stomach rumbled. "Uh, there's more than one? The one near that big church. Calls itself a hub."

"Oh, yeah, see, you'll want the Library of Avalon for folktales and all that. It's on the high street, up by Market Place? Back of the Glastonbury Experience. I mean, I ain't been in there much, but I heard it's where you go for all that mythical stuff." Si slid the contents of the pan onto two plates, and handed one to Zig.

They took them out to the living room and ate sitting companionably on the sofa.

"I saw that Glastonbury Experience place, but I thought it'd be some tourist thing. I'll have to check it out." Zig expected Si to ask why on earth he wanted books of folktales, but Si seemed to accept that was a normal thing to be interested in. It was nice. He ate another mouthful of pasta. "Fuck me, this is good. Family recipe?"

Si shrugged, a little pink. "I found it online. Mum's more into your traditional English stuff. So where else did you get to today?" he asked quickly, like he was keen to change the subject.

Zig didn't like to think why that might be. "She does do a mean bacon and eggs, your mum," he said lightly. "I went up the tor. Flippin' freezing up there. People were saying there's gonna be, like, celebrations for the solstice—you fancy going up for that?"

"Yeah, we could do that." Si's eyebrows shot up, but his cheeks were pinker than ever under the beard. "Would you believe it, I've never been? Always thought I oughtta but never got off me arse to do it."

Zig laughed. "Well, I lived in London all my life, but I ain't never been to Buckingham Palace. Or the Tower, or half the museums. You don't, do you, when it's local? So, you're okay with getting up there for dawn?"

"This time of year? No problem. You want me up there for 3 a.m. in the summer, mind, we might have some issues."

They ate contentedly for a minute or two. Zig felt bold enough to address the elephant in the room. "How was lunch with your mates?"

Si shoved a forkful of pasta into his mouth in the most obvious delaying tactic in the history of the universe.

So, he'd told Adam that Zig was here. And it hadn't gone down well. "Adam all right?"

Si swallowed. "Yeah, he's great. Sorry. He's got this new bloke, Corin. One of they computer wizards."

Good, that'll keep him happy and stop him worrying about me. "You say that like it's some arcane magic. I know you know how computers work."

"Yeah, but you ask him what he's been doing at work and it's like he's talking another language. Or worse, it's the same language, but all the words mean something different. But he's a good bloke. Got a brain condition. Prospo . . . prospag . . . Face blindness, that's what it is. Can't recognise people." Si cocked his head. "Be all right with you, mind. See, the way he explains it, he can see features, but he can't put them all together? But he'd know you, with that hair, and them eyes."

"At least they're good for something, then." Zig's tone was bitter, his dad's voice scathing in his head.

"I like your eyes." Si busied himself getting a precise combination of pasta, sauce, and veg on his fork.

"Yeah, right. Cos one blue and one brown looks so great. It's like wearing odd shoes. Never gonna see that catching on."

Si glanced up. "So, they're different. So what? Be a boring world if we were all the same. And it suits you. Being one of a kind." Then he turned his attention back to his food.

Zig's chest was oddly tight. Like someone was squeezing his heart out to dry.

Maybe he'd better start looking for a room somewhere else sooner rather than later.

That night, Zig was drifting off to sleep on the sofa when his phone vibrated. A flash of alarm jolted through him, and he quickly quelled it. Daft. There was no way Dad—or Trent—could know his number.

Course, Ani had his number . . . No. She wouldn't hand it out to anyone.

Fuck it. Zig grabbed his phone and thumbed it on, finding a text from an unknown number: *This is Kai. You at your mates place?*

Chest easing, Zig smiled and texted back, *Yep. Not sick of me yet. You somewhere warm?*

Im okay. Night :-)

Still smiling, Zig saved the contact. Then he switched off his phone and rolled over.

Chapter Eighteen
Zig

The next day, Zig headed down to the Avalon library. It was easy to find, now that he knew what he was looking for. The entrance was in a small courtyard off the high street, the tiny space adorned with flowerbeds and trees—bare now but promising colour and shade in summer. The building itself was of unknown age, at least to Zig: a hodgepodge of different bricks and stone that might have been patched together over centuries.

It was guarded by the statue of an oriental dragon five or six feet high. There were odd coins in its mouth, and in its coils. Was this like a wishing well? Or an offering to whatever spirits might be around here? Feeling daft, but doing it anyway, Zig put a pound coin at the base of the statue before heading through the low doorway into the library.

Inside, it definitely looked old: the floor was of flagstones, covered with rugs of varying size and pattern, and the white-painted ceiling was crossed by heavy black beams. Off to one side was a large wooden table with chairs arranged around it, where an old man sat engrossed in a book. Most of the chairs looked comfy and modern, but in a corner was a dark oak monstrosity with a tapestry cushion straight out of the Middle Ages. A desk with a computer and printer was occupied by a young brown-haired woman in what Zig was coming to think of as "Glastonbury" clothes—long skirt and a top that laced up the front. She was frowning at her screen, so he didn't like to interrupt her.

Unsurprisingly, bookshelves covered the walls and made inroads into the central space. Zig wandered over to the nearest one and glanced at the contents. Books on dowsing, magic, and astral projection. And Hermeticism, whatever that was. He browsed on, eventually coming to a section on mythology. Here, he found . . . not precisely what he was looking for, but close: books on local legends. Tales of King Arthur, Joseph of Arimathea, and some bloke he'd never heard of called Gwynn ap Nudd. He took a few of the more promising books back to the table and settled in to read.

It was Zig's first shift at the Prince of Wales that night. He made sure he got there early cos he wanted his new colleagues to know he wasn't a slacker. But not too early, cos he didn't want them to think he was a total suck-up. Starting at five meant he had to leave for work well before Si got home, which wasn't great. Si had promised to come to the pub during the evening, but he'd be with his mates, which . . . also wasn't great.

Sod it. It was what it was.

Ange was wearing a tight red dress tonight that showed off her ample curves, with lipstick to match. She seemed cautiously pleased to see him. "Right, then." She turned and raised her voice. "Finn? New boy's here."

A young, slender man with bleach blond hair and gauges in both ears put the bucket of ice he was carrying behind the bar and stepped briskly towards them. "Zig, right? Come this way and I'll get you a shirt."

Right. The polo shirt. Zig had turned up in a black button-up shirt, but he hadn't held out much hope of being allowed to keep on wearing it.

Finn watched him surreptitiously while he was changing, then looked away when Zig caught his eye.

Hah. Still got it. Although he hoped Finn wasn't gonna come on to him, cos that'd be awkward, what with Si—

What with Si not being in any way, shape, or form your boyfriend, you wanker, and not likely to be either. Shit. "You been working here long?" Zig asked, both to be friendly and to gauge staff turnover. But mainly to distract himself from his own thoughts.

"Couple of years," Finn said. "It's a good gig. Pay's all right once your three months are up, and Ange doesn't let anyone take the piss, you know?"

Zig laughed. "Yeah, I got that impression. What are the punters like? Do I need to worry about them getting rowdy? Any troublemakers I need to know about?"

Finn shook his head. "Ange won't stand for any of that. One strike and you're barred. But they're a great crowd here, for the most part. Just want to have a good time, you know?"

"That's locals, though, am I right? What about the tourists? Place like Glastonbury has gotta get plenty of them."

"Not so many round this time of year. And Glastonbury tourists . . . They're not, like, football hooligans or whatever. Worst you can say about most of 'em is that they make half a pint of cider last a night. They're not here to cause trouble. And yeah, festival time's a bit different, but most of them stay on-site over at Pilton." Finn smiled shyly. "You've recently moved here, then?"

"Yeah. How about you? You don't talk like a local."

"No, I grew up in the New Forest. You're from London, right?" Finn added.

Zig took a mo to answer as his head was filled with a mad picture of Finn growing up actually in a forest, like a squirrel or a hobbit or something. "Yeah. Lewisham. So, the New Forest, that's . . .?"

"Marchwood. That's my hometown, if you can call it a town. Near Totton." Finn side-eyed Zig and smirked. "Southampton? Heard of that one?"

"That's where all the cruise ships set off from, innit? Grannies off to sail round the Caribbean." Zig's gran had talked about it once, but she'd never got round to going. Probably never had the money or any hopes of it, now he came to think about it.

Zig's stomach twisted. If only she'd lived longer. Maybe he'd have got a proper job, been able to spoil her . . .

"That's right," Finn said. "And the Isle of Wight ferry," he added as if it was at least as important as all them floating hotels.

"What you doing in Glastonbury, then?" Zig asked, and immediately kicked himself, cos the last thing he wanted was any questions about what *he* was doing here. "Don't you miss the sea?" he asked quickly.

Finn shrugged. "We're close enough here. I can always drive up to Weston-super-Mare if I want to have a paddle. You ready? Time we were getting back to the bar, before Ange sends out a search party."

Huh. If Zig wasn't mistaken, he wasn't the only one who didn't wanna talk about his past.

Zig was getting into the swing of things, reaching for glasses without having to think about it, when he glanced up and saw Si walking in the door. His heart skipping, Zig flashed him a smile, which froze as Adam Merchant stomped in behind him, his chin up and his eyes hard. Wanker.

Yeah, right. Cos it's not like he hasn't got reason to hate you. Whether he knows it or not.

Adam hadn't changed a tenth as much as Si had, since the last time Zig had seen him. He hadn't bulked up or anything, and he was clean-shaven. Still had that arty look about him. No visible ink, though, which, seriously? A tattoo artist with no tattoos? That was like turning up for work a bar wearing an Alcoholics Anonymous T-shirt.

Adam was closely followed by a fit bloke with a worried expression, and a punk girl who looked like she took no prisoners. *She* had ink all right: a wicked death's head hawkmoth on her throat and stuff Zig couldn't make out on both hands. Plenty of piercings, too, and blood-red hair except where it was shaved. She looked like the sort of woman who occasionally made Zig wonder if he might be a bit bi, which, based on past experience, probably meant she was a lesbian. Funny how that always seemed to work out.

Si ambled straight up to the bar, a warm smile on his face. "Going all right?"

"Yeah, cheers. Be with you in a mo—gotta finish serving this gent." He nodded towards his current customer, a fresh-faced young lad who'd shown his ID without being asked. Zig's hands worked on autopilot pouring the drinks, which was just as well as something seemed to have scrambled his brains and tied a knot in his guts. He had to double-check the card reader to make sure he hadn't charged, like, a hundred times too much for a round of beers and one lime and soda.

Finally, he finished with the customer and could turn his full attention to Si. And his mates, who were now clustered around him like feds flanking a VIP. Zig kept his smile steady. "What can I do you for?"

It was the punk girl who answered. "Rum and Coke for me, Diet Coke for Adam, and Corin and Scratch'll have a pint of Becket's each."

Zig cocked his head. "Scratch? Who's Scratch when he's at home?"

"Me, you wally," Si butted in with a laugh. "It's from me name, innit? Si Greczik. Scratchit. *Scratch*. S'what they called me at school. Sash thought it was fun when I told her."

"Did she now?" Nobody got to laugh at Si. *Nobody*.

"You got a problem with that?" The punk girl—Sash?—had her hands on her leather-clad hips and was glaring like she'd deck Zig sooner than look at him.

Good job there was a nice thick expanse of bar between them. "Makes him sound like he's got headlice, don't it?"

She cocked her head. "Yeah? Cos I can only see one kind of parasite round here."

Zig was suddenly one hundred percent convinced he wasn't even a little bit bi.

"Sasha!" Si put a hand on her arm. "Be nice, all right? Zig's an old mate, come to stay."

"Oh, I know *exactly* who Zig is," Sasha said, staring straight at Zig all the time. She didn't actually do the *I'm-watching-you* gesture, but she didn't have to.

Lucky for Zig he'd met plenty of people way scarier than her. "If I'm a parasite, how come I'm the one working here, while you take up my time and stop me serving the punters?"

"Sorry," Si said, like it was him who needed to apologise. "You pour the drinks, and we'll get out of your hair."

Zig couldn't help smiling at him. "No worries. Coming right up."

He got their round ready, forgetting nothing cos he was a professional, all right? Sasha gave him a searching gaze and waved her credit card. "Add one for yourself," she said grudgingly.

Huh. Well, two could play at that game. Zig flashed her his best smile. "Cheers. You have a good night."

She raised a tattooed eyebrow. "I liked you better when you were giving me grief."

She was so sharp she'd cut herself. Or someone, anyhow. Zig gave her a genuine grin. Maybe he was a bit bi, after all. "Sorry, love, catering to your kinks ain't part of the job."

Sasha cackled, then frowned, like she hadn't meant to do that.

"Talk to you later?" Si said, and ushered his mates away.

Zig turned to the next customer.

Chapter Nineteen
Si

Si was about to point out where there was a table available so they could make themselves comfortable, but Adam strode off to the far wall of the pub. They ended up standing by a pillar with a ledge to rest their drinks on. Si took a hefty gulp of his pint. He reckoned he'd need it.

"What was all that about?" Adam demanded, getting in Sasha's face.

"What was *what* about?" She narrowed her eyes.

Adam backed off, but his chin was still up. "You. Buying that bastard a drink."

Si wasn't having that. "Oi. Zig's my mate, so no calling him names, all right? And Sasha can buy drinks for anyone she wants to."

Corin darted glances between them, like he was worried it was about to start kicking off.

Sasha heaved a high-pitched sigh. "Si, I know that. Adam? We're on the same side here, so calm your fucking tits."

Si frowned. "And what side's that?"

"Yours," she said, and gave him a twisted smile. "You know, I can see why you like him."

"You—" Adam's voice cut off abruptly, like maybe someone's elbow had made a short, sharp visit to his ribs.

Si sent Corin a suspicious glance, then mentally shook himself and turned back to Sasha. "You can?"

"Well, yeah. All that cheeky London charm. And the looks don't hurt."

Warmth spread through Si's chest, then cooled as she raised a hand.

"But that doesn't mean I trust him. Not with anything important. Which, in case you ain't realised, you are."

The warmth was back, bringing with it a prickling in Si's eyes. "Sash . . ." he said, and didn't know how to finish.

"As I understand it," Corin broke in, "none of you has seen him since you were all teenagers, is that right? And, well, no offence, Scratch, but teenage romances don't often last. So why is everyone so down on him for a break-up—even a bad break-up—that happened all that time ago? If Scratch is happy to have him here, why can't we all be happy too? Or at least, you know, be friendly?"

Adam got a constipated expression on his face.

Si folded his arms and waited to see if Adam was going to call Zig a thief in front of his face.

"It's . . . complicated," Adam said at last. "It wasn't just a bad break-up, okay?"

"What was it, then?" Corin asked, bless his oblivious little heart.

Si took pity on both of them. "He hung around with a bad crowd, back in the day."

"Yeah, and some of 'em might have ripped off my dad," Adam said.

Si shot him a grateful smile for his restraint.

"Oh." Corin brightened. "But people do change, and if he's moved away from all that . . ."

"We don't know he has, though, do we?" Sasha murmured. "And I can't be the only one wondering why he's turned up here after all this time."

Corin frowned. "But . . . what could he hope to get out of Scratch? No offence," he added quickly.

Seemed like him and Adam both were falling over backwards to give Si no offence, but they were making a right pig's ear out of it. "Maybe he simply needs a place to stay for a while, that's all. For whatever reason," Si said as Adam opened his mouth. "And I'm not gonna turn him away. End of."

Adam still had that expression on his face like someone had shoved a bung up his arse. "Just . . . don't get involved, all right? Promise me that. Whatever shit he's in this time, however much you like him—and I *know* you still like him—don't get involved. Please?"

Sasha nodded. "What he said. Looks and charm aren't gonna make up for him being a shit to you."

Si's chest was tight. "I'm not gonna, all right? I ain't daft. Not that daft, anyhow. I know me and him, it's not . . . But I ain't gonna turn him away. Not if he needs me."

Adam and Sasha shared a glance. It wasn't a happy one.

Sasha put a hand on Si's arm, sending him a wistful smile. "You wouldn't be you if you did, would you? But remember we're here for you."

For when it all goes tits up, she didn't say.

Si did his best not to think about that.

The others left after last orders, but Si was determined to wait for Zig to finish work. It took a while—Si had never realised how much clearing up there was to do—and he dithered over whether he should offer to help. Deciding he'd only be in the way and would be breaking the terms of their insurance anyhow, he'd found himself a chair. He was nodding off in it by the time Zig swept over to him.

"You waited? You shouldn't have. I know me way home."

Home. He'd called it home. Treacherous warmth spread through Si at the thought. "What kind of a gentleman would I be if I let you walk home alone?"

Zig raised an eyebrow. "Gentleman, eh? Haven't met one of them in a long while. Should I dye my hair blond?"

"Nah, the blue suits you. Brings out your eyes. Well, one of 'em."

"Like that's a recommendation." It came out like it was second nature for Zig to do himself down, and Si hated that.

He put a hand on Zig's arm. "You know I like your eyes. I told you, didn't I?"

Zig looked away. "Yeah, well, takes all sorts. We oughtta be getting home, yeah? You had an early start this morning."

Si heaved himself to his feet, and they set off, Zig calling out a farewell to Ange as they went.

The air outside was chill after the warmth of the pub. Si wished he'd brought a warmer jacket. He sent a sidelong glance at Zig, who was shivering in a Prince of Wales polo shirt with a black button-up shirt on top. "Ain't you got a coat?"

"It's fine. It ain't that far."

"You daft bastard. You'll catch your death." Si slipped off his leather jacket and went to sling it around Zig's shoulders.

Zig dodged. "Oi, no way. You put that back on."

"Got me beard to keep me warm. And there's nothing of you." Si lunged again.

Zig danced away. "A bloke could get a complex. Just cos I ain't got muscles growing out of me muscles."

"Put the bastard jacket on. You think I'm going to nurse you through double pneumonia?"

Zig grinned as he finally let Si drape the jacket over his shoulders. "I bet you've got a great bedside manner." He slipped his arms into the sleeves, and somehow Si wasn't cold anymore neither.

"Don't you believe it. You catch some lurgy, you'll get nothing but tough love from me."

"Yeah?" Zig's grin widened. "Long as it's some kind of love, I don't give a monkey's."

Si had to take a deep breath. "Stop arsing about and let's get home, all right?"

Chapter Twenty
Zig

Six years ago

After he'd said his final goodbye to Si, Zig walked away from the Dog and Duck with a spring in his step and didn't look back. Not a care in the world. The fucking *world*, okay? He didn't need a naïve fucking farmboy from Mummerset *ooh-aar*ing in his ear every time he fancied a shag.

Who the hell did Si think he was, acting like he was better than Zig and his dad just cos they had to grift to make a living? Making such a big thing out of a little scam that the insurance was gonna cover anyhow? Didn't he know everyone in this fucking country was on the make?

Except Si . . . Zig shook his head. Fucking Trent. How many building sites were there in south London? Why the hell couldn't him and Dad have picked one of the other ones?

Cos then they couldn't have used Si to get the gen on the site, could they? Idiot.

No wonder they hadn't hauled Zig in on the job. He should have known.

Some arse had left their wheelie bin out, perfectly placed for Zig to catch his foot on the wheel and almost face-plant on the pavement. Zig gave the bin a vicious shove, snarling a smile when it tipped over into the hedge, all the rubbish inside falling out onto their stupid fucking metre square of lawn with a rosebush in the middle. A nappy sack caught on the thorns and ripped, displaying its stinking contents. Fucking *good*.

Then he had to leg it when a six-foot DILF came slamming out of the house yelling about what he was gonna do to Zig when he caught him.

Zig lost the git by ducking down an alley, then leaping over a fence. He doubled over, wheezing, his hands on his knees in some other sod's garden. Christ, he needed to stop smoking.

Or not. What the fuck did it matter anyhow?

When he finally made it home, Dad was in the living room, watching sport on the telly, a beer in hand.

"Did you put him up to it?" Zig demanded.

Dad put his beer down. "Who's crawled up your arse?" Then he laughed harshly. "Thought you liked that kind of thing."

"Trent. Pumping Si for info so you and him could do over his boss's building site."

"Si. That your little boyfriend, is it? So what if he did?"

"For fuck's sake, Dad. You don't shaft your mates!"

Dad stood up slowly, and Zig took a step back. "He's no mate of mine. Some rich bastard raking it in from other men doing all the work? Or do you mean the little tosser you've been panting after? I wouldn't let him in the house."

"Si's a good man!"

Dad sneered. "Too good for you, then."

It hit Zig like a slap to the face, and he reeled from it.

Dad gave a satisfied grunt. "If I've got to have a fairy for a son, I might as well get something out of it, eh?" He sat back down and picked up his beer.

Zig blinked at him a couple of times, his throat tight. Then he hurled himself up the stairs and into his room, slamming the door behind him. He threw himself down on his bed. The sheets were crumpled and needed a wash.

Zig buried his face in the pillow. Was that all he was worth to his dad? A way of making money?

Well, duh. You've always known the bastard don't give two shits about you, you stupid wanker. It's not as if he thinks you're a real man. Not like Trent.

Dad and Trent. Working together, like always. And now they'd lost him Si.

Except they hadn't, had they? Zig had done that himself, spouting off all that crap Dad always came out with. Justifying himself. Making out like he was so clever, beating the system. Jesus, he'd even defended Trent for shafting both of them.

Sod it. He'd always known it wasn't gonna last, him and Si. It wasn't like they had much in common. Si had his nice home in the country to go back to, with his nice mum and dad, probably a granny or three somewhere who knitted him sweaters at Christmas . . .

Fuck.

Zig got out his lighter and a ciggie, but his hands were shaking and everything was all blurred. He threw them across the room instead.

Chapter Twenty-One
Si

Present day

Saturday morning they both got up late, as Si wasn't working this weekend and Zig wasn't due in until six.

Si had made cocoa when they'd got back from the pub, to warm up from the chilly walk home. It'd been nice. Zig had sat close to him on the sofa, their shoulders and thighs touching, but he hadn't tried it on or made any flirty suggestions. He'd acted like a mate. That'd been a relief, what with Si newly determined not to get involved. Definitely.

All right, it'd been a bit of a disappointment too, but that was hearts for you, wasn't it? Never on the same page as your brain. Si had gone to bed after they'd finished their cocoa, and Zig had settled down on the sofa, and that had been that.

So what if he'd maybe dreamed about Zig? Dreamed about holding him. Kissing him. Doing more, too, like they had back in London all them years ago.

Subconsciouses were tricky buggers. Everyone knew that. Si had had dreams about walking in the dragon procession stark-bollock-naked, but it didn't mean it was something he actually wanted to *do*.

Si shook off the dreams with the duvet and padded into the kitchen to boil the kettle sometime after ten. He brought Zig a mug of tea and sat next to him on the sofa, hoping to rekindle the easy atmosphere of the previous night. "Fancy a proper breakfast today? There's eggs and bacon in the fridge."

Zig stretched and, in the process, moved a couple of inches away. When he took the mug Si held out to him, he shifted over farther. Si's chest hurt. He told it not to be a daft bastard.

"Cheers. Whatever you're having." Zig's voice was flat. He seemed to notice, cos he roused himself to give one of them easy smiles he was always flashing around. "Appreciate it."

Si hated those smiles. There was nothing behind them except Zig wanting to make everyone like him. As if he was worried what might happen if they didn't. "You'll be washing up after, mind," he said. "And that pan's a bugger to get egg off of."

Zig let out a startled laugh, and this time, the joy on his face was real. Si basked in it.

"Gonna make me work for me keep, are you? Fair enough." Zig paused. "Listen, I'm earning now, so I'll chip in, yeah?"

"Ain't got paid yet, though, have you? Talk to me again after you get your first wage packet."

"Don't wanna be a parasite."

Zig's face had fallen, and Si thought brief uncharitable thoughts about Sasha for her words last night. "You're a mate, not a flea or a tick or a bloody headlouse. I ain't so hard up I can't feed you for a few days." He sent Zig an encouraging grin.

Zig nodded and sort of shrugged. "Maybe I could take you out after I get paid? Buy you dinner. Say thanks, you know?"

"You don't have to do that," Si said, touched.

"Maybe I wanna."

And there was nothing Si could say to that except, "Well, all right, then."

They'd just finished eating their breakfast when Zig looked up, head cocked. "That your phone?"

It was. Si put down his fork and headed back into the bedroom, where he'd left his phone on charge, but Sod's law, it had stopped ringing by the time he got there. He unplugged it and carried it back into the living room. "Huh. Mum. Better call her back. You know what mums are . . . Shit." He gave himself a hefty mental kick up the arse. Zig's mum was *dead*. Si had known that almost as long as he'd known Zig. "Sorry. Forgot for a mo. Didn't mean to be a bastard."

Zig sent him a weird, intent look, then got up jerkily from the sofa and went to stare out of the window. "I tracked her down," he said.

"You what?" Si asked, confused.

"My mum. After you left London."

Si's forehead creased up so much it was gonna give him a headache. "But you said—"

"Told you she died when I was four, didn't I? Hah. Guess what? I lied. She left us."

There was a stab of hurt, which melted into worry when Si realised how Zig was standing. He was rigid, hunched over, and somehow brittle. "'S okay. That's gotta . . . I mean, I can get it's not something you'd wanna talk about."

"It was in the summer sometime." Zig's voice sounded remote. "She took me round the neighbours' to play in their garden, then buggered off and never came back. Dad was well pissed off."

Fucking hell. Si got up, trying to make some noise about it, like Zig was a cat fresh from the shelter who'd bolt if he was spooked. He stepped over to Zig and placed a hand on his shoulder for a mo. This was all right, wasn't it? Mates touched, didn't they? And hugged, come to that, and gods, if he'd ever seen anyone in need of a hug, it was Zig right now. Si gently slid his arms around Zig's waist.

Zig started, then relaxed into his hold. "Don't you ever get mad about anything?"

"You ain't been living here long. Just wait till you leave the top off the toothpaste." Si went on, "What happened, then? You and your mum, when you tracked her down?"

"She was a hairdresser. Still is, I s'pose. Maybe? I dunno. It's been years. That's how I found her, asking around people in the trade. She was working in this posh salon in the West End, the sort where it costs you a fucking kidney for a dye job. Had a fake posh accent to go with it and all. Still pretty." Zig's voice faltered. "I reckon Dad knew where she was. Always had."

"He never told you?"

"It was more like, 'You go whining about your mum again and I'll give you something to fucking cry about.'" Zig's voice was under control again, like he was talking about the bloody weather, but his body had gone all tense.

Si squeezed him tighter. "But you found her?" he prompted.
"Yeah."

He didn't say more, but Si was sure in his gut Zig wanted to. He'd never have brought the subject up if he didn't. All he needed was a bit of help. "What happened?" Si asked gently.

"She said she had a new life. A new bloke, who didn't have her looking over her shoulder all the time." Zig barked out a bitter laugh. "Fair enough, that was. She . . ." He drew in a breath. "She said she didn't have nothing for me. Told me to go back to me dad."

"Fucking *hell*." It burst out; Si couldn't stop it. If this had been soon after Si left London, Zig would've still been in his teens. A *kid*.

Like he'd been when they'd split up. A kid, still believing what his dad told him. Still trying to please his dad, and gods knew, that couldn't have been easy, from what Si had heard about the bastard and his digs about Zig's sexuality. Bloody hell, was his dad the reason for Zig always being down on himself?

A pang of sorrow shot through Si for the kid Zig had been, all them years ago. It felt natural to drop a kiss on Zig's shoulder, so he did.

Then he tensed, cos what might Zig think about that? But Zig leaned back against him and put his hands on Si's where they lay around his waist, so that was okay. "Guess I know how to get you to kiss me now. Tell you about my shit life." He looked back over his shoulder and flashed that cocky smile of his that could charm the pants off a bloody stone statue.

Suddenly awkward, Si let his arms fall and took a step back. Then he pulled himself together. This wasn't about him, was it? "You can tell me anything," he said sincerely.

Zig's smile froze. "Anything?" His voice was no more than a whisper.

Chapter Twenty-Two
Zig

"**Y**ou can tell me anything," Si had said.

Like it was so easy, baring his heart so that Si would hold him again. Kiss him again.

But if you tell him, at least you'll know. And fuck, what kind of a cunt was Zig, trying to get Si to love him again without telling him the truth?

He'd lain awake half the night on Si's sofa, thinking about how right it'd seemed, coming home with him. How he'd yearned to put his arm round Si as they sat on the sofa drinking cocoa. Wanted to kiss him. Take him to bed.

He'd stopped himself from trying any of that, partly because he'd been scared to break the mood if Si wasn't up for it. But mostly because he didn't deserve it. Seeing Adam again last night at the pub . . . it'd brought it all home. Made it real. Si and his mates, they were decent people.

Not like Zig. He belonged with people like Trent and bloody Dad.

"Ain't you ever wondered what I've been up to since you last saw me?" Zig asked, his tone rough in his own ears. "I know what you were up to. Learning a trade. Making a life."

"I s'pose I reckoned you'd been doing bar work?" Si said slowly. "You know. Learning how to make all them fancy cocktails. Juggling with shakers like in some eighties film." He smiled weakly, like maybe he was expecting Zig to carry on the banter. Tell a few funny stories about working behind a bar.

Zig couldn't stand it. "I was in prison."

Si stilled and pressed his lips together. He didn't say anything. No swearing, no gasp of horror. His eyes didn't widen. Like Zig's news came as a jolt, yeah, but maybe not a surprise?

Which, why the fuck would it be, moron? Si must have known Zig was dodgy. Him, and his dad, and the blokes he hung around with. He'd as good as confessed they'd done over Adam's dad's place, way back when. How much of a stretch would it be to imagine him ending up doing, hah, a stretch?

Fuck, Zig hated himself. "Ain't you gonna ask what for?" It came out bitter.

"You wanna tell me?" Si asked, his tone cautious. "Cos, like, you don't 'ave to."

"Not worried you're sharing your flat with an axe murderer?"

"Nah. You'd've got longer than six years for that. Least, I'd bloody well hope so."

Zig laughed, despite himself. "You'd be surprised. Robbery."

Si nodded absently, like he didn't know he was doing it. "Got unlucky?" he asked in a horrible, fake cheerful voice. Zig could feel him drawing away, closing himself off. Reminding himself Zig was no good. Would never be any good.

Zig hated that even more. "No," he said harshly.

Si blinked.

"There was this job," Zig forced himself to say, each word like acid in his throat. "Not long after you left London. Construction company. Who'd have thought it, eh? Didn't go quite how we planned it."

He swallowed, then took a deep breath and started his tale.

It was just Zig, his dad, and Trent on the job. Dad had fallen out with a couple of the other guys—accused them of having sticky fingers, which was fucking rich—so he'd kept them out of the loop on this one.

It was supposed to be easy, mind. Quick in and out. Trent had been scoping the place out, said the security was shite. And true enough, it was a piece of piss getting in.

Everything was still and quiet, which was what you'd expect at 3 a.m. The management had left a few lights on to make it look like there was someone at home, but they weren't fooling anyone with that tired old trick.

Dad was sorting something out in the van, so Trent and Zig went on ahead. None of the internal doors were locked. Nothing to keep them from getting to the good stuff.

"I'm gonna start here," Trent whispered, his eye on some sweet, sweet tech in a large open-plan room. "You check out the director's office."

"Got it." Zig left him to it and set off down the corridor, resisting the urge to whistle cos he knew it'd get him a bollocking.

He rounded a corner, and his stomach lurched.

There was a guard there, an older bloke with grey hair and a paunch. Zig froze, panicked. There wasn't supposed to be anyone here.

Shit. Time to get out of sight—

"Oi! What are you doing in here?" The guard stomped towards Zig, flat-footed and fumbling at his hip for something.

Zig couldn't move. Christ, it's all going wrong.

Out of nowhere, Trent darted in, fist swinging.

The old guy went down heavy, his head bouncing off the desk on the way to the floor.

Trent barely broke stride, making for Zig and grabbing him by the shoulders. He gave Zig a good shake. "You stupid fucking idiot. Do you want to get caught?"

Zig tore his eyes from the still body on the floor. "Is he dead?"

"Who gives a fuck? Come on, *you moron." Trent strode off without looking back. Like Zig was his dog and would walk to heel when ordered.*

The old guy wasn't moving, and there was blood on the desk where he'd caught his head. Zig's heart was trying to beat out of his chest. Christ, that could be someone's grandad.

Without consciously deciding to, Zig knelt down by the body. Pulse, pulse, how the fuck do you take a pulse? *He reached out a hand, half-afraid to touch the old guy. When the man shifted and groaned, Zig nearly shat himself. The guard didn't open his eyes, though, and his head was still bleeding, thick and red.* He needed help. Now.

This wasn't what Zig had signed up for. Nicking stuff, yeah—from posh wankers who had way too much already, and would claim it all on the insurance anyhow—but hurting people?

Zig had always wondered if he had, like, a moral compass. Something to show him where the lines were. Turned out, seeing that old man lying on the floor ... Zig remembered Ray, his gran's old boyfriend. He'd cried at her funeral, and Zig hadn't known how to handle it. Because grown-ups didn't cry, right? Especially blokes. Dad never cried, and he hated Zig crying. Shed a tear and get a smack round the ear. That was how it worked.

But Ray had wept like it wasn't anything to be ashamed of, and he'd given Zig a hug so tight it'd hurt. That had been the last time Zig had seen him, cos he'd moved to Sussex to be with his family. He was probably dead now, but Zig could still remember his face. And it wasn't much different from this bloke, lying on the floor in front of him, bleeding from a head wound one of Zig's so-called mates had given him.

That was it. That was the line.

There was a device on the old guy's belt, the side he'd been reaching for. It was smaller than a phone, black plastic with just two buttons. One had a telephone symbol; the other SOS.

Zig hesitated. If he pushed that button, the guy would get help . . . and Zig, his dad, and Trent would get caught.

If he didn't, the old man might die.

Zig pushed the button. Then he scrambled to his feet and walked slowly after Trent.

Zig came back to the present to find Si was gripping his hand, tight. It felt like an anchor.

"Was he okay?" Si asked. "The old man?"

Zig nodded. "Yeah. Maybe he'd have been all right anyway, but I couldn't— I couldn't risk it."

Si's whole body had relaxed. "No. No, course you couldn't."

Jesus, how could Si just *say* that? Like he knew Zig was always gonna do the right thing?

That was more than Zig had known. Way more.

Si smiled crookedly. "Guess I know why you and your dad had that bust-up."

"Well, yeah, but I never said anything. I let 'em assume the guard had set off the alarm before Trent decked him."

"You didn't try to make a run for it? Get away before the police turned up?"

Zig stared out of the window and into the darkness. "Think I wanted to be caught. Wanted Trent to be caught, anyhow."

"Always knew he was a bastard," Si said. "You did a good thing, there."

"Got me own dad banged up."

"And yourself." Si's tone strongly suggested he didn't give a monkey's about Zig's dad.

Zig shrugged.

"What was it like?" Si asked softly. "Being inside?"

It was shit, was the first response that sprang to mind, but that had been down to what had been going on inside his head as much as prison life. "Wasn't great. No booze, and I didn't wanna touch the drugs. You never knew what you were getting into. You lose all control over everything—what you eat, what you do most hours of the day. And you're stuck inside with all these other bastards, half of 'em blokes you'd cross the Thames to avoid on the outside. Can't get away from them, even the ones who're fucking psycho. Safest thing is to keep your head down. Not get noticed." Zig laughed bitterly. "You wouldn't have recognised me in them days. Had me hair natural colour and everything." Some days, he hadn't even known if he was still *him* or if he'd actually turned into the drab, colourless drone he saw in the mirror and would stay like that forever.

Si squeezed his hand. "Sounds rough."

Was that pity in his eyes? Zig didn't like it. Didn't deserve it. He lightened his tone deliberately. "Could have been worse, though. I went to a better nick than me dad or Trent did. First offence, see? There were lots of educational courses you could sign up for. Read a lot of books to pass the time after lock-up."

"Yeah? What did you read?"

"Old books, mainly. Classics." Zig found himself smiling. "Stuff like me gran used to read. Oh, she liked her Mills and Boon, don't get me wrong, but she had a load of books by Dickens and Thomas Hardy, Jane Austen, Laurie Lee—that sort. Got them all in them cheap editions they sell for a quid a throw. She reckoned they weren't that different, a lot of 'em. All about love and marriage. Only in bigger words, and more of 'em."

"You didn't have one of these modern prisons, with a telly in your cell?"

"Oh, we had a telly. Me cellmate didn't read, though, so I let him choose what was on. Then I'd open me book and tune it all out, cos there's a limit to how many reality shows I can take."

"He didn't read, or he couldn't read?"

"He could read a bit. But not enough to want to read a book, you know? Dunno if he was dyslexic or what. He was older, older than me dad, so maybe he never got diagnosed. He used to get me to read stuff to him—letters and that." Zig laughed. "Asked me to read from me book, one time, but it was *Jude the Obscure* so I wasn't that surprised he never asked twice."

Si scratched his head. "Not read that one. Too obscure?"

"Too bleedin' depressing, more like. It's about a bloke who never gets to live his dreams. Only worse. I'd tell you the worst bit, but then you'd be depressed and all."

"I'll pass, ta. What are you reading now?"

Heat rose in Zig's face. "*Pride and Prejudice*. For like the six millionth time." So he'd felt the need of a comfort read. So what?

Instead of the derision Zig had half expected, Si cocked his head to the side. "I remember my mum watching that on the telly. Have you got to the bit where he rips half his clothes off and dives in the lake?"

"Hate to break it to you, but that's not in the book."

"No? Ah, well. Probably works better on screen anyway."

"You're not wrong there." Zig paused. "Are you okay about this, then? Me being an old lag?"

"You ain't that old," Si said vaguely, like he was still considering the question. Then he took a breath and looked Zig in the eye. "Way I see it, you done your time, haven't you? Paid your debt to society, all that bollocks. And you saved that bloke's life, maybe. So yeah, I'm okay with it. Long as you're out of all that now?" His eyes turned pleading, and he swallowed.

Zig's heart clenched so hard he could barely breathe. "Yep. Well out of it all." And he was. He was never going back to that life, not even if Dad turned up on their doorstep and—

Nope. Not gonna think about it, cos that wasn't gonna happen. How would Dad find him here? Zig forced his body to relax.

Si was smiling at him, and that helped. It helped a lot. "Well, then. Reckon we're okay." He reached over and squeezed Zig's shoulder.

"Now, I'd better call me mum before she sends a search party, but it ain't likely to take long. How about I take you out afterwards? We can head off on the bike, get some lunch out somewhere."

Zig's smile came easier now. "Sounds great. Apart from the helmet hair."

Si laughed. "If there's anyone who can make it work, it's you."

Zig's insides warmed. "You call your mum. I'll sort this lot out." He picked up their plates—the remains of their breakfasts now cold and congealed to the point he'd probably need a chisel to wash up— and headed into the kitchen.

"You don't have to—" Si started.

Zig shoved both plates into his left hand so he could flip a middle finger up at the daft bastard with his right. "I think you meant, 'Cheers, mate, you're a star.'"

He made plenty of noise filling the sink and clattering the pans around, partly to give Si some privacy for his call but also cos he didn't fancy having to listen to Si's side of the conversation. His mum would most likely be giving Si grief over Zig's continued presence. The thought of it was enough to harsh the buzz he'd been feeling since telling Si the worst and not being chucked out on his ear. But only a little.

And he wasn't gonna feel guilty. Si knew everything now, and he still wanted Zig around.

Okay, maybe he felt a little bit guilty. Because Si deserved so much better.

But he was a grown man, now. Capable of making his own decisions.

Chapter Twenty-Three
Si

Standing in his bedroom, Si fought the urge to cross his fingers as his mum answered his call. "Mum? You called?" He lowered his voice, despite the closed door and all the clattering and splashing sounds coming from the kitchen. "If this is about Zig again—"

"It's not. Well, it is, but . . . Your dad's been telling me I've been coming on too heavy. Turning up at your work like that. Says I'm treating you like a child."

Si could hear his dad's voice in the background, saying, "Too right!" He bit back a laugh, and his tone was gentle when he answered. "Well, I'm not gonna lie, it coulda been a bit awkward, Mum. What if one of the lads had been there to hear you?"

"You know I'm only thinking of you. I don't want to see you get hurt again."

"I know, Mum. And it's not . . ." Si lowered his voice even more. "Zig's changed. He really has. He came from a bad place, but he's put all that behind him now. You don't need to worry about him leading me astray or nothing."

"What about him leading you on, though? Strikes me, the sort of man who turns up with no warning is the sort who'll disappear just as easily."

Si couldn't help the chill that ran through him at the thought of Zig leaving. "That ain't fair, Mum. He ain't got no obligations to me."

"*Hasn't*," Mum corrected absently. "As long as you keep that in mind, love. Don't let yourself get drawn in deep only to find he leaves you without a thought."

Si did laugh that time. "Mum! When have you ever known me to get *drawn in deep* by a man?"

"Once only, my lad. Once, and that was enough."

Si winced. "It ain't like that this time," he said weakly. "Listen, I gotta go, all right? We're heading out."

"Fine. But you call me, Simon Greczik. I want to know how you're getting on."

Si said his goodbyes and took a deep breath, then opened up the browser on his phone.

Ten minutes later he headed into the kitchen, finding it spick-and-span with everything dried and put away.

Zig was in the living room, thumbing through his phone. He looked up as Si entered, his expression wary. "Everything okay?"

Si nodded. "Crackin'. Right, you ready to go?"

Zig grinned. "Me? I'm always ready. Let me get me coat."

It was a short walk from the flat to the lockup garage where Si kept his bike. The sun was shining, and the air was bracing.

Zig was animated, almost dancing around him as he tried to get Si to say where they were going. "C'mon, give us a hint."

"Nope. My lips are sealed."

"At least tell me what sort of bike you've got these days, then. I hope it's a bit bigger than the one you had in London. There was barely room for the two of us on that, and you're about twice the size now you were then."

Si smiled enigmatically. Well, that was the intention, anyhow. Gods knew what it actually looked like. "Maybe. You'll see."

He unlocked the garage door and threw it open with a flourish. "Big enough for you?"

Chapter Twenty-Four
Zig

Zig stared in admiration. Then he whistled.

Si's old bike had been a crappy little thing, barely better than a moped, but riding on the back of it, his arms around Si's waist, Zig had felt . . . looked after, somehow. Like when he'd been a kid and his gran's bloke had driven them around in that old Morris Minor he'd somehow kept going for, like, a century or something.

But, bloody hell, this was something else. Si had an honest-to-god Harley-Davidson now, a great monstrous thing in black and chrome.

"What do you think?" Si asked.

"I think I'm in love," Zig answered honestly.

Si just laughed, which was . . . probably for the best. Then he tossed Zig a black helmet with blue flames painted on the sides. "There you go. Matches your hair. Put that on and we'll take her out."

They climbed on the Harley, Zig sitting snug behind Si. There was no bar behind him to hang on to so he slung his arms around Si's waist and that familiar feeling of safety came flooding back, bringing with it a curious pain in his chest that Zig did his best to ignore.

Si started the engine. It roared like a fucking tiger, all muscle and power. Then he hit the accelerator, and they sped down the road.

The ride took them out of Glastonbury into open countryside, past farmers' fields and through villages and small towns, all brightly lit and decorated for the season. The ends of Si's hair hung below his helmet and danced wildly in the strong wind.

After they'd been riding for around an hour, as good as Zig could guess, Si brought the hog to a halt on a quiet country lane and they got off, removing their helmets. Zig tried to fluff up his hair in a wing mirror, but it was a lost cause. He scowled at his reflection.

Si laughed. "Don't worry, you're still pretty."

Zig straightened, brandishing an eloquent finger at him. "So where are we now?"

"Wessex," Si said proudly.

"Uh-huh. You know that ain't a real county, right? Thomas Hardy made it up."

"I know it ain't called that in real life, but I looked it up, and it's all based on real places. See, first I reckoned I'd take you to Bath, cos of Jane Austen, you know? But then I checked to see if there was anything going on, and it's the last weekend of their Christmas market *and* there's a match on, so it'll be heaving. Not that it ain't always. So I thought of Wessex. And here we are."

"I can't believe you remembered I said I'd read Thomas Hardy."

"You only told me it this morning."

"Yeah, but . . ." Zig shrugged, not sure how to explain. "You like all that science-fiction stuff. Comic books and that. Modern stuff. All them dead authors I read—I didn't think they'd mean enough to you to stick in your head."

"Course they did. You like 'em."

Zig's rib cage was doing some weird thing that made it feel two sizes too small. "So what part of Wessex is this, exactly?" he asked, keeping it light.

"You'll find out. Come on, we got a bit of walking to do. It ain't far."

Si led the way down to the end of the lane, then got out his phone and frowned at it a bit. Zig tried to see what he was looking at but the bastard danced out of his reach, moving lightly for such a big bloke. "Ah ah ah! It's a surprise."

"What am I, five?"

"You ain't never too old for a surprise," Si said firmly, putting his phone into his pocket.

"Depends on the surprise," Zig muttered darkly, then couldn't help flashing Si a smile.

They walked on until they came to an ancient stone bridge. It was long, with several arches over the water, and bulged out at intervals with what Zig could only imagine were places for ye olde peasants to stand while crossing so they didn't get in the way of any carts or carriages coming the other way.

"See that?" Si pointed to a big old house—mansion, really—with steep pointy gables and three unreasonably tall chimneys, like the people who'd built it were too posh to breathe their own smoke when they popped outside to check the gardener wasn't slacking. "That's Woolbridge Manor. Or Wellbridge, if you ask Thomas Hardy. From *Tess of the D'Urbervilles*."

Zig blinked. "That's where she and that bloody hypocrite Angel Clare went to stay after they got married."

"That's right. Least, that's what the internet's been telling me. It ain't got much about this Angel bloke, though. Why's he a hypocrite?"

"You know the story of Tess, right?" From Si's look, Zig realised he didn't. "She's this innocent country girl who gets date-raped in her teens by a posh bloke and has a kid out of wedlock. Years later, she meets this so-called angel and marries him. On their wedding night, he confesses to her he's had a lover before her. So she's all, 'Thank God, I can tell him what happened to me.' Except he then throws a massive wobbly and basically tells her she's dead to him cos she's not a virgin. And then it all goes downhill from there."

Christ, what if Si had reacted like that when Zig told him about being inside? How many blokes would want a convicted criminal taking up house room? Zig couldn't take his eyes off the house, and found he was hugging himself.

Then a thick, leather-clad arm draped over his shoulders and squeezed him. Was Si maybe thinking about Zig's confession too?

"Bastard," he rumbled in Zig's ear. "Guess I shoulda read up on that one a bit more before bringing you here."

"No—no, it's good. I mean, yeah, it's sad, and it makes me fucking mad, but it's amazing, seeing the actual place he had in mind when he wrote it. I always thought it was smaller, you know? Dunno why." Warmed by Si's embrace and hoping it'd never end, Zig shook his head, then he laughed. "Weird to think of the bloke going round scouting out locations. Wonder what the people who lived there then thought about it?"

"Now *that* the internet didn't tell me. But guess who used to own it? Family called Turberville."

"No way!"

"Way. Not since the eighteenth century, mind."

"So, Hardy went around borrowing places and names and only changing a letter here and there? Huh. And here was me thinking writers actually made up stuff."

"Well, I s'pose they gotta get inspiration from somewhere."

Zig pulled out his phone and took a couple of pics of the manor. Then he swung and took one of Si, who was leaning on the parapet of the bridge and gazing into the water. Si glanced up and smiled, and Zig caught it on camera with a twist in his gut that was half pleasure, half pain. "Any more book locations around here?"

Si scratched his beard. "Well, there are, but it's a bit of a trek. We can do it another time. You gotta get back for work, and there's one more place I wanted to take you today."

"Yeah? What's that— No, don't tell me, it's a surprise?"

Si grinned. "You're learning."

They retraced their steps to the bike and got on. Si headed more-or-less back the way they'd come, riding for around half an hour before he turned into a National Trust car park and stopped the bike. He pulled off his helmet, his hair and beard springing out and fluffing up in the breeze.

Zig followed suit and ran a self-conscious hand through his hair as they got off the bike. "What are we here for?"

"To see a bloke who was around in Thomas Hardy's time. And maybe a few thousand years before that." Si cocked his head towards a neighbouring hill.

As he did, a pale sunlight broke through the clouds, illuminating a massive line drawing carved into the chalk of the hillside. It showed a man with a raised club—and that wasn't all that was erect, either.

Zig blinked. "You brought me here to show me a giant prehistoric dick pic."

Si nodded solemnly. "Classy, that's me."

Zig cracked up. After the sombre thoughts Woolbridge Manor had roused, seeing a gigantic chalk carving with a massive stiffy seemed bloody hysterical.

"Thought the Cerne Abbas giant might cheer you up if all the Tess stuff got too depressing," Si said with a smile.

"Not gonna lie, giant dicks have been known to have that effect. Course, they're better in real life." Zig cast a sidelong look at Si.

He got a raised eyebrow in return. "I ain't getting mine out in public. For starters, it's gotta look a bit small in comparison. Specially in this wind."

"Eh, don't sell yourself short." From what Zig could remember very well indeed, Si didn't have anything to worry about in that department. To cover all the weird mixed feelings that recollection stirred up, Zig jogged over to an information board.

Si followed him and read over his shoulder, his beard tickling Zig's ear. "Says the giant's 180 feet tall. So by my reckoning, that's a 40-foot dick, give or take. And that, my lover, I cannot compete with."

"Fair enough." Zig leaned back into Si's solid warmth, just a little, hoping Si might take the hint and put his arms around him. It wasn't crazy to hope, was it? Zig had been in the West Country long enough to know that Si calling him *my lover* meant absolutely nothing, but he'd brought him here, hadn't he? To see the world's biggest dick pic, and if that wasn't flirting, what the hell was? And that was after taking him to see Tess's honeymoon hotel.

It had to mean something, didn't it?

Chapter Twenty-Five
Zig

As he leaned back against Si, Zig's stomach rumbled loudly, breaking the mood.

"C'mon," Si said easily, stepping away from him. "Let's go find some grub, yeah?"

With a twinge of regret for lost chances, Zig followed him back to the Harley, and they rode the short distance to the nearby village.

Cerne Abbas village was old and postcardy, with some proper ancient buildings. There was one that looked like the sort of place Shakespeare might have visited if he'd been out this way, all Tudor beams and mullioned windows. The pub in the centre of town looked almost brand-new by comparison, but it still had a thatched roof and stone walls that were disappearing below a thick coat of ivy. Inside, the low ceiling was crossed by black beams and a log fire blazed at one end, making the place warm and inviting. It was, of course, done up for Christmas, with a tree in the corner and tinsel round the specials board. Most of the specials had been wiped off—looked like the lunchtime trade had been brisk.

Now, a few groups of people still sat at tables, lingering over their drinks, but most of the lunch crowd had been and gone. The sign said food was served all day, though, so they were golden.

"You going to be all right for getting back if we eat here?" Si asked with a glance at the clock behind the bar. It was gone three.

"Yeah, no worries. I don't have to be in until six this evening. Don't wanna be late, though," Zig added, to be clear. He wasn't going to balls up his job on the second day.

"Course not. Nah, that's good. Gives us some extra time."

They ordered their meals—steak and ale pie for Si, and a halloumi burger for Zig—and got some drinks in, then found a table. Si took a swig of his Diet Coke and looked wistfully at Zig's cider. "Burrow Hill. That's proper stuff, that is."

"Yeah? I thought it sounded like something a hobbit would drink. Go on, you can have one sip. Just one, mind. You're driving."

Si laughed. "Nah, I'm good. You enjoy it. Bet you don't get that in London."

"Not in any pub I've worked in."

"What was it like, the place you were working in before you came here?"

Zig shrugged. "You know. Like any other pub. Some of the other staff were pretty okay," he added, thinking of Ani. Then he cursed mentally and braced himself for the inevitable *Why did you leave, then?*

It didn't come, although their food did, and there was a break in the conversation while plates were handed out and sauces provided.

Si didn't let the subject drop, though. "What about at the Prince of Wales? You getting on with them all right? Ange is great, ain't she?"

"Didn't know you and her were mates." Zig took a bite of his burger. Not bad, with plenty of mushrooms.

"Not mates as such, but I'm a regular, ain't I? Think she's got the wrong impression of me, mind. She seems to reckon I'm some kind of Lothario." Si frowned. "Is that the bloke I mean?"

"If you mean a bit of a player, then yes. Guess I'm lucky I caught you between boyfriends." All right, so Zig was fishing for info. Why the hell not?

Had Si's face gone a bit pink? "Not really had any," he muttered, and ate a forkful of pie.

Zig put his fork down in surprise. "Not *any*? In six years? A fit bloke like you? Come off it." That couldn't be right. "What, you decided hookups were the way to go, then?"

"What? No." Si stared at his plate. "There just ain't been anyone, that's all. Not since you. Never really been anyone I wanted to, you know. Go out with. Mates, yeah," he added quickly. "Nothing more than that."

"Bloody hell. I know it's a small town, mate, but seriously? No one you fancied at all? Ain't you ever heard of Grindr?" Zig's chest was tight with way too many emotions. Shock, with a touch of guilt on the side. Incredulity. Pain, for Si being all on his own. And, cos he was a bastard like that, a shameful bit of pleasure that Si had, what, waited for him? *Yeah, right. Get over yourself.*

Si shrugged. "Don't really get Grindr. How do people look at a picture on their phone and want to get naked with the bloke? They don't even know him. He could be a proper dickhead."

"Most people on Grindr aren't too bothered about personality," Zig said wryly. "But there's other dating apps, ones that are more about actual dating. You could chat for a while, get to know the bloke, and . . ." And why the hell was he trying to persuade Si to find blokes who weren't *him*? He had another bite of his burger to shut himself up.

Si paused, a forkful of chips halfway to his mouth. "S'pose. It all seems a bit of a palaver, though. And chatting online, it ain't like meeting someone for real."

Zig grinned. "You're an old-fashioned gentleman at heart, aren't you?"

"Oi. No taking the piss. You see if I hold any doors open for you now. But what about you? Bet you've had dozens of boyfriends since we were together in London."

Did Si's voice sound sad, under the surface cheer? It was hard to tell, and he'd bent his head to his food once more so Zig couldn't see his eyes. "Not so many, as it happens. Turns out the dating pool in prison ain't that great," Zig said with painful honesty.

He didn't usually talk about his time inside. It was no one's business. But with Si . . . With Si, he felt he could stop trying to pretend it'd never happened.

Si had gone still. "Zig . . ."

Zig cocked his head. "What's up?"

"You didn't, like . . ." Si's voice oozed unhappiness. "You know. Get attacked?"

"What? Shit, no. *No.* It ain't like all them stories you hear about US jails. And I was in a good nick. Nobody even got shivved, not while I was there, anyhow. Worst thing that happened was a fistfight over *Britain's Got Talent.*" Zig grinned. "Turns out some people *really* like dog acts. And some people really, really don't."

Si smiled at his pie. "I'm glad. That it weren't too bad for you."

"Some people would say I got off easy." Dad would, no doubt about it. Him and Trent had both got longer sentences in worse jails. Thank God they didn't know he'd raised the alarm, or they'd have spent their years inside plotting bloody revenge—

Zig startled as Si's large, warm hand landed gently on his arm.

"Sorry, didn't mean to make you jump." Si lifted his hand, but Zig grabbed it and held it tight.

"Nah, I'm good. Was miles away." Zig took a deep breath. "It means a lot to me. You accepting me, after everything. Most blokes wouldn't. At least, not for any longer than it takes 'em to get off." Then he wanted to kick himself, because seriously, whose side was he on?

"What, like give a dog a bad name and hang him? I told you. You done your time, and now it's in the past." Si squeezed his hand.

Zig's eyes prickled weirdly as he squeezed back. "You're all for second chances, then?" For a moment he had a crazy, wild hope: maybe Si would be willing to give *them* a second chance?

Should he say something? Ask Si outright if he'd be willing to try getting together again?

But then Si dropped his hand and glanced at his phone in a way that seemed somehow staged. "If you're finished, I reckon we'd better be getting back now. Otherwise Ange won't be giving you no second chances."

"Right. Yeah." Zig forced a smile. "I'll get me coat on."

It was probably better like this anyway. This way, nobody got hurt. *Yeah, right.*

Chapter Twenty-Six
Si

S i drove carefully along the country lanes, keeping to the speed limit despite how he wanted to open up the throttle and let the Harley roar. Zig's arms around him were making his whole body fizz, half in pleasure and half in pain. Close as they were on the bike, he wanted to be closer. To hold him, touch him, make love to him.

He hadn't felt like this since . . . since he'd been with Zig in London.

Sitting there in the pub, holding Zig's hand, Si had come *this* close to asking him out. Suggesting they get back together properly. He hadn't meant to. All he'd wanted was to give Zig a fun afternoon: seeing stuff from a book he liked and then going on to the Cerne Abbas giant, which was always good for a laugh.

Course, it hadn't occurred to him until they were there that the itinerary could be seen as a bit suggestive. Not that Woolbridge was romantic, exactly, but the giant—he wasn't so much suggesting stuff as hollering it out across the countryside. Zig had noticed, Si could tell. He'd been like Si remembered from their time in London, when it was only the two of them. He'd stood closer, touched Si more. Not in a sexual way. In a wanting-to-be-close way.

Si had wanted it too. He'd forgotten how much he loved doing stuff with Zig. Seeing him smile properly. Laughing with him. Then when they'd been in the pub, bellies full and warmed by the fire, the conversation had turned intimate. Si had gazed into those odd-coloured eyes, shining in the firelight, and he'd barely been able to stop himself.

Had he made the right decision? To back off, lose the moment? Si wasn't sure. In fact, speeding along the road to the end of their afternoon together, he was starting to wonder if backing off had been the worst decision he'd made in his life.

Zig had changed. The old Zig would never have talked about second chances with a tear in his eye. The old Zig would have expected all the chances as his gods-given due, and sod anyone who disagreed. Although Si hated to think of him locked up in prison, it was like it'd knocked the sharp edges off of him. Or was it down to what happened on that last robbery and the decision he'd made then? Any road, he'd grown up; they both had. Si wasn't the naïve kid he'd been back then, believing the best of people cos he cared for them.

In so many ways, though, Zig hadn't changed. Still the same smile, the same glint in his eye that made Si melt inside. The same leggy sprawl whenever he sat on a sofa, a bench, a barstool. The same vulnerability in his body language, although Si hadn't recognised it as such way back when.

Si forced himself to concentrate on the road, ignoring the yearning to stop the bike and take Zig in his arms. After all, maybe that was his dick talking? For an organ that didn't usually have a right lot to say for itself, it was being proper gabby right now. Si didn't know what to think, and he didn't have a clue who he could ask about it. If he went to Adam to ask if he ought to get back with Zig, he knew what sort of answer he'd get. Mum? There'd probably be pitchforks involved. Sash . . . She'd be less stabby, but there wasn't much chance she'd give him her blessing either.

Esme? Now he really was clutching at straws. *She* might tell him to go ahead, but that was only cos she didn't know about the past.

And at the end of the day, did Zig feel the same way? Si wasn't daft, at least not more than fifty percent of the time, and he could tell Zig had been into the idea of them having a second chance. But what did that really mean for Zig? A second chance to get his end away?

No, it'd been more than that. Si had seen it in his eyes, right before he'd bottled it and said it was time to go home. He was sure of it. Then again, they'd spent that afternoon together, after a morning of Zig baring his soul and obviously expecting a bad reaction . . . Si felt a weight crushing him, so heavy he was surprised the Harley wasn't sinking into the tarmac. Of *course* Zig's feelings had been intense after all that.

Give him a couple of days to get over it all and he'd probably think he'd had a lucky escape. Avoided any complications that might stop him moving on when he felt like it. Si had done the right thing.

It didn't make him feel any better as he parked the Harley in front of the garage. Zig gave him a fake smile as he handed back his helmet, and Si's heart clenched.

"You coming back to the flat, or are you heading straight over?" he asked, not sure what answer he wanted to hear.

"I'll go straight on. No harm in getting there early," Zig said, and Si realised that definitely wasn't the answer he'd hoped for.

He nodded mechanically. "Have a good night."

"Yeah. You too." Zig turned to go, and Si closed his eyes for a moment in something like despair. Then a hand touched his arm, and he opened them, startled.

"Si? Thanks for this afternoon." Zig's expression was weirdly intent. "I mean it. And— And for everything. It means a lot. Even if . . ." He didn't finish the sentence, just half laughed and shook his head. "I'll see you tonight."

"Yeah. Tonight," Si said, having to clear his throat as Zig walked away.

Chapter Twenty-Seven
Zig

Zig walked along the street with his hands in his pockets and his head down, the cold biting into him now that he was no longer pressed against Si. He felt chilled inside, too, and empty. It had been the perfect afternoon, right up until the end.

At least now you know where you stand, and it's freezing your bollocks off out in the cold on your own. It ain't gonna happen, you and Si getting back together.

Si had been tempted, Zig was almost certain. That moment in the pub when they'd held hands and talked about second chances. It hadn't all been Zig's stupid, hopeful imagination wanting them to get back to how they used to be. Si had been thinking about it too. Wanting it, even.

But then he'd thought about it some more, and he'd made sure things didn't go any further. Because, face it, Si was smart enough to know he didn't need a fuck-up like Zig ruining the life he'd made for himself here. With a good job and mates who cared about him. Close to his mum and dad—decent people who obviously loved him to bits.

Zig ought to be happy for him. And he *was*. But he couldn't help wishing Si's life could include him, that was all. Because it was clear, now, that Si wouldn't want him staying in his flat much longer. He'd have to move out, find his own place somewhere. Some boxlike room in a shitty shared house, like he'd had in London. And yeah, he'd still see Si. Friday nights, when he came in with his mates for band night. Around town. Maybe Si would let him come to the flat for pizza and a *Doctor Who* marathon every now and then. But what they'd had today—the closeness they'd shared—that wouldn't be repeated. Si would drift away from him.

Zig had lost him.

He made it to the Prince of Wales, having barely noticed the route he'd taken. There must have been other pedestrians, cars on the roads he'd crossed, but he couldn't have remembered any of them to save his life. He should probably feel grateful that his subconscious had had enough sense of self-preservation to stop him from walking under a bus, but it was difficult to muster the energy to care.

Standing for a moment outside the pub, gazing at the already-familiar black-and-white exterior, Zig squared his shoulders, took a deep breath, and struggled to find a smile. Punters didn't like a miserable sod behind the bar, and Ange wouldn't thank him for chasing off trade. It was time to put his game face on.

When he walked in, Finn was behind the bar and flashed him a smile. It helped.

"All right, mate?" Zig greeted him.

Finn glanced at the clock on the wall. "You're early. Sucking up to the boss, or could you not wait to see me?"

"You got me. I've been pining for your presence. Be back in a mo, once I've got me shirt off." Zig headed into the back room to change into his regulation polo shirt. He'd been issued with two, and the one he'd worn last night was snuggling up to Si's undies in the laundry basket back at the flat.

Way to go, Zig. Jealous of your bloody uniform shirt.

Ange waltzed in while he was mid-change without so much as a by-your-leave. "Well now, my lover, *that* I did not expect."

Zig rolled his eyes—it was safe; he was facing away from her. "Shocked by how fit I am?"

"Surprised by your taste in ink, more like. I wouldn't have put you down as the flowery sort."

He pulled on the shirt and turned around, blocking her view of the tattoo on his shoulder. "Me gran's name was Rose, and they were her favourite flower."

Ange's expression softened. "You were close, were you?"

Zig shrugged one shoulder. "Didn't have a mum, so yeah, I guess." No guessing about it. Everything had been better before Gran had died. Even Dad had watched how he spoke and acted while she was around.

"Well, it's a lovely way to remember her. Now go on, don't let me keep you. There's thirsty people out there. Although I hope you're not expecting to be paid for the extra fifteen minutes."

"Hadn't crossed me mind," Zig said honestly and headed out to the bar.

Ange hadn't been wrong about the thirsty punters. The pub was busy enough, although it was a different crowd from last night. Zig let himself fall into the rhythm of serving drinks and taking payment, adding a bit of banter when it seemed called for.

None of Si's mates had turned up by ten o'clock, which probably meant they weren't coming. Zig was grateful. He wasn't sure he could take any of Adam's digs tonight.

Or, for that matter, the reminder of how badly he'd fucked up back when he'd first known Si. Christ, what if things had gone differently, back then? What if he'd distanced himself from Dad earlier? Told Trent to sod off when he came sniffing round Si at the pub? Maybe him and Si would've stayed together. Zig would never have gone to prison. He might have joined Si in learning a trade. Got a job that paid more than minimum wage.

Maybe he'd be happy now. Although he might have the odd scar from the beating Trent would've given him.

"All right there, my lover?" Ange's sharp voice cut into his thoughts. "You're away with the fairies this evening."

"Sorry." Zig dragged up his best smile. "Did I miss something?"

"I was saying, we've got a barrel needs changing. Go with Finn, and he can show you where everything is."

"Course." Zig nodded to Finn, and they headed out back while Ange took up her station at the bar.

"You don't really need me," Finn said as they jogged down the stone stairs to the cellar. "It's all pretty standard down here."

Zig grinned. "Yeah, but for all Ange knows, I lied about me experience. I could end up swapping stout for cider."

Finn laughed. "No way, mate. I've seen how you move around the bar. You've got plenty of experience." His shoulder bumped against Zig's as they reached the empty barrel.

"Hey, fake it till you make it." Zig was only half-joking. Wasn't that what he was doing now? Acting like there was nothing wrong, while inside his heart was aching?

"Go on, then. Show us what you've got."

Zig raised an eyebrow, then set to it. The new kegs were clearly marked and stored, he found, in date order, so it was easy to select the oldest. Shifting a full barrel of beer the few feet necessary was more about technique than muscle, and he could have done it in his sleep. With the new barrel in position, he flipped the valve controlling the gas supply to the empty, removed the coupler, checked the seals, coupled up the new keg, turned on the gas, and watched the chamber fill. Then he straightened. "We're good."

Finn nodded approvingly and patted Zig on the back. "Nice. First time I did one of these, I sprayed a couple of pints all down myself."

"Hey, turns out I wasn't lying about my experience after all. Right, we'd better get back before Ange sends out a search party."

"Guess so." Finn sounded disappointed for some reason.

Nah, that was crazy. Zig was imagining stuff.

At the end of the night, after they'd cleared up, Zig went out back to pick up his jacket and the shirt he'd changed out of. He'd have to do some laundry tomorrow; no way was he turning up to work in a polo shirt he'd sweated in all night. Pulling it off felt good for a moment, an acknowledgement work was done for the day.

Then reality dropped back on his shoulders like a yoke. What did the end of the working day mean, except time to think about how much Si didn't want him?

"Nice."

Finn's voice jarred him out of his thoughts, and he spun. "What?"

"Just admiring your . . . tattoo." Finn grinned slyly. "Want to come back to mine for a drink or something?"

"Uh . . ." Generally speaking, Zig was a lot smoother when someone tried to pick him up. But he was the sort of bone-deep tired that came from emotion, not exertion. "It's a bit late."

"Yep. That it is. Might have to head to bed soon. *Really* soon." Finn winked. "So, how about it?"

For a wild moment, Zig was almost tempted. Si didn't want him, and here at least was someone who did. Someone who'd hold him, touch him, the way he wanted Si to . . .

Christ, no. Bile rose at the thought. "Sorry, mate. I'm sort of taken." Because he was, he realised. Even if the bloke who had his heart didn't want it, and who could blame him?

Finn grunted through tight lips. "That hairy biker who was in last night?" His tone was resigned.

It was easier to go with that than to explain. "Yeah. We're, uh, living together."

"Thought you only got into town a few days ago?"

Zig laughed in a faintly hysterical way. "What can I say? I'm a fast mover. Nah, me and him, we go way back. Been picking up where we left off." His stomach was hollow as the truth in it hit him like a gut punch. *Yep: right back with Si deciding I ain't worth the aggro.*

"Okay. Well, if you change your mind . . ."

"You'll be the first to know." Zig mustered a cocky grin from fuck knew where, waved at Finn, and went to say goodnight to Ange.

Then he walked back to Si's flat, feeling as cold and empty as the streets half an hour after closing time.

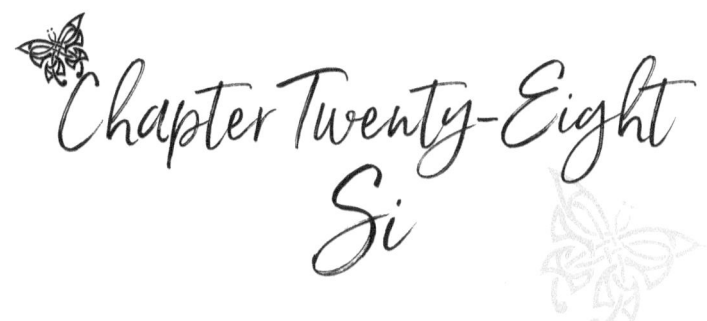

Chapter Twenty-Eight
Si

S i's Saturday night had been, objectively speaking, a bit on the sad side. He'd stayed in. Watched a couple of episodes of *Doctor Who* on iPlayer. Realised he'd watched them out of sequence. Thought about cooking dinner but hadn't been that hungry since they'd had lunch at three, so had made himself a slice of toast and marmite and called it a day. Thought about playing a game, but hadn't been in the mood.

Had phoned his mum.

"Simon, love. I thought you'd be out. With that boy." Her tone darkened several notches on the last bit.

"He's working tonight. And it ain't like, you know. He's not my boyfriend." Si's heart clenched, because saying it out loud only rubbed it in. *He could have been.*

No. No, he couldn't, cos what Si wanted from a boyfriend and what Zig wanted were two very different things. He had to remember how Zig had been when they'd broken up—it'd been water off a duck's back, hadn't it?

Except Zig never lets anyone see he's hurt.

"Well, I can't say I'm not glad to hear that. How long is he staying with you?"

"I dunno. Till he gets himself settled, like." Gods, *would* he get settled? Or would he be moving on once he'd got enough cash from his new job?

"Well, don't you let him take advantage of you."

"Mum!"

"I don't mean like *that*. Although it's a valid point, now you've mentioned it. There's such a thing as being too easygoing, you know. Don't let him leech off you."

"Zig's not leeching. He's offered to pay rent."

"Did you accept?"

"Well, no. He ain't been working long enough to get paid yet."

"And *that's* what I mean. You're letting him take advantage."

"It's not taking advantage. It's being a mate." There was a knock on the downstairs door. Zig must be back. "Mum, I gotta go. You take care, all right? Give my love to Dad."

"You can give it to him yourself. Come round for lunch tomorrow."

"On me own?"

She sighed. "No, you can bring your *friend*, all right?"

"What, so you can have a go at him? Mum, I need to get the door."

"I won't have a go. You be here tomorrow, Simon. With or without."

"I'll let you know. Bye, Mum."

"Love you." She ended the call before he could say it back.

Si put his phone down and hurried downstairs. Zig looked like he'd had a long night, Si thought as he let him in. "Work all right?"

"Yeah. Busy, but you know."

Si wasn't sure what he was supposed to know.

"You have a good evening without me?" Zig asked.

Si shrugged. "Quiet." He mustered a laugh. "Must be getting old."

Zig smiled weakly. "Me too. Think I'll turn in early tonight, if that's okay."

"Yeah, no problem." Si could wait until tomorrow to mention Mum's invitation.

Si got up early on Sunday, but he tiptoed around the flat so as not to wake Zig. How could anyone appear tired while actually asleep? Course, Si didn't see a right lot of sleeping people, so maybe everyone did? Any road, Zig probably needed his rest after working till nearly midnight.

He put a load of washing on, did a bit of cleaning, and managed to nip out to the shops for some groceries before Zig blinked awake sometime after eleven.

Zig sat up, glanced at his phone and scrubbed his face with his hands. "Christ, did I really sleep that long?"

"Yep. Wasn't sure if I oughtta wake you or just knock the dust off. You okay? Not coming down with something, are you?" Si peered at him with concern.

"Nah, I'm good." Zig yawned. "S'pose I've missed breakfast."

"Pretty sure we can rustle up a slice of toast for you. You, uh, you might not want to fill up too much," Si said cautiously. "Mum's invited us round for Sunday lunch."

"What, me too?" Zig's voice rose an octave.

"Yeah, of course. Her and Dad do a nice roast. So, are you up for that?" Si mentally crossed his fingers. The more he thought about it, the more he wanted this: Zig and his family having a meal together.

Even if it wasn't like he was bringing a boyfriend home.

There was a pause. "Can't. Gotta work."

"At lunchtime? Thought you only did evenings."

"We're short-staffed. Ange asked me to come in." Zig didn't meet Si's gaze.

Si's heart fell. Which was daft, really. At least this way they wouldn't have to worry about Mum forgetting her promise and causing any aggro. "That's a shame, then. Maybe another time."

"Yeah." Zig stood up and stretched. "I better hit the shower."

"I'll put the kettle on for when you've finished," Si said.

Chapter Twenty-Nine
Zig

The hot water did its best to unthaw the chill in Zig's bones he'd been feeling since yesterday. He made his shower last as long as he reasonably could.

Si had seemed disappointed Zig wouldn't be sitting down to a nice cosy family lunch with him and his parents, and he felt bad about that. But, Christ, it would have been awkward enough at the best of times—what did Zig know about cosy family meals and how you were supposed to behave?—but coming after Si had oh-so-gently dashed all Zig's hopes of them ever getting back together . . .

Nope. No way. He'd rather stake himself out on the tor naked and wait for the crows to peck out his eyes. And any other soft bits they fancied. Zig gave his hair a vicious scrub, then turned the water temperature down for a cold rinse off. He felt worse than ever, lying to Si about having to go to work, but telling him the truth would've only made him sad. This way, Si could go off to his mum and dad's with a clear conscience.

Course, it left Zig with a day to fill on his own, but that was hardly new. He dried off, his hair leaving blue streaks on Si's towel. Bugger. Better shove that in the wash before the stain dried in.

When he came out of the bathroom, Si broke into a smile.

Zig felt off-balance. Self-conscious. "What?"

"Your hair's all fluffy."

"Oh." He'd have to gel it for tonight, but he couldn't be arsed right now. "Yeah, uh, the colour's run and all." Guiltily, Zig held up the streaked towel.

"No worries. Chuck it over, and I'll bung it in the machine." The corners of his eyes crinkled. "Don't matter if it don't come out. I always reckoned these towels were a bit boring."

Did he have to be so bloody *nice*? It really wasn't helping.

"Right. You up for that toast? Kettle's boiled, so I can make you a coffee in a jiff—"

"It's okay," Zig cut him off, unable to stand it any longer. "I'm heading straight out. Need a bit of fresh air before work, yeah?"

"Oh, right. Course you do. I'll, uh, see you after work, then?"

"Yeah. Have a good time with your folks." Zig grabbed his phone and his jacket and practically ran out of the flat.

There was a biting wind outside. The icy chill of his still-damp hair on his neck told him he was an idiot for running out like that, but then Zig knew that already. He'd spent the night lurching from one dream to another, all of them featuring Si. In some of them he'd held Zig, kissed him. In others, he'd told him plainly he wasn't good enough. Zig wasn't sure which ones had been worse.

It'd been torture to be in Si's flat and have him acting like he cared. *Except he does care, doesn't he? He just doesn't want you.* Maybe if he got cold enough, the pain from that would distract him from the aching hollow in his chest?

Zig snorted, his breath steaming in the air. Yeah, right. *Pull yourself together, you tit. Time to stop the self-pity party and think about getting somewhere warmer. Or at least getting some food inside you.*

It being Sunday, the libraries wouldn't be open, though the shops mostly were. Not that Zig wanted to buy anything. No point accumulating stuff he'd have to shift out of Si's flat all too soon, and it wasn't like he had cash to spare in any case.

On the other hand, he was bloody starving.

He nipped into the small supermarket on the high street and picked up a meal deal of sandwiches, fruit juice, and crisps that'd serve as brunch. Then he picked up another, checking the dates to make sure things would keep if Kai already had food for today. At least lack of refrigeration wasn't going to be a problem in this weather.

Then he set off on the way to the tor, hoping Kai would be there.

At least here his luck was in. Kai greeted him with a smile, then a suspicious look. "You okay? You look like you came out in a hurry."

Zig ran a self-conscious hand through his ungelled hair. "This mate I'm staying with—it got a bit awkward."

Kai frowned. "Have they been telling you it's time to move out?"

"Nah, fuck no. Not that it ain't." Zig dropped to his haunches beside Kai. He'd have sat down, but he didn't have a sleeping bag and the ground looked fucking freezing. "Just, I thought me and him were . . ." He shook his head. "We went out yesterday. On his bike—fucking monster, that thing is; it's well cool—and he was so . . . It was like it was a date, yeah?"

"But?" Kai prompted.

"Wasn't, was it? He made that pretty clear in the end."

"Bugger," Kai said sympathetically. "He's not, like, homophobic, is he?"

"He's me ex, so no."

"Doesn't always follow."

"Si's not phobic about anyone. He's a good bloke. The best." Zig sighed. His kneecaps were slowly turning to ice. If he stayed crouched down too long, they'd probably snap when he tried to get up. He should probably care about that.

"That sucks."

Zig gave them a look.

"Well, I mean, if he was a total shit, then you could feel good about not getting back together, couldn't you?"

"Fair enough." Zig had to laugh. "He deserves better than me anyway."

"You seem all right to me."

"Tell that to Si. Or rather, don't bother cos he knows the truth about me."

"But he still likes you as a mate? That's something, innit?"

Zig nodded. "Yeah. Yeah, it is. But . . . I got me hopes up, you know? I mean, I didn't know I was doing it, but when he . . ."

"Made it clear?"

"Yeah, that was when I realised how much I wanted it. Wanted him. And I don't mean only sex, okay?"

"Do you love him?"

Icy shards pierced Zig's battered heart. "Yeah. I do." Funny how he'd known that, really, but putting it into words hurt so fucking much.

"Does he know that?"

Zig stood up, his frozen joints protesting. "Don't think it matters."

Chapter Thirty Si

Si's mum had made an occasion of lunch with wine at the table and proper coffee afterwards. Even a box of chocolates she'd got in the Secret Santa at work. It was a real shame Zig hadn't been able to come.

Mum didn't say word one about Zig once Si had explained he was working, so maybe Dad had been having a go at her again. Si found himself wanting to bring up the subject out of sheer perversity, but he wasn't quite that daft. Instead, he talked about work, and family, and Mum's Pilates classes.

It was a while before Si was able to leave for home. And okay, maybe he hadn't fancied going back to the empty flat too soon anyway. When he finally left, Mum gave him a big hug and told him to take care with an emphasis that showed she hadn't forgotten about Zig. Or maybe he was reading too much into it.

Would Zig be working the evening shift as well? Si wondered as he walked along the street, his comfortably full belly a contrast to the weird emptiness in his chest. He might only get to see Zig for an hour or so between shifts. Or not at all. It didn't feel right, after yesterday.

Sage & Seer was still open when he got back—the shop closed at four on Sundays—but there were no customers at the mo, so Si popped in to see Esme. She was restocking the crystals.

"All right, Es?"

Esme glanced up. She was in crimson today, some sort of knitted dress that looked grand on her. "Oh, hello, you. Mislaid your shadow?"

"Zig? He ain't me shadow. Hardly see him, most days."

"Oh, dear." Esme frowned in concern.

Bugger. "It ain't like that," Si protested.

She cocked her head. "But you'd like it to be?"

Si opened his mouth, then closed it again. He'd thought talking to Esme about Zig was a nonstarter cos she didn't know about their past. But then, wasn't that what he wanted? Someone who wasn't biased?

"Simon Greczik, are you trying to put me off by doing goldfish impersonations?"

"No—I'm thinking, all right? Gimme a mo."

"Take several." The bell over the door rang and a couple of teenagers stumbled in, laughing. Esme stepped forward. "I'm so sorry. We're closed now. Do come again tomorrow."

Somehow, the teenagers ended up outside without complaint. Esme bolted the door behind them and turned the Open sign to Closed. "Now, I'm all yours."

Si took a deep breath. "I dunno what I want. I mean, I know what I *want*, but I dunno if it's a good idea."

"Come through and I'll make a pot of tea."

"Long as it's not that roo-ee-booze stuff."

"It's pronounced roy-boss. And it's good for your heart."

"Could do with that, I'm not gonna lie. Bring it on, then," Si said, resigned, and followed her into the tiny kitchen area. He stood there, hands awkwardly shoved into his jeans pockets, while she boiled the kettle and steeped the rooibos tea. Then he accepted the mug she handed him, took a sip, grimaced, and set it down carefully on the draining board.

Esme sipped her own tea with obvious enjoyment. "Now, tell Aunty Esme all about it."

"Ain't nothing to tell, really."

She gave him a steely smile. "Tell me anyway."

Si drew in a long breath and let it out slowly. "See, me and him? Back in the day, we was more than mates. We was, well, lovers, I guess. And it didn't end well. But now I'm thinking—and I'm pretty sure *he's* thinking it and all—maybe we could get back together."

"Hmm. And it would be different this time because?"

Si found himself picking his tea up and taking another swallow. It wasn't any better than the last. "Zig's changed since then."

"Has he? Or does he just want you to think he has?"

"No—I mean, I know he has." Si thought furiously. "Look, there's stuff I can't tell you, cos it wouldn't be right, but the last six years, they ain't been easy for him."

"Family troubles?"

"Kind of. See, Zig's dad . . . He's a bit of a bastard, from what I heard. Now *and* then, like. And Zig, well, he decided he didn't want no part of that no more. But it cost him, getting out. And that's what I mean about him having changed. Old Zig wouldn't have stood up against anything his dad said or did. Specially not if it meant him going to j— Uh, forget that bit." Si winced, guilt rising.

"Forgotten." Esme's tone was firm, with a hint of smug. "Now, you said you think he's changed, and for the better. So, what *is* worrying you?"

"I dunno what he wants," Si blurted out despairingly. "He turned up on me doorstep and it's brought out all kinds of, well, *feelin's*. For me at any rate. I don't know what it means to him, though. I know he fancies me, and I'm pretty sure he likes me, but . . . I don't want to have, like, something casual. I ain't built like that." *I don't think I can survive it if we get together again and he leaves me.*

Esme patted his arm. "Of course not. So, what did he say when you asked him about it?"

Si stared into his mug. "Uh . . ."

"You *did* ask him?" Esme's tone was arch, and she didn't wait for an answer. "I hear words can be quite effective as a means of communication."

"It ain't so easy, all right?" Si had probably gone as red as his tea. "What if I ask him and he says he don't want nothing serious? Gonna feel a right numpty then, ain't I?"

"As opposed to the way you'd feel if you *didn't* ask him, never got together, and found out on your deathbed he was in love with you all along? Faint heart never won fair maiden—of any gender."

Si laughed despite himself. "If there's one thing I know about Zig, it's that he ain't no maiden."

"But you would like to win him, yes? So think about it. And then ask him." Esme stood up. "I like him. Although perhaps you shouldn't take that as a recommendation; I've always had terrible taste in men."

"I've never seen you with a man," Si said without thinking.

"Never let it be said I don't learn from my mistakes. Now, finish your tea and away with you. I've got a till to cash up."

Si chugged the godsawful stuff down in one and headed up to his flat, trying not to gag.

When eight o'clock rolled around and Zig still wasn't back from work, Si had to face the fact he'd be spending the evening alone. Maybe it was a good thing, though? It felt like they needed some space from each other. Time to think about what they both wanted.

Trouble was, Si *missed* him. Was worried about him too. It couldn't be good for him to work such long hours. Was Ange taking advantage of him? Course, he'd have the week to recover, assuming he didn't pick up any more extra hours. He could sleep in while Si went to work.

It was like tag-team flat-sitting, this was, Si thought with a sigh.

When Adam rang, it was a welcome distraction.

"All right, mate?" Si answered eagerly.

"Yeah, I'm good. How about you? Still got your house guest?"

"Yeah, but he's working tonight."

"How's it going?" Adam's voice sounded a bit off, but Si couldn't work out what the subtext was. Assuming it wasn't just a bad line.

"His job? Good, I think."

"I meant you and him."

"You know we ain't together, right?"

"Right." There was a pause. "Had a good weekend?"

"Yeah. Took Zig out for a ride on the Harley." Si decided not to mention the honeymoon hotel and the giant dick pic.

"Uh-huh."

Si was suddenly tired of trying to read Adam's tone of voice without any accompanying visual input. "You fancy going out for a quick pint?"

All right, maybe the flat was a bit depressing tonight with only him in it too.

"Bit cold, innit?"

"Don't be a wuss. A bracing walk'll do you good."

"Fine. Where?"

"Prince of Wales?" At least he'd get to see Zig. Check he was okay.

"If you want." Adam didn't sound exactly keen, and Si could guess why, but sod it, it'd been their local for years. If Adam didn't want to see Zig there, he could sit with his back to the bar.

"See you there in twenty."

In the end, Si bumped into Adam on the corner before the pub. He was on his own. "No Corin?" Si asked as they headed down the street.

"No, he's working out." Adam looked into the middle distance and smiled, presumably at the thought of his bloke with his muscles all pumped up.

Guilt twinged in Si's chest. "Sorry to drag you away from him."

"Hey, you're my best mate. Course I'm going to be here for you. Let's get inside, though. It's bloody freezing."

Pushing open the door of the pub, Si was hit with warm, beer-scented air and the buzz of conversation. Even on a Sunday night, the place was busy, although not packed. His gaze darted to the bar, but he couldn't see Zig there. "Pint of Becket's?" he asked Adam.

"Cheers, mate." Adam followed him to the bar, where they got served almost immediately.

The barman was tall, blond, and fit in a lithe, skinny way. The sort of bloke Si could easily see Zig with, which hurt a lot worse than it should have.

"Oh, it's you." He looked at Si strangely. Unhappy, but resigned, maybe? Si was still wondering what that was all about and if he was imagining it, when the barman spoke again. "Zig's out back. I'll tell him you've come."

Then he loped over to the door to the back and called out, "Zig? Your boyfriend's here."

Beside Si, Adam went still. "Boyfriend?"

"What? No. I told you, we're just mates." Si wasn't sure how convincing he sounded, which was rich seeing as it was the truth, but hearing himself called Zig's bloke had done weird things to his insides that were putting him off his game.

"So why does Blondie seem to think you're an item? Mate, you *know* it's a bad idea. I can't believe you—"

He broke off as Zig appeared behind the bar, looking flustered. "All right, Si? Adam? What can I get you?"

Si took a breath, but Adam got in there first. "How about an explanation of what your mate there called you?"

Zig smiled nervously. "What, Zig?"

Adam darkened, leaning over the bar to get in Zig's face. "Don't try to be funny. He said you were Si's boyfriend."

"And what did Si say about that?" Zig's gaze turned to Si, so intense it made him totally lose his train of thought.

It didn't help that Blondie, as Adam had called him, was standing two feet away staring at the lot of 'em. *Gods help anyone who wants to get served in this pub tonight*, Si couldn't stop from thinking.

It seemed he wasn't the only one. Ange marched over from the other end of the bar. "Is this a pub or some kind of reality soap opera? No, don't tell me, I don't want to know. You"—she glared at Blondie—"get back to work. And you"—she turned her steely eye on Zig—"if you're having a domestic, you have it outside. You've got five minutes."

Zig nodded and left the bar. Si stared after him, then roused himself. Zig would be going out the back, so if Si nipped out the front and round the side, he could meet him in the back alley. He hoped.

Adam's hand caught his arm before he'd gone two paces. "What the hell are you doing?"

"Having a domestic?" Si tried to smile. "I dunno what's going on, all right? Gonna talk to Zig."

Adam shook his head wildly. "Why would you tell me you're not—"

"Cos it's true! Cross my heart. Look, I gotta go. He's only got five minutes."

This time, Adam let him go, and Si made it out of the pub and round the corner fast as he could.

Chapter Thirty-One
Si

Si found Zig leaning against the wall next to the bins, his arms wrapped around himself, looking so vulnerable it made Si's heart ache. Si slowed his pace, not wanting to spook him. "Zig?"

"Sorry." Zig stared at the ground.

"Right. Uh, what are you sorry for?"

Zig looked up then, his face unreadable this far from the streetlighting. "I let Finn think you and me were together."

"Oh." Si's chest felt weird, and he really wished he'd had a chance to get a drink in. The alley wasn't the greatest place for a heart-to-heart. The best thing that could be said about it was that the bins didn't stink, although someone had definitely had a pee here in the not-too-distant past. Muted sounds of conversation and laughter drifted out to them from the pub. "Why?"

"He came on to me, didn't he?"

"Oh." Of course he had. Si felt flat, like a pint of beer left out for a week. Then he frowned, honestly puzzled. "Don't you fancy him, then?"

Zig laughed, but he didn't sound happy, and he was back to staring at the ground. "He's okay. Not really feeling like being with anyone right now."

Si hated the way he sounded. Like his heart had been ripped out from the inside. He moved closer and took Zig gently by the shoulders. Under his hands, Zig's body shook. "Zig? Tell me why you ain't all right."

Zig looked up again, and his darker eye gleamed. "Fucked up, didn't I? Met this great bloke, but it turns out he's not daft enough to want me back." He shook his head. "I'll move out. Soon as. Get out of your hair."

Si's chest was doing more of that weird stuff, and his ribs felt too tight. It almost sounded like Zig really cared about him. Had been crushed by Si's implicit rejection yesterday afternoon. But that couldn't be true, could it? "You don't have to move out. I like having you around," he added with a lopsided smile.

"Don't say that if you don't mean it."

"Course I mean it." Si struggled to get his thoughts in order, a desperate hope fizzing in his veins. "Zig, you know I like you. Always have." *Always will.* "I don't know what you want from me, though."

"What I want? I want you." Zig's voice cracked on the last word, wrenching Si's heart.

"What does that mean, though? You want to be, what, friends with benefits or something?" Si wasn't sure he could survive that.

Zig didn't answer immediately. Then he shook his head. "Sorry. I'm a greedy bastard. Always have been. I want everything. I want to sleep with you. Cook with you. Watch crap shows on Netflix with you. Christ, I even want to put up with your best mate looking daggers at me every time we meet if it means I can be with you."

Si had once had a near miss when he was out on his bike and a container truck turned without signalling. Right now, he had a pretty good idea of how it would've felt if the truck had ploughed into him. "You mean, like . . . boyfriends?"

"I mean I love you." It sounded despairing, which was all wrong, because Si was flooded with a heady, disbelieving surge of elation.

Zig *loved* him? "Why?" he blurted.

Zig sobbed out a laugh. "That. That's why. It's okay. I get it. I fucked up last time. You've got no reason to—" His voice cut off with an *oof* of breath as Si threw his arms around him and hugged him tight.

"I've got every reason," Si said into Zig's hair, his voice hoarse. He pulled back a bit and looked Zig in the eye. "You ain't the boy you were six years ago. Nor am I. Reckon we've both grown up a bit. Changed for the better. Thing is, though . . . I loved that boy back then. No, wait," he added quickly, cos Zig had started to pull away. "I ain't finished. I loved you, yeah, but I couldn't be with you. Not the way you thought in them days. But I reckon you've changed your mind about a few things since then."

"Haven't changed me mind about you," Zig whispered. "You were always the one that got away."

Si tightened his arms around Zig's trembling frame. "I ain't going nowhere," he said softly, his heart singing. "Not this time. And I hope you ain't, neither."

Zig clung to him and then sobbed out a laugh. "Except maybe back to work. Pretty sure it's been more than five minutes."

"Ah, Ange'll let you off," Si said carelessly, light-headed over the amazing turn this evening had taken. "She's an old romantic at heart."

"Speak for yourself, lover-boy." Ange's voice cut through the still of the alleyway like a well-sharpened, but not unsympathetic, axe through firewood. "Zig? Everything sorted?"

Zig sniffed loudly and stepped back from Si. "Yeah. All sorted." He turned to Si with a look of open wonder. "See you at home?"

Si nodded, then cursed. "I'd better go get Adam first, though. Or he'll be accusing you of doing away with me."

"I'll send him out, love." Ange sighed. "I can see I'll get no work out of this one while you're here."

"One sec," Zig blurted, then he seized Si's face between his hands and kissed him.

Si melted. Zig tasted fresh like mint tea and warm like sunshine. His lips were soft, and after the first fierce grasp his hands were gentle.

Ange cleared her throat pointedly, and Si congealed again as Zig let go of him. "See ya," he said with a crooked smile, and followed his boss back into the pub.

There was a tug in Si's heart at the thought of leaving now, but Ange was probably right. If Si stayed, he'd spend the night leaning on the bar making googly eyes at Zig, which would probably be a bit distracting while he was trying to work. And Adam wouldn't take too kindly to it, either.

The butterflies flitting around Si's insides stuttered in midair. Oops. He was going to have to explain this to Adam. And with the thought, the man himself appeared.

He didn't look happy. Although he didn't look *un*happy, Si thought with relief. More sort of confused.

"Scratch? What the hell is going on? Are you and Zig together or not?"

Si took a deep breath. "Well, we weren't . . . But yeah, we are now." He couldn't stop the grin from breaking out over his face.

Adam grimaced. "I bloody knew it."

"Dunno how, seeing as I didn't," Si said firmly.

"You realise you're making a mistake, right?" Adam kicked at a screwed-up leaflet that'd blown in from somewhere. "It's gonna be history repeating itself."

Si folded his arms. "No, it ain't. He's changed."

"Has he?" Adam's voice dripped with scepticism.

"He's grown up and stopped listening to all that bollocks his dad used to tell him." Si held Adam's gaze. "You gotta remember, we were all kids back then. I know you looked up to your dad."

"Still do," Adam confirmed defiantly.

"So, it took Zig a while to realise his dad's a wrong'un. And I know what you think you know about Zig, but that break-in at your dad's site? Zig didn't have nothing to do with that."

"And you believe that?"

"I do. It was all his dad. Well, and that mate of his. You remember him, right? Trent. Nasty, slick little bastard." Si gave Adam a sharp look. "And even if it weren't true, Zig ain't the same man he was then."

"How can you be sure?" Adam threw up his hands. "You can't be sure! He's only been back on the scene for a matter of days."

"Cos he's told me other stuff. It ain't mine to share, but gods, if you'd been there, you'd have believed him too. I know he don't always tell the truth, but this weren't him lying. It weren't slick or nothing. It was raw. Like open bloody heart surgery."

Adam shook his head. "Listen to yourself. Five seconds ago you're admitting he's a liar, but *this*, this we've gotta believe him on?"

"Adam, you know you're my best mate. Always have been. So don't take this wrong. But it don't matter what you believe, cos I trust him." Si gazed at him sadly. "I hope this don't mean we can't be friends no more."

Adam was still shaking his head. "I can't . . . Look, I gotta go. I'll call you. Take care, okay?"

Si watched sorrowfully as he walked out of the alleyway and was lit, briefly, by the streetlamp before disappearing into the dark.

Chapter Thirty-Two
Si

Si headed home alone, caught in an unholy battle between elation and sadness. And a hefty dollop of nerves, he wasn't gonna lie, cos what if Zig had second thoughts by the time he finished his shift?

No, that was daft thinking. Zig had said he loved him. Elation surged to a victory, and Si practically skipped round the corner. All he needed was an umbrella and a sudden downpour, and he could reenact the "Singin' in the Rain" bit from that film his mum was so keen on.

Course, it'd probably look a bit different with a large, hairy biker doing it. Might get him a few funny glances, and his mates would piss 'emselves if they saw it.

Sadness rallied. Adam hadn't been happy with the news. Should Si have said what he had to him? He'd made it sound like he didn't care what Adam thought, which was bollocks. Si *cared* all right. He just wasn't gonna live his life by it.

Maybe Adam would come around? Be okay with things, once he'd had time to get used to it all? Once he'd got to know Zig—the new Zig—better? That was never gonna happen, though, if Adam refused to take the chance. Well, there was nothing Si could do about that right now.

Si let himself into the flat, took off his boots, and grabbed a beer from the kitchen. The place felt empty without Zig in it. Too quiet and definitely not colourful enough. He sat on the sofa. Zig's bedding was rolled up at one end. Si smiled. Might as well bung that in the wash. Zig wasn't gonna be needing it anymore.

Or was he? Maybe he'd still want his space, despite them being together now? They hadn't actually talked about what that meant. Si had been assuming it meant sharing a bed, but he shouldn't go taking Zig for granted, should he? He took a contemplative swig of beer.

It wasn't like they'd ever actually *slept* together before. Even when he'd sneaked Zig into his room at Adam's dad's, Zig had always left before morning, joking about his dad changing the locks if he stayed out all night.

Course, maybe it hadn't been a joke after all. There wasn't a lot Si would put past Zig's dad, despite never having met him. He didn't want to; he'd heard enough to know that. Zig was well away from that bastard.

Si took a hefty swig of his beer and wished he could fast-forward time to when Zig would be home. He nodded at his twelfth Doctor figurine. "Bet you never had this problem when you were waiting for River. Lucky bastard."

Chapter Thirty-Three
Zig

Zig knew he'd had a stupid smile on his face the rest of the night. Every time he'd fixed someone a shot, he'd seen it in the mirrored back wall of the bar. He'd tried to tone it down around Finn, cos he wasn't a bastard, but it kept creeping back up on him.

Si was going to give him another chance. Si believed he'd changed, and for the better. Zig hadn't been fooled by all that *we've both grown up* stuff—that'd just been Si being tactful. Si hadn't changed, not in who he was. Okay, maybe he'd got a little more cautious, but hadn't that started six years ago, when he'd told Zig to piss off? The actual growing up, though, that was all Zig. *Thank God you finally managed it.*

He'd never had so many people buy him a drink.

One of them was a middle-aged woman who'd come in with a crowd of cronies, all of them dressed to the nines. "You look like the cat that's got the cream," she commented as she paid. "Won the lottery?"

Zig grinned at her. "Something like that."

One of her mates broke in with an excited "Ooh, what did you win?"

"Big hairy biker with a Doctor Who collection and a Harley-Davidson."

"Aw, bless!" They gave him matching soppy looks. Come to that, Zig was probably wearing one too.

"Don't suppose he's got a mate who likes older women?" asked the lady who'd ordered, a bit wistfully.

"Why, is your mum looking for a bloke?" Zig sent back.

Both women laughed raucously. "I hope that poor boy knows what he's let himself in for with you," the second woman teased, as they gathered their drinks and walked away.

Yeah, Zig thought. *He does, and he still wants me. How the fuck did I get so lucky?*

After they'd closed up, he went to have a word with Ange, despite being desperate to get back to the flat. To Si. "Sorry about tonight. Won't happen again."

She actually gave him a fond look. "You're only young once. But next time, save the drama for when you're off the clock."

"Cross me heart." Zig grinned at her.

"Now get off home to your young man."

He didn't have to be told twice. Zig grabbed his jacket and left, still in his Prince of Wales shirt.

The cold was bitter outside, but it didn't seem to penetrate his clothing. Zig was walking on air. Him and Si were back together. He'd told Si he loved him and Si . . . Well, Si hadn't said it back, but it'd be crazy to expect that so soon. He'd said he didn't want him to leave, and that was the main thing, right?

A shiver of doubt crept in, like an icy finger of mid-December night air down the neck of his jacket. Si hadn't said what else he wanted, had he? Zig's memory of their conversation was a bit jumbled, but he reckoned it'd been all him saying what he wanted, not Si.

But then again, Si hadn't said no to any of it, had he?

He knocked on the door to the flat and waited, stomach churning, feeling a lot like he had when he'd first come here—Christ, had that really been less than a week ago? For a moment it all felt unreal.

Then Si's footsteps sounded on the stairs, and the door opened, letting out a welcoming breath of warm air. Si stood there on the doormat: big, solid, and smiling gently behind that beard. "All right? Come on in, it's perishin."

Zig stepped inside and wrapped his arms around Si's waist. He heard a surprised *oof* and then strong arms were hugging him back. "Been a long shift," Zig mumbled into Si's beard, every part of him going boneless in that warm embrace.

"Too bloody right," Si muttered back. "I hope Ange ain't gonna take advantage of you like that too often."

Guilt twinged in Zig's gut. He'd almost forgotten the lie he'd told Si about working this afternoon. *Never again*, he told himself fervently. *One hundred percent honesty from here on out.* He looked up, flashing Si a cheeky smile. "Only one person gets to take advantage of me from now on."

Si laughed. "C'mon, let's get you properly inside before we have any more of that sort of talk." Stepping back, he took Zig's hand and led him upstairs like they were a couple of kids.

It was really fucking charming.

There was a moment, after they'd closed the door of the flat behind them, that they stood and gazed at each other, still holding hands.

Then the moment broke, and Si surged forward to take Zig's face in his hands. "Gods, I've missed you," he said hoarsely, and then they were kissing like the world was about to end.

Chapter Thirty-Four
Si

Si's whole body was ablaze. The bits that touched Zig—and there were plenty of them—were incandescent. Zig felt so right in his arms. More than that. It was like part of Si had been missing, ever since he'd left Zig in London, and now he was whole again.

Si tried to be gentle with his kisses, but Zig was like he'd been starving for this. Like he wanted to eat Si up, and fuck knew, Si was on board with that. He let Zig push him up against the wall, and if he was honest, he was grateful for the support. His head felt like it was about to float off and his knees didn't seem all that reliable right now. Zig had both hands shoved down the back of his jeans now, holding him tight while they kissed, tongues getting everywhere.

Si had a stiffy the size of St. Michael's Tower, and it felt like it'd been neglected for centuries too. He couldn't help moaning into Zig's mouth.

Zig shivered and broke the kiss. "Jesus, fuck, you don't know what you do to me."

"Hope it's something like what you're doing to me," Si told him fervently.

"I never . . ." Zig stopped, his face contorted. "Never thought I could have this again. I've missed you so fucking much."

Si couldn't stand the look on his face, so he kissed him again, hard. "You can have anything you want. Anytime."

Zig half sobbed a laugh. "Sure about that? I might have got into some kinky shit while we were apart."

"Eh. I'm open-minded." Si gave him a gentle and hopefully reassuring smile. "Come to bed and we can talk about safewords and stuff." Then he hesitated. "Uh, that is, if we're heading to the bedroom? Cos we can totally stay on the sofa if you'd rather . . ."

Zig's laugh sounded happier this time. "Bedroom. Unless you don't wanna? Cos honestly, you're a big bastard these days. If we start on the sofa, I guarantee we're gonna land on the floor sooner rather than later."

Si beamed. "Well, what are you waiting for, then?" He pulled Zig into the bedroom, and somehow they ended up on the bed, fully clothed. Boots and all. "Is it a leather fetish you've got into?" Si managed to ask. "If you give me a mo, I can get me biking gear—"

Zig silenced him with a kiss, one hand tangled in his hair. "No fetishes," he said shakily when they paused to draw breath. "All I want is right here. Although it's got way too many clothes on," he added, and now the old glint was back in his blue eye.

"Could say the same for you," Si countered. Then he sat up and pulled off his shirt.

"Fuck me," Zig breathed, staring at his chest.

Si looked down a bit self-consciously. "Hope you don't mind a bit of hair. Never could see the point of waxing and that."

"You're perfect." Zig buried his face in the fur between Si's pecs, which did all sorts of things to Si's heart rate. Then he looked up and grinned. "Can floss me teeth while I'm here."

Si laughed. "Come on then. Show us what you got."

Zig gave an awkward little half shrug. "Hasn't changed much since the last time you saw it."

He peeled off his work shirt, and Si drank in the sight. He was still slender but not as waifish as he'd been as a teenager. The planes of him were harder but still with a hint of vulnerability. Si raised a hand and gently stroked the bared skin. "You're beautiful," he breathed.

Zig's brown eye was almost black. "I'd do anything for you, you know that?"

It made Si's heart hurt, and his voice was hoarse when he said, "You ain't gotta do nothing."

"No?" Zig's voice was a whisper. "Cos I want to do everything with you."

And then Si could hardly keep track of what was going on, how they got their kit off and who was on top of who, cos his heart was the size of a harvest moon and all his thinking was going on below the belt, not that he was wearing one no more.

They kissed, and touched, and neither of them had the patience for anything fancy. When Si gripped their dicks in one hand, fireworks going off in every nerve, Zig let out a strangled moan. It wasn't long before they were both crying out and spilling all over each other, their come mingling together, never to be separated.

Si was panting like he'd run a bloody marathon as he drew Zig close, not giving a damn that they'd end up stuck to each other. "So bloody glad you came back," he whispered into blue-tinted hair. "No buggering off now, all right?"

"You got it," Zig whispered back, and there wasn't a trace of a lie in his voice.

Finally, Si could trust him.

Chapter Thirty-Five
Zig

The next week passed like a dream. Si was working days, of course, but Zig found ways to occupy himself. He picked up a few extra shifts at the Prince of Wales, as one of the barmaids was off sick, and spent some time in the library or wandering around town. There was some wicked street art around.

Evenings—when Zig wasn't working—were spent together in the flat, watching old *Doctor Who* episodes, playing two-player games, or getting frisky on the sofa. Zig had never been much for cosy evenings in, before. Turned out he simply hadn't had the right bloke to share them with. Who needed to go out when being with Si was enough? More than enough.

More than he deserved. Si had even cut Zig a key to the flat. He'd presented it to him Monday night, on a keychain with a Tardis fob. Zig had felt like he'd won the bloody lottery.

Things weren't totally perfect. One of the nights Zig was working, Si had gone round to his mum and dad's, and Zig had been shitting bricks all night that he'd come home and find out Si's mum had convinced him to break up. In the end, though, Si had said, "I told 'em we're together. It could've gone worse." Then he'd smiled and kissed him.

Zig could tell Si was worried about his friendship with Adam, who hadn't yet made that call he'd promised. Still, it was early days. Zig also knew he needed to increase his hours at the pub or get another job, despite Si insisting it didn't matter that he wasn't bringing in much money. He wanted to pay his way. So, he kept an eye on job adverts, but this time of year, it was all short-term gigs in shops and restaurants over the holiday season. And a lot of it was evening work. Call him selfish, but he wasn't prepared to sacrifice his time with Si for a few quid more in his pocket. He'd only just got him.

London, Dad, and Trent seemed a world away.

During one of his jaunts around town, Zig saw a poster for an upcoming Yuletide Fayre at the weekend. Si wasn't working—he had to do some Saturdays, but Sundays were always free as the locksmith's shop was closed—and so, after a morning spent in bed, they headed into town.

There were stalls all along the high street selling seasonal decorations with a pagan flair. People had dressed up for the event too: there was a higher-than-usual proportion of cloaks, weird headgear, and face paint.

Zig frowned. "Think we're a bit underdressed." In both senses of the word—as per usual, he was shivering in his black jeans and leather jacket. Still, it gave him an excuse to keep Si's warm, solid form close.

He had a feeling Si might be planning to buy him a winter coat for Christmas. Zig hoped not. He'd probably be hurt if Zig kept accidentally leaving it at home so he'd have a reason to snuggle.

"These things are come-as-you-want," Si said. "Not that you wouldn't look good dressed up, mind."

"Reckon I'd suit a cloak?" Zig asked, seeing a particularly swish one in green wool swoop on by.

Si laughed. "You can make anything look good. If I put on a cloak, I'd look like Father bloody Christmas."

"No way. Santa's much cooler little brother, maybe." Zig grinned wickedly. "If I'm good, will you let me sit on your lap tonight and whisper what I want in your ear?"

The few square inches of Si's face that were bare of beard turned a seasonal red. "Maybe," he muttered. "But not if being *good* means you keep on getting me hot and bothered while we're out in public."

He walked on briskly. Zig followed, laughing.

There were fire jugglers performing outside St. John's Church, and further on, a band playing folk music. Zig watched them for a mo. Then, with a start, recognised the musicians he'd seen up the tor. Instead of a pom-pom hat, the bearded guitarist was wearing a sort of crown made of holly, with antlers sticking up from it. And the woman in the shapeless orange coat was transformed: in a flowing, form-fitting dress topped with a woollen cloak and a crown of ivy leaves and flowers, she looked like a medieval dryad. Next to them, a man in rough clothes of earthen colours used a short, double-ended stick to beat on what looked like a large tambourine without any bells.

Zig nudged Si. "Is that a bodhrán?"

"Yeah, that's right. How'd you know that?"

"Saw them up on the tor. Hey, we should definitely go up there for the sunrise on solstice day. They're gonna be there for the celebrations."

Si smiled fondly. "On the twenty-first? Yeah, we can do that. Anything you want."

Zig's heart sang in time to the music as they ambled through the crowd.

As they reached Market Place, Zig tensed. A couple of uniformed coppers were standing on the corner—the first Zig had seen in Glastonbury. He told himself furiously that they didn't know who he was, or what he'd done, and it was all in the past anyway. They wouldn't take a blind bit of notice of him walking down the street with his boyfriend.

Then the bloke glanced their way and recognition showed in his face. Zig froze, but Si was striding forward with a grin.

"All right, mate? Haven't seen you in a while." He clapped the man on the shoulder.

"Been working county lines the last few months. How are you doing? Broken into any good houses lately?" The copper laughed.

Si laughed too.

Zig looked from one to the other, trying not to show his nerves. At least the young woman officer seemed as baffled as he was.

"Rob, this is Zig," Si was saying. "He's from London."

"Good to meet you." The copper held out a black-gloved hand.

Zig shook it disbelievingly. "A copper called Rob? That's like calling a cat 'Mouse.'"

Rob groaned. "And I've never heard that one before. Hope you've been keeping our lad here on the straight and narrow."

"Uh . . ." It was painfully obvious the bloke didn't know the first thing about Zig.

"Rob here nearly arrested me," Si said with a grin. "Caught me bang to rights, breaking into a semidetached in broad daylight. And that, by the way, is why all my work shirts have *LOCKSMITH* on the back of 'em in large, friendly letters."

Rob nudged his colleague. "Thing is, he was wearing one at the time. And the neighbour *still* called us in."

"Well, like she said," Si added, and they chorused together, "'Anyone can buy a T-shirt!'"

They all cracked up, even Zig, although it felt a bit surreal. He'd learned from an early age that the filth were the enemy. It didn't sit right, sharing a joke with them. *Better get used to it*, he told himself.

"Staying here long?" Rob the Copper asked.

Zig glanced at Si. "Hope so."

Si sent him a tender look, and the female copper cooed, *Aw, bless* at them.

Then they went their separate ways and Zig could relax, thank God.

Si leaned in close. "He's a decent bloke, Rob is. Not one of them racist bastards you hear about. Saw him at Pride this year with rainbow face paint."

"There's a Glastonbury Pride?"

"Course there is. We had a brunch this year, with a blessing by a priest of some gay Roman god."

"There's gay gods?"

"Blimey, where you been? Course there are. All over the place. Romans, Greeks—especially the Greeks—Egyptians, Hindus, probably a shedload I don't know about and all."

"Huh. I need to get back to the library." Zig huffed a laugh. "All them old British classics I've read, they weren't big on diversity."

Si grinned. "We gotta broaden your horizons, then."

Zig reckoned that was happening anyhow, simply by being here. Funny how he'd always thought London was as broad as it could get, but somehow, Glastonbury was making him think about stuff like he never had before. Like, London might contain multitudes, but it was easy enough to spend a whole life in one small corner. Here, they didn't have the space to separate everything out. It was all mixed in together, King Arthur legends rubbing up against *some gay Roman god*. Zig liked it.

Zig kept an eye out for Kai, thinking they might have come to the Fayre. He didn't see them, but there were a couple of other rough sleepers tucked discreetly around a corner. One of the men called out, "Merry Yuletide!" as they passed, and raised a steaming takeaway cup to them. Zig grinned and crouched down. "Same to you, mate. What are you drinking? Smells good."

"Mulled wine, from the lovely lady on the stall over there. Go buy some, it'll warm your cockles."

"Thanks for the tip. You have a good day, mate." Zig passed him a fiver, then rose and returned to where Si was standing watching a bloke in medieval gear doing tricks while riding a unicycle. "You up for a mulled wine?"

"Course I am." Si slung an arm around Zig's waist and squeezed him.

"Wait here," Zig said, extricating himself with regret. "I'll grab us a couple."

The mulled wine stall was next to one selling German Christmas cookies. Zig stared at the selection, which included Lebkuchen, Spekulatius, and Zimtsterne, and opted for the least pronounceable for the hell of it. "A couple of . . . paffeffernusses, please?"

"*Pfeffernuesse*," the young girl corrected him with a smile as she served them.

"Feffernyooser," Zig repeated dutifully, and turned to go.

Only to find himself looking straight into the eyes of Si's mate Adam. He swallowed.

"Quick word?" Adam's face was unreadable.

Zig pasted on a smile. "Course." He was glad he hadn't got the wine first, so he still had one hand free. Then again, hot beverages could be a useful makeshift defensive weapon . . .

Get a grip. He's not gonna deck you in the middle of a family crowd. Probably.

He followed Adam to the edge of the crowd and couldn't help noticing they'd moved farther away from Si and out of his sightline.

Pushing down his nerves, Zig decided to get the first shot in. "I'm not messing Si around, all right? And I'm not gonna hurt him. I love him."

Adam's eyes narrowed. "Right, cos no one's ever hurt the one they love."

"Hurting Si's the last thing I want." Zig put every ounce of the sincerity he felt into his voice.

Was that a softening in Adam's face? He sighed. "It's not a question of you *wanting* to. But you and me both know it's gonna happen. Like it did last time. Because of who you are."

"And who am I, then?"

"You're a chancer. You think the rules don't apply to you."

And here it came. "Thinking of any rules in particular?"

"Since you ask, yeah. The ones relating to property ownership, for a start. Come on, are you seriously gonna deny you were one of the bastards who did my dad's site over?"

Part of Zig, the side of him that always came out when he was with Trent, or Dad, or anyone he wanted to impress, wanted to say, *Oi, that was six years ago. Let it go, already, can't ya?*

He didn't like that side of himself very much, so he took a breath before he spoke, and let the honesty come out. "All right, so I was a bit of a shit when I was a teenager. But for what it's worth, I didn't know about the raid on your dad's until afterwards. Swear it. On Si's life, and you know that's an oath I wouldn't take in vain."

"Do I?" Adam countered, but it sounded like he was going through the motions. He sighed again. "Swear to me you're not involved in anything illegal anymore."

"Hand to heart." Zig smiled wryly, holding his bag of pfeffernuesse to his chest. "Learned me lesson, didn't I?"

"Did you?"

"God's truth." He meant it too, and maybe that came across, as the tension in Adam's frame relaxed.

"Guess I'll see you around, then." Adam turned and walked away.

Zig let out a ragged breath and went back to the mulled wine stall, needing a drink more than ever. Juggling his purchases in hands that, okay, might have been a little shaky, he returned to Si, who flashed him a fond smile. "Bit of a queue, was there? Shame. You missed him standing on his head on that thing."

Zig shot the unicyclist a frankly disbelieving look. "How does that even work? Never mind. Here, have a feffernoose."

The cookies he'd bought, which were round and covered in an all-over dusting of icing sugar, turned out to be sweet and spicy, with a tart orange flavour, and went well with the mulled wine. The food and alcohol doing their calming work, Zig glanced over at Si, and huffed a laugh, his breath steaming in the cold air. "You've got icing sugar in your beard."

Si laughed too. "Can't take me anywhere, can you?"

Zig wanted to take him *everywhere*. "Come here." He gently dusted the white specks away from around Si's lips, and then, because he could, dropped a kiss on them.

There was a soft *Awww* from a girl standing next to them. Smiling, Zig took Si's arm and they turned to walk on—only to find themselves faced with Adam, now joined by his bloke, Corin.

Si breathed in audibly.

Nobody spoke. Zig could feel the tension in Si's body; Corin's face was twisted in discomfort. Adam looked confused. Zig gave a mental eye roll, guessing they were pretending that little heart-to-heart hadn't happened. "All right, you two?"

It broke the spell. "Yeah, we're good," Adam said, still staring at them oddly. "Uh, you?"

"Never better," Zig said with a tight smile. "No Sasha tonight?"

"She's still working. Didn't want to close the studio early."

"Nice of her to let you out to play, then."

Adam nodded. There was a brief silence, and frankly Zig thought he'd done his bit. Up to the rest of them if they wanted to break it.

"Are you working tonight?" Corin asked awkwardly.

Zig nodded. "No rest, and all that. See you in there later?"

Corin brightened. "Maybe. We haven't really made plans."

"Uh . . ." Adam's gaze darted to Si and then back to Zig. "Not tonight. Another time, though. You, uh"—and now he was looking at Si again—"you take care, okay?"

"Right," Si said. It came out hoarse, maybe cos he'd been silent so long. "You too."

Adam nodded, and he and Corin walked away.

Zig slipped an arm around Si's waist. "That wasn't so bad, was it? You okay?"

"No. I mean, yeah, that could have gone worse. I'm okay."

"I don't wanna come between you and your mate," Zig said, the words like knives in his chest. Because he *didn't*, but he was a selfish bastard and he didn't want Si to leave him, either.

"You ain't gonna," Si said firmly. "He'll come around."

Zig wished he could be so sure.

Chapter Thirty-Six
Si

Si would have liked to have been as certain as he'd made himself sound that his and Adam's friendship wasn't broken, or at least in serious need of repair. Zig had been due at work soon after they'd all met in town, so Si had been left to go back to the flat on his own.

He'd switched on the telly but couldn't focus on anything. Should he give Adam a call? Build on the brief contact this afternoon? But if Adam still needed time to come to terms with him and Zig being back together, Si didn't want to ruin things by rushing him.

He just hoped Adam didn't need too *much* time, that was all. Cos the longer they stayed out of touch, the easier it'd be for Adam to let it all slide. Decide he didn't really need Si in his life, like he'd done after Si had left London all them years ago.

Bugger. Si had told himself he wasn't going to dwell on the past. It was water under the bridge, and didn't they say you could never cross the same river twice? Si hoped they weren't wrong about that.

He hadn't liked that river much.

When the phone rang, he jumped a mile. *Too bloody broody by half.* It was Sasha.

"All right, Sash, me love?" he asked heartily. "Didn't see you at the Prince of Wales last night. You missed a good band."

"Like I wanted to spend the night playing gooseberry to you and your London lover-boy. How's that going, then?"

"It's good. Really good." Si couldn't help breaking into a smile. Then his mood sobered. "Worried about Adam, though. Not sure how he's feeling about things right now."

"Hah. Be grateful. I've had him bending my ear all week about you and your bloke."

"Yeah? What's he been saying?" Si held his breath.

"He's worried about you, babe. Scared you'll get hurt again. That's fifty percent of the time. The rest of it is all about him feeling guilty for being a terrible mate." She paused. "Which to be fair, he was a bit, after you broke up with Zig the first time."

Si frowned. "The first time? When do you reckon the *second* time I break up with him's gonna be?"

"I meant, the first time you went out with him! Jeez, don't put words in my mouth. I hope you'll be disgustingly happy with him and die old and wrinkly in each other's hairy arms, okay?"

"Sorry, Sash. You're the best. How's things with you, anyway? Still in touch with what's-her-face?"

"Gone a bit quiet on her end." She sighed. "So bloody well sort things out with Adam, yeah? I need some good news in my life."

"I'll do me best. Promise. Maybe I'll give him a call tonight."

"You do that."

When Si hung up, he noticed he'd missed a call while he'd been talking to Sasha.

It had been from Adam. Si swallowed, and hit Call.

Adam's voice was breathless when he answered. "Si. Thanks for calling me back."

That sounded a bit formal and had the added disadvantage of not giving Si clue one as to what Adam had been calling to say. "All right, mate?"

"Yeah, I'm good. Zig at work now?"

"Yep." Did that mean Adam wanted to say stuff he didn't want Zig to have any chance of hearing? Si's heart sank.

"Cool. Fancy heading to the Isle of Avalon for a quick pint? Me and you, like the old days, yeah?"

Si scratched his beard. "Uh. Gotta be blunt, if this is gonna be you getting up my arse about Zig, I ain't exactly in the mood."

"No, it's . . . Look, just meet me, will you? Promise I'm not gonna have a go at you."

Fifteen minutes later, Si took a long draught of his pint of Becket's, and set it firmly down on the table. "What's this all about, as if I couldn't guess?"

Adam sighed and put down the menu he'd been browsing. "Look, I wanna clear the air, okay? I know I've been pretty down on Zig, but if he makes you happy, I guess I'm gonna have to live with it."

"Cheers for the ringing endorsement." The sarcasm came out on automatic, but inside, Si's heart lifted in hope. Cautious hope, mind. "So, not to look a gift horse in the mouth, but what's brought this on? Bit of a change of heart from last week."

"Yeah . . ." Adam hung his head. "Look, I dunno if he told you, but I had a word with him this afternoon. Before we saw you."

Si swallowed. "No. He didn't mention that."

"And I think maybe—*maybe*—you might be right, and he's changed? Like, I'm not saying he has, but it's possible." Adam's cheeks reddened. "Saw the way you and him were together, and all."

"Okay." Si's voice came out hoarse.

"And I had a chat with Corin about it. And Sasha. Mostly Sasha, if I'm honest. Made me see I'm not being supportive. Not being a good mate. Like, I gotta let you make your own decisions, and be there for you when—uh, whatever happens."

When it all goes tits up, you mean. Si couldn't help the warmth that flooded through him, regardless. It was more than he'd hoped for, Adam saying all this when he clearly thought it was going to be an epic disaster. "Cheers, mate. And yeah, he does."

"What?"

"Make me happy."

"And you're certain he's not into anything dodgy?"

"Course I am. Wouldn't be with him if I weren't." Si rubbed his beard, trying to think how to convince Adam without betraying all of Zig's secrets. "Look, he had a . . . an experience with his dad and that cockweasel Trent, about five years ago. It showed him what they were really like, and he knew he didn't want no part of it. They ended up in jail, cos of Zig. Cos he stood up for what was right."

Adam's eyes widened, and he put down his pint. "Seriously?"

Si nodded and took an angry swallow of his beer. "And I'll tell you this, if I ever meet that father of his or see that Trent again, them and me are gonna have words."

"Sounds like they'd be the ones wanting to have words with Zig," Adam said grimly. He sat there a moment, then took a draught of his beer. "Okay. I'll give him a chance. But if he ever . . . If you ever get worried about him or think something's dodgy, you tell me, okay?"

His heart melting, Si reached over the table and grasped Adam's arm. "I won't have to. But yeah, I will. Cross my heart."

"Cheers, Si. Makes me feel a lot better." Adam ducked his head. "I've been feeling like I failed you, the first time round, you know? I should have been a better mate."

"What? That's bollocks, that is. You've always been my best mate."

Adam laughed. "Don't let Sasha hear you say that."

"What? She knows. I love her to bits and then some, but you and me, we go way back, don't we?"

"Yeah. Yeah, we do, and I never should've let you come back here on your own without making sure you were okay."

"I survived, didn't I? And you had a lot going on, what with uni and that. And gods know, with your mum."

"Still should've kept in touch better."

"You're here now, ain't you?" Si found himself examining the rings on the table, a memento mori of pints long passed through drinkers' bodies and out the other side. "And it means a lot, you looking out for me. Even if it pissed me off, you being so hostile to Zig. I know it came from a good place." He frowned. "But, you know, don't do it again."

Adam laughed. "I won't. Well, I'll try not to." He sighed. "You're a good bloke, you know that? Not sure I could be so forgiving, if it was me."

"Oi. Thought you weren't gonna slag Zig off no more?"

"I wasn't!" Adam hung his head. "Well, okay, maybe I was a bit. But the rest of it was about me."

Si smiled softly. "Give it a rest, you daft bastard. We were all kids back then, weren't we?"

"Yeah. Look at us now, all grown up." Adam laughed. "Dunno about you, but I still don't feel like I've got a clue what I'm doing half the time."

"Mate," Si said seriously. "You honestly think anyone does?"

Chapter Thirty-Seven
Zig

Walking over to the Prince of Wales, Zig wasn't sure what to think about their encounter with Adam at the Yuletide Fayre. The bloke hadn't been outright hostile, at least, which was better than he might have hoped for. Maybe meeting up this afternoon would prompt Adam to get back in touch with Si. That would be good, right?

Yeah, good for Si. Probably not for you, though. Zig winced as his mind helpfully suggested what Adam might be whispering in Si's ear right now.

No, that wasn't fair. Adam wouldn't whisper. He'd come straight out with it if he reckoned Si should tell Zig to piss off back to London. Which he probably *did* reckon.

Si wouldn't let himself be persuaded, though.

Would he?

It had been so good, the last few days, him and Si. Like back when they'd been kids. *Better, in fact, cos face it, you didn't have a clue back then. Strutted around thinking you were God's gift to all men gay, straight, or otherwise, and all the time you were looking over your shoulder at Dad. Trying to make him proud of you, like that wasn't the most pathetic aspiration in the entire history of the world.*

But Si cared about him, despite everything. Had done then, and still did, God knew why.

Zig would just have to trust in that.

Work helped, keeping him too busy to brood on things. It wasn't until he was on his way back home after his shift that Zig checked his phone and saw he'd missed a call a couple of hours ago. It'd been from Ani back in London. There was a text from her too: *Call me*. That was potentially worrying. Telling himself he shouldn't be paranoid, Zig hit Dial.

She answered straight away. "Zig, thank God."

Okay, now it was *definitely* worrying. "Hey, babe, what's up?"

"Are you still in Peckham?" Ani's voice was high and breathy.

Unease prickled at Zig's neck, and his pace slowed. "No, why?"

"Oh, thank God. That's all right, then."

The prickling intensified. Zig stopped under a streetlamp. "Ani, what's happened? Did Da— Did that bloke who was asking after me before come round again? Did you tell him that's where I was going?"

"No! I'd never, but there was this other bloke came in last night. Younger. And he seemed really nice, you know? Worried about you, cos he knew there were people looking for you. He said he wanted to make sure you were safe, so I thought you and him must be friends or, you know, more."

Zig's throat went tight. "What did he look like?"

"Good. I mean, I could see you and him together, he was that fit. Nice skin. Um, he was white, with light brown hair. Cut short and combed back, old-fashioned, like. Broad shoulders. Had one of those sailors' coats on—peacoat, I think they call it? Looked smart. Does he sound like anyone you know?" Ani's tone was pleading now.

Christ. Trent, it had to be. God knew he could put on the charm when he wanted to. But that was only one of his ways of getting people to do what he wanted. "He didn't threaten you, did he?"

"No! Nothing like. I told you, he was nice. It was only after he'd gone that I started thinking it was a bit funny. Zig, I'm sorry. Did I fuck up?"

"What did you tell him?" Zig's voice sounded rough in his own ears.

"Only what you said about going down to Peckham for a family emergency."

Zig's stomach lurched. If they knew he'd gone to Peckham . . .

"Zig, is everything okay? Did I screw up?"

"No," he forced out, and tried to inject a bit more cheer into his voice as he stepped out of the way of a young couple who were loved-up and clearly boozed-up, weaving across the pavement. "Don't worry about it. But if he comes round again, don't tell him anything else."

"I don't know anything else, do I? Zig, who is he?"

"No one you want to know. Don't tell him we've been in touch, or that you've got my number, okay? If you've gotta tell him something, tell him you were glad to see the back of me."

"I'm a bit crap at lying."

"Then tell him them pints won't pull themselves and you've gotta get on with work, okay?"

"Okay. Zig, I'm really sorry." She sounded it too.

He couldn't be mad at her. "Nah, it's okay. Not your fault. You take care, okay?"

"Yeah. You too."

Zig jammed his phone back into his pocket so hard he felt a stitch go. *Fuck*. He forced himself to calm down. Keep on walking. As he turned into the street where they lived, Zig thought he heard footsteps behind him. Heart pounding, he whirled, but there was no one there.

Jesus. Get a grip. You're getting paranoid.

Then again, it wasn't paranoia if they were really out to get you, was it? But Dad and Trent couldn't have traced his steps from Peckham, could they? No, he was being daft. Nevertheless, Zig quickened his steps.

He looked around once more as he reached their flat but didn't see anyone that time either. His pulse still racing, Zig put his key in the door and prayed his life with Si wasn't about to come crashing down.

Chapter Thirty-Eight
Si

After he'd said goodbye to Adam, Si had damn near floated back from the pub. He'd gone there expecting to have to fight Zig's corner, and instead he'd got Adam's blessing, or good as.

It was like . . . It was like opening a lock for a client who'd gone out and left their keys in the house, and that sweet, sweet moment when the last of the tumblers fell into place. It was like finding the last rare figure to complete a collection, or going for a ride and hitting the perfect combination of clear roads, good weather, and the bike purring like a well-fed cat. He had Zig back in his life—and his heart—and his best mate was okay with that. It was so much more than he'd have hoped for only a few days ago.

He couldn't wait for Zig to get home.

Si didn't have to wait that long, as it happened, which was good cos he hadn't been able to settle to anything, not even old *Doctor Who* episodes on iPlayer.

When Zig opened the door to let himself in, his frown was a minor dampener on the mood. "Rough shift?" Si asked sympathetically.

"What?" Zig blinked at him. "No. It was fine."

Then he smiled one of those fake smiles of his.

Minor became major, and Si's heart plummeted. "Right. You, uh, want a drink, or sommat?"

"Cheers. Beer's good. You having one?"

"No, I had a couple already. I'll put the kettle on."

Zig didn't follow him into the kitchen, and he didn't ask how Si's evening had gone, either. Si tried not to let it get him down as he grabbed a beer from the fridge and made himself a hot chocolate. Zig was tired, that was all. And working in a pub, he probably had to smile at wankers all the time. He just hadn't switched that off yet.

When Si took the drinks into the living room, Zig was sprawled on the sofa typing into his phone. He stopped abruptly when Si appeared in his line of vision and shoved his phone into his pocket.

Well, that ain't good.

But there's no proof it's bad, neither.

Si considered Zig. Zig seemed to shrink, somehow, the longer it went on, and Si's heart clenched. "Zig, mate. I'm not daft. I know something's changed since this afternoon. Is it about Adam? Cos you ain't got nothing to worry about there. I met up with him tonight, and he said he's gonna give you a chance—"

"He did?" Zig blurted out.

Si wondered how much of it was about Adam's change of heart, and how much was because he'd been thinking about something else entirely. "Yep. In them words exactly."

"Why?" Zig went on.

"Cos he's not a bad bloke?" Si reached out and pulled Zig towards him. Zig came readily, so he probably wasn't having second thoughts about them being a couple. "And I ain't either, so are you gonna tell me what's bothering you? We're in this together, you and me."

Zig's body tensed in Si's arms, then slowly softened again, although he still didn't seem relaxed exactly. "You sure that's what you want? Plenty of people would tell you I'm trouble."

"Are you?"

Zig gave a laugh that was almost a sob. "Fuck, yeah. I don't wanna be," he added in a whisper.

Si kissed him on the top of the head, tasting hair gel and getting a faint whiff of beer. "Whatever it is, I'm pretty sure we can handle it together. You wanna tell me what it is?"

"I . . ." Zig sniffed. "It might never happen."

"Still. Problem shared, problem halved and all that bollocks."

"Dunno what I did to deserve you," Zig mumbled against Si's chest.

"Must have been something pretty bad."

"Fuck off. You're the best thing that's ever happened to me."

Warmth spread through Si. "Same here."

He wasn't prepared for Zig to slip out of his arms and stand, running his hand through his hair. "We oughtta turn in, yeah? You've got an early start in the morning."

"We've got time to talk if you need to. You've hardly touched your beer." His own hot chocolate was still sitting sadly in the mug, having lost all right to the first part of its name.

Zig didn't turn to look at him. "Sorry. Not thirsty after all. Nah, I'm good. I just need to get my head round some stuff. Sort out what I need to do. It's nothing you need to worry about."

Bugger it all to hell and back. Si took a deep breath. No point pushing. Zig clearly didn't want to share whatever was worrying him. But it hurt being shut out like that. It was still early days, though. Si had to remember that. "Right, then. You coming to bed?"

There was a horrible pause. Then Zig said, "Course I am," and Si could breathe again.

Chapter Thirty-Nine
Zig

Z ig stayed in bed long after Si had left for work. He'd slept badly, and several times considered leaving Si's embrace for the cold comfort of the sofa, but somehow he hadn't been able to. *Too fucking selfish.* Si had held him all through a restless night, not asking for anything more.

Zig wasn't sure what had kept him awake the most: the worry about Dad and Trent tracking him down, or the guilt that had punched him in the gut when Si had blithely said, *"Same here"*—like Zig could *possibly* be the best thing that'd ever happened to him. Worst thing, more like. They'd barely been back together a day and already the crap in Zig's life was threatening to overwhelm them.

Maybe he should say something to Si? The reaction to that was swift and visceral. *I'd rather chew off my own arm.* He couldn't bear the thought of ruining Si's happiness. Christ, how could Zig even *hope* to make up for all the hurt he'd caused Si already?

All the hurt he might yet cause?

Sod it. He wasn't gonna do it by moping in bed. And it might all be nothing. He had to remember that. Zig forced himself to get up, and checked his phone to see if Kai had answered his hurried text last night.

For fuck's sake, his own message was still there, cursor blinking at him. Looked like he'd missed when he went to hit Send. Too busy trying to stop Si seeing the message: *You ever worry your past's going to catch up with you?*

He deleted it, not feeling like sending it now, and then went looking for stuff that needed doing around the flat. He put on a load of laundry but failed to find anything in need of cleaning, Si clearly not believing in the stereotype of bloke-living-on-his-own slovenliness. The fridge was well stocked too.

Giving up, Zig grabbed his jacket and headed downstairs. Maybe a walk would clear his head.

Esme, dressed today in a smart navy trouser suit with a cropped jacket, caught him before he could set foot outside. "You're looking a little peaky this morning. Too much bed, not enough sleep?"

"Something like that."

Zig's face must have given away more than his words, as she replied with, "Oh, dear. Tell you what, if you mind the shop for a minute, I'll pop out and get us some coffees."

He couldn't have heard her right. "What?"

"You: shop. Me: coffees. Capisce?" She gave him a motherly smile that almost, but not quite, took away the sting of her patronising tone. "You work in a pub, so I'm assuming you know your way around a till."

"Ain't you worried I'll nick something?"

Still smiling, Esme pointed to a sign hanging up behind the counter: *Shoplifters will be cursed.*

Zig had to laugh. Like he needed that on top of everything else. "Fine. But if the punters are put out that I don't know shit about this stuff you sell, that's on you."

"Oh, I'm sure you can spin them a line if you put your mind to it." She marched out of the shop, nodding en route to a couple of twentysomethings who came in past her.

Zig winced and nipped behind the counter so as to look like he belonged here. Although, come to think of it, his all-black combo of jeans and long-sleeved shirt probably made him look more the part than Esme herself did.

He'd sold six packs of incense and a book on the healing power of crystals before it occurred to him that Esme hadn't asked how he liked his coffee. Maybe she could tell by looking at him that he wouldn't be fussy.

Some candles, an amulet, and a divining pendant later—how far had she gone for this coffee? Bristol?—Esme was back with two large cups with no logo. "I got you white with an extra shot. That okay?"

"Yeah, that's good. Ta." Zig took the cup, then couldn't resist adding, "Was that what my aura told you?"

"Mm, no. The white was Si buying more milk than usual, and the extra shot was the bags under your eyes."

"Cheers." Zig toasted her, with a grimace. "You always keep an eye on your tenant's shopping?"

"Not generally, but it's hard to ignore when a large, hairy man runs through your store muttering, 'Bugger, bugger, bugger, run out of milk already.'"

He had to laugh. "Fair enough."

"How's the job going?"

"What, the bar work, or this unpaid job you got me doing?"

"Excuse me, I've remunerated you with a very decent and not inexpensive cup of coffee. Which, I might add, you haven't so much as tasted."

"Gimme a chance." Zig made a show of bringing the cup to his lips and taking a sip. Then he took a larger one. It was, actually, bloody good coffee. "Not bad. Still it oughtta be, for over a fiver."

"And how do you work that out?"

"Minimum wage, and I've been minding your shop for half an hour—"

"Twenty minutes, if that." She smirked at him over the top of her coffee cup. "Sell much?"

Zig reeled off a list of the items he'd sold.

"Not bad."

Zig was almost, but not quite, certain she was mocking him. "The crystal book was an upsell too," he went on, cos he'd been proud of that one. "I noticed she was wearing one of those tree of life necklaces, the ones made of wire and crystals, so I gave it a go."

Esme raised an eyebrow. "You know, if you wanted to make this a regular thing, I might see my way to paying you actual money."

"Huh. Seriously?"

"Seriously. Think about it. Now, if you'll excuse me . . ." Esme put down her cup on the counter and slunk over to a shy couple loitering by the spellbooks.

Zig took his chance to escape, taking his coffee with him. Should he take Esme up on her offer? It'd been okay, manning the till and talking to the customers, he thought, as he walked down the street dodging the shoppers and their dogs. It shouldn't conflict with working the bar on weekend nights. And it'd mean, for some days at least, that his hours would line up better with Si's.

And if Dad turns up and you have to do a runner, that'll be one more person you've let down.

The coffee turning bitter in his mouth, Zig chucked the cup in a nearby bin and jammed his hands into his pockets.

Chapter Forty
Si

It was just after lunchtime on Monday when the locksmith's shop bell rang and Corin stepped inside, with Adam close behind him. Si broke into a smile, touched they'd taken time out of their working day to check in with him.

Course, maybe they needed a key cut. "All right, mates?" he greeted them. "How's it going in the world of computers?" He hadn't seen Corin to talk to for a while.

"It's, um, good." Corin's gaze was shifting all over the place, like it did when he met someone new.

"It's me," Si said hastily. Maybe the poor sod didn't recognise him in his uniform. "Si. Scratch."

Corin blinked. "I know. You've got a name badge."

"Huh. S'pose I have and all." Si peered down at his chest automatically and read *Simon*, which only his mum ever called him. Or Sasha, when she was narked with him, but then it was always paired with his surname.

Adam stepped forward impatiently. "Where's Zig right now?"

Si was getting a bit uneasy. "Right now? Dunno. He's got an extra shift tonight, and he'll be gone by the time I get home. He said he'd be going for a wander before then, but he didn't say where. What d'you want him for? Cos, not being funny, but it's a first, you wanting him for anything." Si was aware he was babbling a bit, but Adam didn't look happy. Had something happened to make him change his mind on Zig again?

"It's not—"

Adam broke off as Corin put a hand on his arm. "Let me? It's my fault."

At least they didn't seem to think *it*, whatever it was, was Zig's fault. "You know," Si said conversationally, "if the plot thickens any further, we'll be up to our knees in it like cow shit, and here's me without me wellies."

"Sorry." Corin sounded like he meant it. He took a deep breath. "I think Zig may be in trouble," he said in a rush. "And I think I may have made it worse."

Si went cold. "Meaning?"

"It's his dad," Adam burst out. "Come looking for him."

That couldn't be good. Si didn't reckon the bloke would've turned up wanting to play happy families. Not from what he'd heard about him from Zig.

"And I didn't know that was an issue," Corin put in. "Adam and I had arranged to meet for lunch at the Isle of Avalon, and while I was waiting for him, a man was asking around, showing a photo on his phone. Saying he was worried about his son. And of course I only looked to be polite, because I didn't imagine I'd be able to help. But the picture showed his eyes, and the man pointed it out too—one blue, one brown—and I, well . . ." He reddened. "I was so surprised, and pleased, I suppose, to recognise him, that I said, 'That's Zig, isn't it?' And he said yes, that was his boy, and did I know where to find him? So, I told him Zig was staying at Esme's with you. And he'd probably be around during the day, because he works evenings at the Prince of Wales."

Si felt hollow inside. *Knee-deep in cow shit? Up to our bloody necks, more like. And rising.*

Corin's face was twisted with guilt. "I didn't think it could be a problem. I just didn't think," he added bitterly.

"He didn't know there was bad blood between them," Adam butted in, with an unspoken *Don't you dare get on his case.*

Si was quick to agree. "Course he didn't." Corin didn't talk a right lot about his mum and dad, and it was obvious there was some tension there, but it was also obvious he'd grown up in a nice middle-class family planted firmly on the right side of the law. Parents presenting actual danger wasn't gonna be the first thing he thought of. "Well, bugger," Si added, because he was only human.

Corin still looked worried. "So, after Adam told me about the, um, jail thing, we thought we should probably warn Zig that his dad's in town."

"You're sure it was his dad?" Si frowned. "Don't suppose you can tell me what he looked like?"

"Grey hair. Clean-shaven. And a gold tooth. Oh, and the one next to it was chipped. Quite well-built, and smartly dressed for here. Business casual." Corin made a face. "Sorry, that's all. Does that sound like him?"

"Not a scooby. I never met him. Zig always reckoned he wasn't too keen on the gay thing, so he never took blokes home. But that's great, that's loads of info." Much more than Si had dared hope for, what with Corin being face blind. "I'll give Zig a call, put him on guard."

"Tell him I'm sorry."

"You weren't to know," Si said, at the same time Adam came out with, "Not your fault."

Corin looked a bit less unhappy at that. Si only wished he could feel so cheerful.

Adam gave him an intent look. "Let us know if you or Zig need anything, all right? You know. If it turns into a situation."

Si's heart swelled. "Will do. Cheers, mate. I'll owe you."

"No, you won't. We've got to go, but you keep me posted, yeah?"

Si nodded. After they left, he rang Zig straight away, going so far as to hold up an apologetic hand to a customer who'd walked in and mouth, *Be with you in a mo*, at her.

It went straight to voicemail. Si cursed under his breath and left a message. "Call me as soon as poss, all right? It's a bit urgent."

Then he shoved his phone into his pocket and turned to apologise to the lady waiting patiently.

Chapter Forty-One
Zig

Zig sat on the bench at the top of the rise and looked down over the Chalice Well gardens. The trees might have been bare but somehow there was still a rare sense of being among nature, in the midst of living things, here. Well, rare for him, at any rate.

After he'd left Esme and her confusing job offer, Zig had wandered aimlessly for a bit, until he found his feet leading him towards the tor path. Apparently, his subconscious wanted to talk to someone. And . . . it probably wasn't *wrong*. Moping around town on his own until it was time to go to work wasn't gonna solve anything, so maybe talking would help. Not exactly *about* Ani's phone call and what it might mean, but . . . just talking to someone. Someone like Kai, who didn't judge and didn't make conversation like it was a prize fight.

Zig kinda liked Esme, and he definitely respected her, but he felt like he needed to bring his A game whenever they had a chat.

The cold wind was making him regret chucking a perfectly good cup of coffee, and Kai could probably do with something to warm them up, so Zig backtracked to the nearest coffee shop before heading on up to the tor.

He told himself all the way Kai wouldn't be there, but when he got to the gate, there they were, bundled up in their sleeping bag as usual.

"All right, mate?" Zig called, relief making him grin.

Kai smiled in answer. "I'm good. You?"

Zig made a face. "Peachy. You like lattes? Not got any milk allergies or whatever? I've got black if you'd rather."

"Latte, please. I need the calories. Thanks." Kai took the cup Zig held out and warmed their hands on it.

Zig sank down into a cross-legged position next to them, the ground under his bum like a block of ice. Probably seeping damp into his jeans, too, but they were black enough that at least it wouldn't look like he'd wet himself when he got up. "Bit of luck, you being here, and all. I'd have felt a right muppet having to drink two ventis on me own."

"Lose my number, did you?" Kai asked, eyebrow quirked.

"No, I— Ah, shit." Just call him bloody Kermit. "Could have texted you, couldn't I? Asked what you wanted. I am *really* not thinking straight today."

"Got something on your mind?"

Zig took a sip of his black Americano. It tasted bitter. Funny how quick he'd got used to having milk again. "Yeah. Kinda."

"Let me know if you want to talk about it. Or we can talk about something else." Kai shrugged. "Or sit and drink coffee and not talk at all."

A couple in high-tech hiking gear reached them and sent a dirty look their way before walking on, ignoring the mostly empty margarine tub Kai had out with *Thank You* scrawled on it in Sharpie.

Zig coughed. "Wankers," he muttered.

Kai giggled.

A lady in patchwork trousers stopped to drop in a couple of quid. She gave Zig a sharp look. "You ought to wrap up warmer. There's nothing of you. You know you can get warm clothes at the shelter, don't you?"

"Uh, cheers. I'm good, ta," Zig said, embarrassed. Mind, it *was* a bit nippy up here.

"You go to the shelter," she admonished him, like she was worried it hadn't sunk into his obviously thick head the first time, and strode away up the hill.

Kai was laughing into their scarf again.

Zig rolled his eyes. "Think I'd better leg it before she comes back down. She might not take no for an answer next time. Hey, are you all right? Keeping warm enough?"

Kai gave him a side-eye. "I'm fine. *Some* of us know when it's time to go to the shelter."

Zig flipped them a middle finger, feeling better already.

"So where are you off to after this?" Kai asked. "Not up the tor, if you're hiding from the patchwork-trousered philanthropist."

Zig grinned. "The what now? Have you been reading books or something?"

"You oughtta try it sometime. Broadens your horizons, and some of 'em have pictures in. And it's warm in the library, and you don't have to buy stuff to stay."

"Oi, I read books. I've been to *both* the libraries in town." Zig sighed. "Probably end up back in one of 'em after this. That's the trouble with bar work: you get your free time while everyone else is working. There's only so many times a bloke can wander round the shops before they start to think he's casing the joint." He huffed a bitter laugh.

Kai gave him a long look. "If you've got the money, you could go to the Chalice Well. It's quiet there. S'posed to be really spiritual."

"If it's spiritual, how come it costs money?"

Kai shrugged. "It's a garden, innit? Needs upkeep. Spirituality isn't going to weed the beds. Or clean the loos."

"Don't they have, like, acolytes to do that?"

"It's not a religion. It's a peaceful place you can go for reflection. And drink the waters, and wash your feet in them. If you want."

"You've been, then?"

"Once. When I first got here." Kai smiled crookedly. "When I still had some spare cash. It was nice."

"All right, I'll bite. You wanna come with? I'll pay for you."

Kai pursed their lips, like they were thinking it over. "Nah," they said at last. "Better if you go on your own. Then you can concentrate on letting the quiet in."

"You're sure?" Zig stood and stretched, stiff from sitting on the cold ground. "How much is it to get in this place?"

"Five pounds, when I went."

Zig nodded, and pulled out a tenner. "Here you go. In case you want to go some other time."

Kai didn't reach for it. "That's too much."

"No, it ain't. I'm earning, and the daft bastard I'm living with won't let me pay rent. Take it."

"Thanks." Kai squirrelled the money away inside the sleeping bag. "You take care, okay? Hope you like the well."

"Cheers." Zig turned to go, then, recalling his unsent text, turned back. "Kai . . . you ever worry your past's gonna catch up with you?"

"My past don't care enough to catch up with me."

Ouch. "That's a bit shit."

"Or, looked at another way, pretty lucky. Sure you don't wanna talk about it?"

Zig shook his head. "Think I'll try that quiet you mentioned. See if I can get me head straight. Cheers, though. I'll see you, okay?"

"See ya," Kai said.

Zig walked down the path feeling a tiny bit lighter, to Kai's shout of, "Try the water, it's lovely!"

The Chalice Well turned out to be literally about a minute's walk from the bottom of the path up the tor. Zig wondered why he hadn't noticed it before. Was it like one of those mysterious magic shops in books, that only appeared when you really needed them?

Nah, couldn't be. They'd miss out on all the tourist trade that way.

Even on this freezing December day, there were a few people waiting in line to pay their money and get spiritual. Zig joined the queue, which moved slower than he'd expected. Maybe that was all part of the experience—getting out of the pace of modern life. Or maybe they weren't all that efficient.

When he got to the front and paid over his fiver, Zig found that part of the reason for the wait was the mini-lecture on turning off all phones and other devices so as not to disturb the airwaves. Which didn't quite make sense to him—surely the air was full of radio waves whether anyone was receiving them or not?—but he dutifully switched off his phone. In any case, Si was working, and Kai knew where he was. Nobody else was likely to try to call him. At least, nobody he wanted to hear from.

Zig wandered down the path and into the gardens. Down a short slope, there was a man-made pool shaped like a Venn diagram with two overlapping circles. Water fed into it from a sort of rockery, with a staircase of wide, flat stones for the stream to trickle down.

There were people sitting on a bench nearby, talking softly as though they didn't want to disturb anyone listening to the hypnotic sound of the running water. Zig stood there for a moment, taking it in. Was this the peacefulness Kai had been on about? There was plenty more of the place to see.

The water from the pools ran out through a shallow, rust-coloured channel to another small pool and emptied into a drain shaped like a leaf. There was a crescent-shaped stone in the middle, and someone had placed acorns and pine cones on it, like it was some kind of woodland altar. Or a food bank for squirrels, maybe. Did squirrels sleep all through the winter, or did they wake up every so often for snacks? Zig had no clue.

Walking on, through mostly bare trees and empty flower beds, Zig tried to picture the place in summer. It'd be an explosion of colour and growth, most likely. The lawns were well-kept, and the beds weed-free, although it was winter. He found himself liking the barren look it had now, though. The land didn't feel dead—only asleep, and under it all was a sense of potential, waiting for the warmer weather to wake it up and bring it to fullest life. Zig blinked. Huh. *Look at you, being all poetical.* Kai would kill themself laughing. And Si . . . Si would know what he meant. Zig was sure of that. The bloke who'd researched an author he'd never read so he could take Zig on a tour—yeah, he'd understand, all right.

He waited until the couple in front of him had moved on before approaching the spring that trickled down a rough-built stone wall, even rustier than the pools by the entrance. One of them had filled a bottle with the water, which . . . Was that to drink? Zig frowned. Kai had said to try the waters, hadn't they? He bent forward and cupped a cautious handful, bringing it to his lips.

Fuck, that's bitter! Zig swallowed with a grimace, wiped his hand on his jeans, and grabbed his phone to tell Kai they were a git. *Lovely, my arse.* Then he remembered: no disturbing the airwaves here. Right. It could wait. Smiling, he wandered on, up a slope to an area sparsely planted with trees and benches, only one of them occupied, by an older couple so wrapped up they were pretty much egg-shaped.

He could see the tor from here, the tower visible through the bare branches. Somehow it looked farther away than he knew it was. Kai was probably still there, out of sight. Zig hoped people were being generous to them.

Sitting on one of the empty benches, cold leeching through the still-damp seat of his jeans, Zig realised he hadn't thought about his dad once since he'd been here. Even now, the thought didn't bother him as much as it had. The threat—if it was a threat—seemed more distant, somehow. More manageable. After all, what could Dad actually do to him?

Okay, he was probably still bigger and heavier—and meaner—than Zig; prison wasn't likely to have changed that. But he couldn't make Zig do anything, could he? Not now he wasn't a kid anymore, living in Dad's house. Dependent on him.

Zig had a new life now. A better one, with Si in it. *I'm never going back to London*, he found himself thinking, and blinked. Did he really mean that? Teenage Zig would have hated this place, he was pretty sure—too quiet, too rural, too limited.

Adult Zig appreciated the quiet. He liked Glastonbury, tiny as it was compared to where he'd grown up. There was still stuff going on, and more than that, there was a sense of permanence he'd always missed out on before. Like, while people moved on, the tor would still be here, like it had for thousands of years before. London had old bits, yeah, but it was always changing despite that. People moved on; businesses changed owners or were knocked down and rebuilt. It was all bland and commercial.

He'd made a decision. Whatever came, he was going to weather it. If Dad turned up here, for whatever reason, Zig would tell him to sod off back to London. If Trent came with him . . . Well, in the best-case scenario, Zig would take care only to come within a mile of the bloke if there were half a dozen witnesses. Even if the worst came to the worst, what was Trent going to do to him? Zig could take a beating if he had to. Probably. If that was the price of staying here, with Si. The price of happiness.

And then I'll have the feds on 'em so fast they won't know what's hit 'em, he thought with vicious satisfaction.

There was a chill wind blowing, and he'd started to shiver, so Zig rose, reluctantly, and headed back down the slope. Without his phone, he wasn't sure how late it was, but it was probably time to grab something to eat before he was due at work.

Not wanting to face Esme again until he'd had some more time to think about her offer, Zig ate his dinner at a vegan café instead of heading back to the flat. He'd picked up a book called *Normal for Glastonbury* in one of the shops in town, which kept him entertained while waiting for his order. After a bowl of soup so thick and full of rough-cut veg it probably ought to be called stew, coupled with some bread made of spelt, whatever that was, Zig felt ready to face anything.

For a Monday night, the pub was pretty busy, probably due to people getting into the Yuletide spirit with less than a week to go to the twenty-fifth. No wonder Ange had wanted him in for an extra shift. Women were dressed in sparkly tops or warm shades of red and green, with novelty earrings shaped like holly or gingerbread men. A couple of blokes had ugly Christmas sweaters on, and one wore a Santa hat that looked weird with the resolutely drab and normal clothes he had on.

Ange was done up like a Christmas present, in a tartan dress with a bow at her waist. Zig was grateful she didn't insist on festive wear for her staff, just the usual black polo shirts. Although, he noticed Finn had accessorised with a Christmas tree earring. It didn't look that bad, actually.

Finn noticed him looking and turned away with a flush.

Damn it. Zig had thought they'd got over the awkwardness. "Hey, nice earring," he said quickly. "Think I ought to get more festive?"

Finn smiled wryly. "Thought you were too cool for Yule. Won't it mess with the image?"

"Ah, sod that." Zig decided it was possible to worry too much about looking naff. Also, that Finn really didn't know him all that well if he thought Zig was *cool*. "Gotta get into the spirit, yeah?"

After that, the orders came nonstop, and Zig barely had time for a bit of banter with the customers. Everyone was in a festive mood, drinking a little more than usual. Letting their hair down. Tipping more too. It was a good night.

Until Zig turned to face the next customer. "What can I get—" He broke off, his mouth suddenly dry.

His dad gazed at him, a sneer twisting his lips. "How about a word?"

Chapter Forty-Two
Zig

*C*hrist. Zig had forgotten how much bigger than him Dad was. How much meaner, and the way he made Zig feel like a fag-end only fit to be stamped out on the street. It'd seemed so easy to dismiss him when he was sitting in the Chalice Well gardens. So easy to imagine telling him to piss off.

Zig's guts twisted. "I'm working," he said, his voice coming out a lot less firm and confident than he'd wanted it to.

"You can take a break to catch up with your old man. That's all right, ain't it, love?" Dad smiled at Ange, who with some kind of sixth sense for trouble had appeared at Zig's shoulder. "You won't mind giving my boy five minutes with his dad who ain't seen him for years."

Ange looked sharply at Zig. "Is that what you want?"

Zig was tempted to say *No, Christ, bar the bastard*, but it wasn't like Dad would simply disappear. Best to get it over with now. "Five minutes?" he asked hoarsely.

She nodded. Then she sent Dad an insincere smile. "We're a bit busy tonight, so I can't spare him any longer, my lover."

He looked smug. "I'll find us a table."

No doubt by evicting its present occupants with menaces. Zig couldn't stand the thought of that, and he didn't want anyone overhearing whatever Dad had to say to him, either. "No. Outside."

With a depressing irony, Zig found himself in the same alleyway he'd stood in a week earlier, telling Si he loved him. It was dark, with a bitter wind blowing, and Zig shivered in his polo shirt. Dad, in his thick wool coat, loomed larger than ever in the silhouette cast by the streetlight.

Christ, had it been a mistake coming out here, where there was no one around to see what Dad might do?

"What do you want?" he asked brusquely, trying to keep the fear out of his voice.

"Is that any way to greet your old man, when he's travelled all this way to see you?"

"I didn't ask you to come."

"Maybe I wanted to see my only flesh and blood. Wasn't easy tracking you down, you know. Almost like you wanted to hide, imagine that? It was Trent what first got on your trail. Remember him? He remembers you, all right. He had a word with that young lady you used to work with—management said you and her was in tight." Dad laughed nastily. "And we both know it wasn't like you'd be trying to shag her. Not unless she had a dick hiding under them short skirts. She told him you said you were going down Peckham for a *family emergency*."

His tone was full of derision. "And Trent thought, 'Peckham, why's that familiar?' And then he remembered. All them evenings down the Dog and Duck with the brickies, back before that job that went tits up and landed us all in jail. So, he heads over there, and what do you know? They had plenty to say about you turning up like a fucking bad penny. Asking about the boss's nipper's mate—one of your little boyfriends, back in the day, wasn't he? They told Trent he'd moved back to hippie central here." Dad folded his arms, looking smug. "After that, it didn't take long to find you. You've done a piss-poor job of hiding, but then, why should I expect any different?"

Zig felt colder than he had on the tor. "Why, though? Why come all this way after me? Last time we spoke, you told me I was a bloody waste of sperm."

Dad's face turned hard. "Because you owe me, boy."

"I don't owe you nothing." Ice, there was fucking ice clogging up his veins, making it hard to think. *Stay strong. Tell him to eff off and do his worst.*

"That's what you think, is it? I gave you life, you ungrateful little bastard. I gave you life, and I fed you and housed you after your cunt of a mother fucked off and left us, so don't you fucking tell me you don't owe me."

Even as Zig reeled mentally with the blows, the ice melted, a little. *He doesn't know. Thank fuck, he doesn't know what I did on that last job.* "I never asked you to do any of that."

"No?" Dad's tone was steel. "And I never asked you to set off the alarm, grass us up to the pigs, and land us all in jail. But here we are."

The ice stabbed him right in the heart, and bile rose in Zig's throat. He wanted to swallow, but his mouth was too dry. "Who told you that?" His voice shook.

Triumph flashed in Dad's eyes. "I knew it. I fucking *knew* it. Trent swore blind he laid that guard out before he had a chance to reach for his alarm. And unlike some ungrateful pricks, he don't lie to me." Dad's colour rose, but his voice was as quiet as ever. It was somehow worse than if he'd shouted. "Think I'm stupid? Did you think I'd never work it out? You ought to thank your lucky stars Trent ain't put it all together. You'd finally have two matching eyes if I let him loose on you, and that'd be the least of your troubles."

"What do you want?" Zig rasped. *What'll stop you telling Trent?*

"You're going to do a little job for me. And this time, me and Trent won't be coming along, so the only person you can shit on is yourself, you got that?"

"What, and then you'll leave me alone?" *Like hell he would.*

"All I want is you to pay me back for those years inside. So you do this job, and you make it good, and then we're quits, right?" Dad smiled, showing his gold tooth.

There was a lead weight in Zig's stomach. They'd never be quits, not in Dad's eyes. Not unless this *little job* was doing over the Tower of London and making away with the Crown Jewels. No, not even then, cos this wasn't about the money, was it? This was about showing Zig who was boss. Making him do what he was told.

Stay. Fucking. Strong.

"No," he said, but it came out almost inaudible, so he said it again. "No. I'm not doing it. I'm through with all that." A cautious flicker of warmth spread through him. He'd done it. He'd stood up to Dad.

"You're through with it when I say you are." Dad's voice went softer, snuffing out that warmth like a bucket of ice water. "Or do you want me to give Trent your new address? Tip him off about you sounding that alarm? Admitting it to my face? Reckon he'd be *very* happy to see you again." He paused. "'Spect he'd like to meet that bloke of yours too. Rides a Harley, don't he? I saw one parked out back of that shop you live over, and I don't think it's that witch bint who rides it. Terrible dangerous things, those are. So many accidents. I knew a boy came off a motorbike. Skidded on some oil. He spent a year in hospital getting his face pinned back together. Never the same again, poor lad."

The ice was back big-time, and the nausea too. *He'll hurt Si . . .*

Zig couldn't let anything happen to Si. Not Si, with his warm smile and the utter fucking *goodness* of him. "You wouldn't."

"Wouldn't I?" Dad snarled in Zig's face. "You just try me. Now, are you going to be a good little boy, or is the boyfriend going to be trading his Harley for a wheelchair?"

Oh God . . . "One job," Zig found himself saying, though it didn't sound like him at all. "One job, and we're through, yeah?"

"That's it." Dad nodded, like he was satisfied. "Give me your phone."

Numbly, Zig pulled his phone out of his pocket, realising as he did so that he hadn't switched it back on since the afternoon. Dad muttered a few curses while they waited for it to boot up again, then Zig unlocked it and handed it over.

After sending a quick text—to himself, Zig assumed, so he'd have Zig's number—he handed it back, so roughly it almost fell to the ground before Zig could grab it and shove it back into his pocket.

Dad rolled his eyes. "I'll be in touch with the details." Then he turned on his heel and walked away.

Chapter Forty-Three
Si

Si had spent every spare moment of the afternoon trying to call Zig. He kept getting the message "Sorry, the person you are trying to call is unavailable."

Why wasn't Zig available? Si *knew* he'd charged his phone—he'd seen it plugged in by the bed like it was every night. Why would Zig have switched it off?

Maybe the power to the socket hadn't been turned on? Si had done that once or twice.

In the end, he gave up trying to get through to Zig and called Esme.

"Es, is Zig there? I can't get him on his phone."

"No, I haven't seen him since this morning. But—"

"Has a bloke been round asking after him?" Si cut her off.

"I *was* about to mention that. I see those psychic abilities are coming along nicely."

"No—look, Es, it's important. Was it an older bloke, uh, with a gold tooth?"

"Yes. He said he was Zig's father and that he'd heard Zig was living here. I didn't much like the look of him, to be honest, so I simply said that any guests you might have were none of my business, there was nobody in the flat at the moment, and I couldn't say when anyone might be back. I invited him to leave a number, which he declined."

"Es, you're a treasure."

"*Is* he Zig's father?"

"Seems so. But he's bad news."

"I could have told you that. I had to burn sage to cleanse the atmosphere after he'd gone."

"If he comes back, call me. If you can't get me, call someone else. Or . . . or the police. I mean it, Es. He ain't good news."

"Noted. And if I see Zig, I'll tell him to call you."

They said their goodbyes and hung up. Si's stomach was churning. It was killing him, being stuck at work while Zig could be in trouble. Thank the gods he wasn't out on calls this afternoon—or would that have been better? Maybe he could have kept an eye out while he was on his way around?

A customer came into the shop, and Si forced himself to focus on home security. Once they'd gone, he checked the time. Almost five. They closed at six; should he beg off early? Say it was an emergency? Another customer came in before he'd come to a decision.

Sod it. How much harm could Zig's dad do in—Si checked— three quarters of an hour? It'd take most of that for anyone to get here to cover him. Course, he could close the shop early . . . but that wouldn't be fair on the customers. Or the boss. And for what? A vague presentiment of doom?

Every second seemed to take an hour to tick by as he watched the clock—when he wasn't dealing with customers or answering the phone. When Si finally looked up from the last call, it was two minutes past six. He surged into action, flipping the sign to Closed, locking the door, cashing up, and finally, *finally* grabbing his coat.

Si only stopped at the flat long enough to be certain Zig wasn't there, then he headed out to the Prince of Wales. Gods, the streets were *full* of people. He wanted to shout at them to get out of his way. Didn't they know this was an emergency?

Could be nothing, though, a voice in his head kept on telling him. It sounded a bit like Sash. *Could be Zig's dad found him, Zig told him to piss off, and everything's hunky-fucking-dory*. Si wished he could believe it.

He was so lost in his thoughts, he didn't notice Adam until he'd practically walked slap bang into him coming out of the pub.

"You've spoken to Zig, then?" Si blurted out, taking a step back. It was decent of Adam to come out to warn him.

"Yeah . . ." Adam's tone was grim.

It worried Si. "And?"

"He's not inside. I asked at the bar. They said he'd gone out the back to talk to this older bloke who came in asking for him."

"You mean his dad." Si took a step towards the side alley.

Adam grabbed his arm. "Right. Look, maybe hold back a mo?"

"Why, for gods' sake?"

"Well, for a start, if you go barrelling in there in the mood you're in right now, you might end up starting a brawl. Zig ain't gonna thank you for losing him his job."

"I ain't in a mood," Si growled out.

"Mate, you look like you're this close to punching someone."

"I can control myself."

"Can you? And . . ." Adam made a face. "You're not gonna like this, but . . . Zig told you him and his dad had fallen out, right? That he sent his dad to *jail*. So how come when I stuck my head round the back, I saw them having a cosy little conversation like nothing's wrong?"

"That's . . ." Si's brow creased. "Hang about. I don't think his dad knows it was Zig that got them banged up."

"Huh." Adam paused. "In that case, all the more reason not to barge in like you think his dad's about to deck him or worse. You don't wanna give the game away, do you?"

"S'pose not." Gods, Si's knees went weak at the thought of putting Zig in danger.

"Right. So there's no need for the rescue mission. He's not a bloody damsel, and he doesn't look all that distressed to me. We tried to warn him, and we didn't make it, but it looks like he's handling it on his own just fine. So we let them have their chat. Chances are, Zig's gonna tell you all about it when he gets home, yeah?"

Si wasn't daft. He knew what Adam really meant was, *See if he tells you about it, then you'll know if he's been honest with you.* Half of him wanted to say bugger that—he trusted Zig—but the other half, the shameful half that remembered all too well the pain after they'd split up six years ago, seemed to be in charge right now.

It wasn't a betrayal of Zig's trust, was it? It was simply giving Zig an opportunity to be open with him.

"Fine." Si's heart clenched painfully, and he let Adam lead him away.

Chapter Forty-Four
Zig

Zig didn't hang around after his shift. He cleared up in record time and was out the door while Ange was still saying goodnight. No way was he hanging around chatting when Si would be all on his own back at the flat.

Who knew where Dad had disappeared off to after he'd left the pub? Zig didn't trust him any further than he could throw him. It'd be just like the old bastard to cause trouble and make sure Zig didn't forget who was in charge.

Christ. Tears pricked at the corners of Zig's eyes. He'd thought he was free. Thought he could be happy. Now . . . Zig couldn't see any end in sight. It wouldn't be only one job. He'd be sucked back into Dad's life, and Si would never be safe.

He stopped dead on the street, gut-punched by a realisation. If he wanted to get out, he'd have to leave Glastonbury. Leave Si. If Zig wasn't there, Si would be safe.

Or would Dad hurt him in revenge? God, if only he could *think*. Misery spread through his entire body. He'd never get out. He'd never be free because he was too fucking *stupid*.

Zig balled up a fist and punched the nearby wall. It hurt like fuck, and it didn't do a thing to distract him from the pain inside. *Stupid.* Zig's internal voice was sounding like Dad again.

"Are you all right, my lover?" A large woman in long skirts was peering at him in concern, while her bloke, who was even larger, hovered protectively.

Zig wanted to burst into tears. He managed to dredge up some kind of a smile instead. "Yeah. I'll live. Been a day, you know?"

"You go home and get some ice on that hand," she told him firmly. "Have a hot drink, and watch something nice on telly. And make sure you call someone before you go doing any more damage to yourself. Samaritans, if you don't want to talk to anyone you know. Google them. Now, are you going to be okay getting home?"

Zig nodded. "It ain't far."

"We can come with if you want," she insisted. "So you're not on your own."

"Nah. I'm good. I've . . . I've got someone waiting." His heart broke again at the thought of Si. "I better go."

"Well, I hope they take care of you. Remember what I told you, won't you?"

He nodded again and strode away, head down, before she could kill him with any more kindness.

Zig took a deep breath and pasted on a smile as he put his key in the door to the flat. *Gotta act normal.* He couldn't tell Si what had happened. Si's world was good, and kind, and decent. Dad, and his crimes, and his fucking vengeance couldn't be allowed to taint it. *And what about you, then?* an inner voice demanded. *Aren't you tainting Si's world by being in it?* Zig felt sick. *I'll sort this out,* he told himself desperately. *I'll think of something, and Si will never have to know Dad was here.*

But he needed time to get his head round it all. To work out what the fuck he was going to *do.*

He kicked off his trainers and walked through to the living room, where Si was on the sofa nursing a can of beer.

"You all right there, my lover?" Si asked.

Was he giving Zig a searching look?

Nah, your guilty fucking conscience is seeing things. Zig laughed awkwardly. "Sounds bloody weird you calling me that. Seeing as it's actually true."

Si blinked. "That how you think of me, is it? Your lover?"

Ah, fuck. "Well, you know. We're shagging, ain't we?" *And so maybe you ain't my lover, but I'm bloody well yours.*

There was a pause. "You have a good evening at the pub?"

Fucking terrible. "It was okay. Busy, though. I'm run off me feet." Zig flopped down onto the sofa next to Si. Not touching, simply . . . there.

Side by side, there wasn't the pressure to look Si in the face.

"No trouble, I hope?" Si asked.

Was there something significant in his tone?

"Nah. Nothing. Dead boring, really."

There was another pause before Si spoke again. "I tried to ring you, earlier, but couldn't get through. Problem with your phone?"

Zig frowned and pulled it out of his pocket. "Shit. Forgot to switch it on again, didn't I? I was up at the Chalice Well this afternoon. You been there? It's a technology-free zone." He grinned and thumbed it to life. "Huh. Three missed calls. Was it something urgent?"

"No, it was— Here, what've you done to your hand?" Si grabbed his right hand, the one that'd lost the argument with the wall.

Fuck. Zig should have known he'd notice the swelling knuckles. "Nothing! Uh, slammed the hatch on it. You know, the one that lifts up to let you out the bar? Ange went through to, uh, talk to some regulars, and she left it open. Then Finn came over and shut it, but I'd, uh, left me hand there." Zig's laugh sounded fake even to him. "Felt a proper numpty, didn't I?"

"You ought to ice that. You sit there, and I'll get the frozen peas." Si disappeared into the kitchen, coming back with a bundle wrapped in a tea towel.

Zig's heart clenched. "You're too good to me, you know that?" He took the parcel and applied it to his throbbing hand. It didn't exactly make it feel better, but he knew it'd reduce the swelling.

"You want a beer with that?" Si asked. "Or some painkillers?"

Zig thought of the motherly woman in the street. "How about a cup of cocoa? And maybe we could watch some more *Doctor Who*?"

"Yeah, course." Si went off to the kitchen again, and the kettle began to boil.

The TV remote was harder to work with his left hand, but Zig managed to navigate to iPlayer. Si came back with two steaming mugs, sat down on the sofa, and put his arm around Zig's shoulders.

Zig sank into his embrace, wishing to God that the world would bugger off and leave them alone.

Chapter Forty-Five
Si

In the early hours of the morning, when they'd finally gone to bed, Si lay with his arms around Zig. He could have wept, except he was a big boy now, wasn't he? Any road, this was good, wasn't it? Zig showing his true colours again. Like, before Si got in too deep with him.

Hah. That horse had bolted clean across the Welsh border and would be booking a crossing to Ireland right around now.

Zig had lied to him. He'd lied about seeing his dad—maybe not explicitly, but he'd said there hadn't been any trouble at the pub. Si wouldn't call the sudden appearance of Zig's estranged, criminally minded bastard of a dad *no trouble*.

Or maybe he'd lied about being on the outs with his dad? Gods, had that whole story about getting him sent down been a lie?

Maybe it hadn't, though, cos what about that hand of his? Lie number . . . Si had lost count. It'd been a rubbish lie. Who had Zig been punching, to bruise his knuckles like that? His dad?

But why wouldn't he tell Si about it?

That bit about his phone being switched off had been a lie too. Si knew how long it took for a phone to restart. So, he must have seen the missed calls. And ignored them. Si was losing him.

His arms tightened reflexively around Zig, who shifted and rolled out of his grasp. "Sorry. Can't sleep. Gonna watch telly for a while."

Again? They'd watched two episodes of *Doctor Who* already. "Want some company?"

"Nah, you get your rest. I'll be good."

Will you? Si pulled the duvet tighter around himself, but somehow he still felt cold.

Chapter Forty-Six
Zig

Waking up the next morning was worse than the worst hangover Zig had ever had. And he'd only been drinking bloody cocoa the night before. He wished it'd been something stronger. Maybe there might have been some lingering effect to numb the pain and the anxiety that came crashing down on him along with the memory of the night before. God knew how much sleep he'd managed—two hours? Three?—by the time Si's alarm went off and, from the next room, roused Zig from his uneasy dreams of Dad and prison.

Si seemed subdued too. Well, they'd both had a late night. Zig tried to be helpful but found himself staring at a running tap while the water went down the sink instead of into the kettle he held.

A large, gentle hand took the kettle from him, filled it, and switched it on. "You go get some more rest," Si murmured. "Looks like you could use it."

Zig tried to smile. "Nah, I'm good. Need some caffeine in me, that's all."

"You got plans for the day, then?"

Did Si's voice sound a bit off?

Zig was in no condition to judge. "Might hit the library. Still ain't checked out all them gay gods of yours."

As Zig walked through town, all he could think about was his dad and what the hell this *one more job* was gonna turn out to be. Another building site? Couldn't be. Glastonbury, from what he'd seen, didn't have the sort of construction projects to make it worth it. Zig passed an antiques shop, and shivered. Dad could have picked up a whole new skillset in jail. New contacts. There was a jeweller's down the street. How much could you get from doing that place over? Course, they'd lock away all the stock overnight, so it'd have to be a daytime raid.

Armed robbery. Zig felt sick. He couldn't do it. *Wouldn't* do it.

Then a picture crashed into his head of Si lying in hospital after an "accident" on the Harley, and he felt even sicker. He had to stop for a mo, head down, resting his hands on his knees.

"Are you all right, my lover?" a woman asked, sounding concerned and oddly familiar.

Zig looked up and nearly shat himself. It was Si's mum.

"Zig?" she asked, her eyes widening and her voice a bit sharper than before.

"Di," he said weakly. "Good to see you. How's Bob doing?"

"He's fine, but you still haven't told me how you are." She frowned. "Hangover, is it?"

So, she still wasn't keen on him. It was no more than Zig deserved. "Something like that."

"Hmph. Do I need to get you some water?"

Zig straightened and shook his head. "Ta, but I'm good. Listen, I'm sorry I didn't, you know, tell you the whole story when I came looking for Si."

She softened a little. "Well, I can see why you wouldn't have wanted to. And Simon does seem happy with you. I'd begun to wonder if he was ever going to find someone."

Guilt twisted a knife in Zig's guts. "He's a great bloke," he managed to say. "Deserves to be happy."

Di smiled then. "That he does. Now, I haven't said anything to Simon yet, but I hope we'll be seeing both of you on Christmas Day?"

Jesus. That was, what, a week away? Zig couldn't begin to think that far ahead. "That'd be great, thanks." He dredged up a cheeky smile. "Can't wait to eat some more of your cooking."

"Who says I'll be the one cooking?" There was a twinkle in her eye now. "But you go easier on the booze between now and then, or you won't be in a state to appreciate it."

Zig nodded. "It's a promise."

"Good. We'll see you then. Now, you go get yourself a hot drink and something to eat. That'll take the edge off it." Di gave him one last smile, then strode off down the street, her tall figure drawing glances as she went.

Zig wanted to cry. Mums giving out hangover advice and invitations to Christmas dinner . . . This wasn't his world.

He couldn't do this. There was no way on earth he could do what Dad wanted him to, and then go home to a decent bloke like Si. There was even less way he could then let Si take him round to his mum's for Christmas.

But if he didn't go along with Dad, Si would never be safe. Not with Zig in his life.

A vast hollow opened up in Zig's chest. The solution was obvious, wasn't it? Zig had to get out of Si's life. With Zig gone, there'd be no point in Dad threatening Si.

He should never have come here. Should have kept going west until he fell into the bloody sea. Si would've been safe, then. Safe from Dad, and safe from the hurt Zig was gonna cause him.

Again.

His heart breaking, Zig turned back towards the flat. It was time to pack his things and go. This time, forever.

Chapter Forty-Seven
Zig

It took longer than it should have for Zig to get all his shit together. Mostly because packing his bag felt like hammering nails into his heart. He didn't want to go. He hated the thought that he'd never see the flat again.

Never see Si again.

Deliberately, he made himself think of Si in hospital, and while it hurt like fuck, it gave him the determination he needed to finish the job.

He wrote Si a note: *Sorry, you're better off without me. I love you.* Then he crumpled it up and chucked it into the bin.

He left his key on the kitchen counter, took one last look around, and left.

Zig had to wander around town for a bit. Let the cold air clear his head and make his eyes less watery. Only then did he feel up to walking through the door of Furious Ink.

Sasha looked up from the client she was applying a transfer to. "Zig? Come to get some ink?"

"No." It came out hoarse, and Zig cleared his throat. "Need a word with Adam, if he's here."

She assessed him for a long moment. "He's out back. Sit down, and he'll be out in a mo."

Zig couldn't settle on the sofa in the window. He picked up a folder of tattoo ideas and leafed through it, not seeing the designs.

"What did you want to talk to me about?"

Zig jumped badly and covered it by getting to his feet. He hadn't even noticed Adam walking up to him. "Uh . . ."

Adam's eyes narrowed as they took in Zig's backpack. "You're leaving?"

Zig laughed unhappily. "Thought you'd be pleased about that. Yeah. I'm going. Not sure where."

"And you're telling me because?"

"I need you to look after Si. Make sure he's okay."

Adam stepped closer and hissed into Zig's face, "He's not going to be fucking *okay*, you bastard. Christ, you haven't even told him, have you? You're sneaking out while he's at work. You make me sick."

That made two of them. Zig tried to pull himself together. "I can't— I can't say goodbye to him. If he was here, I wouldn't be able to hack it."

"So, why the fuck are you leaving, then? Got a better offer, did you? Your dad tempt you with easy money?"

Zig froze. "What do you know about my dad?"

"I know he's here, and you and him had a cosy little chat last night. Made up your differences, did you? If they ever existed. Fuck, you've been lying all along, haven't you? Making out that you're one of the good guys now. Well, sod off, then. Back to easy street, ripping off honest people. Hope it makes you happy, breaking Scratch's heart. Again. You fucking *cunt*."

Zig flinched. His head was dizzy. "Does Si know Dad's here?"

"Course he bloody knows. You're the only one who lies to him around here. Keeps secrets from him."

"I never meant to hurt him," Zig insisted desperately. "You've got to tell him that."

"I don't have to tell him anything you say. Why the fuck should I? I always knew you were a waste of space."

That old insult again, only not from Dad this time. Anger and misery rose in Zig's throat, nearly choking him. "I'm doing this for Si!"

"What?"

"My fucking dad. He threatened him. Said he'd make him have an accident on his bike if I didn't work for him again. I can't . . . I can't do it. I don't wanna be in that life anymore, and it'd kill Si if he knew I was breaking the law. I ain't gonna lie to him about it, neither. But I can't risk him getting hurt. Not Si. He don't— He deserves everything good, not shit like that happening to him. That's why I'm leaving. Not cos I wanna go work for my dad. So I can get the fuck away from that bastard, and get him away from Si." Zig wrapped his arms around himself, feeling like if he didn't, he'd probably fall apart right there.

Adam was staring at him. "Why haven't you told Scratch all this?"

"He's a good bloke. The best. He shouldn't have all this shit in his life." Zig laughed bitterly. "Shouldn't have a waste of space like me pulling him down."

"You know what he ought to have?"

"Yeah?" Zig braced himself for more hard truths.

"He deserves to make his own decisions about who he wants in his life." Adam's voice was quieter now. Almost gentle. "And the chance to protect the man he loves. Cos he does love you. Has done for years. He never stopped."

"Fuck knows why," Zig whispered.

Adam huffed. "I'm starting to get an idea. A very faint one, mind. Look, put your backpack down. You're not leaving. We're gonna sort this out."

Chapter Forty-Eight
Si

Si jogged down the street to Furious Ink, misgiving churning in his guts. *"Come over to the studio as soon as you finish work,"* Adam had said on the phone. *"Don't go to the flat first. Do not pass Go; do not collect £200."* And when Si had protested about Zig expecting him home: *"No, he ain't. He's here."*

Then he'd refused to say any more and hung up, cos sometimes Adam was a bastard like that.

When he burst through the door, the first thing Si saw was Zig, sitting on the sofa with his knees drawn up and his arms wrapped around them. He wasn't wearing his Converse, and his feet looked weirdly vulnerable in a pair of Si's Tardis socks.

The second thing he saw was Zig's backpack, on the desk with a hard-faced Adam standing between Zig and it. Si's heart sank. No wonder Adam hadn't wanted him to go by the flat and find all Zig's stuff gone.

"Gonna tell me about it?" he said with a sigh.

Zig glanced at Adam, then nodded jerkily, uncurling himself from the sofa and standing up.

Sasha appeared from the back room. "You can come in here. I've made tea for you. It's in there." She was holding two mugs, which she brought out for herself and Adam.

Zig took a step, then faltered. "Not sure I can do this." He glanced at Adam again.

"Yeah, you can. Tell Si what you told me. About your dad, and what he wants you to do."

What the hell was going on? How come Adam knew all about it and not Si?

Didn't Zig trust him enough to tell him? But then why would he talk to Adam? They weren't exactly besties. Si felt hurt, and bewildered, and really fucking worried.

He followed Zig into the back room. As Sash had promised, there were two steaming mugs of tea in there on the counter. Zig picked one up, wrapped his hands around it, then put it down again.

Si looked him in the eye. "What are you gonna tell me, then?"

Zig took a deep breath. "Adam said you know my dad's here. That we talked." He swallowed and picked up the mug again.

Was he waiting for an answer? Si nodded, not trusting himself to say anything without going off on one because whatever this was, it couldn't be good.

Zig lifted the mug to his lips but didn't drink. He put it down again. "Dad said . . . He said I gotta do one more job for him. You know. Nicking stuff."

All the tension in Si boiled over. "I defended you!"

"What?"

"All this time, everyone's been telling me you're no good. Mum and Dad. Sasha. Adam. Even bloody Corin, who don't know anything more about you than what Adam's told him. And here was muggins, telling 'em all to lay off. Saying they shouldn't go hanging dogs by giving 'em a bad name."

"Huh?"

"Told 'em, it was six years ago you broke my— broke up with me, and you can't judge a man by what he was like as a teenager. Told 'em to give you a chance, and you'd surprise 'em. Well, more fool me. Guess I'm the only one surprised, as it turns out." There was a great hollow cavity in Si's chest, and it hurt like nothing had ever hurt before.

Zig's eyes were wide. "No, wait. I'm not gonna do it!"

"How come you're leaving me, then? Cos don't try to tell me you ain't. You'd be halfway to gods know where by now if it hadn't been for Adam and Sash." Si's eyes prickled, and he blinked furiously.

"I didn't know what to do!"

"From the look of that rucksack, you had a pretty good idea." Si folded his arms.

Adam poked his head round the door. "He's buggering this up, isn't he? For fuck's sake. Si, I can't believe I'm saying this, but he was actually trying to be noble. His dad threatened you."

"Me?" Si turned to Zig. "Is this true?"

"He said he'd make sure you had an accident on your bike." Zig's voice was high and breathy, and getting higher. "I couldn't risk you getting hurt, but I couldn't go along with him; it'd never have ended, and fuck, you'd have hated me for it anyhow—"

Si grabbed hold of him and held him close until the panicked babble subsided and Zig was taking deep, shaky breaths in his arms. "You daft bastard," Si murmured fondly.

Zig sobbed and said something indistinct into Si's chest, which had somehow filled up so fast his ribs felt tight.

"Was that you going, 'Yes, Si, I'm a daft bastard'?"

Zig pulled back and gave Si the shakiest smile he'd ever seen, those mismatched eyes glistening. "Something like that. But what are we gonna do? I can't let him hurt you."

"Zig, love. You don't have to sort it all out by yourself. I know he's your dad and he's messed with your head all your life but, well, he's only a petty criminal, ain't he? They have coppers to sort them out. Like the one I'm mates with, remember?"

There was a penny-dropped look on Zig's face.

"And if the coppers can't sort him, you've got me. And Adam, and Corin, who's a black belt in the old martial arts. And Sash, and let me tell you, I wouldn't wanna be the one who's threatening anyone she cares about. But it ain't gonna come to that. Chances are, your dad's breaking all kinds of parole conditions being here. He ain't gonna want to risk going back to jail."

"And Trent? He's worse than Dad, seriously—"

"Same applies. All I gotta do is have a word with Rob the copper. And maybe some of the lads I work with. Just in case." Si pulled Zig in close once more and kissed him. "We'll sort it out. You don't have to worry no more. Now come on, let's get you home."

"You sure you wanna? All the trouble I cause you . . ."

"Ah, but I heard you don't mean to," Si reminded him, his voice gruff. "You go grab your shoes from wherever you've left 'em."

Zig's laugh was small, but it was there. "Sasha nicked 'em. Said if I was gonna run out on anyone, I'd have to do it in me socks."

"They ain't your socks," Si pointed out fondly. "Look good on you, though."

"Wanted something to remember you by." Zig sniffed.

"That forgettable, am I?" Si teased gently.

"I never forgot you. Not once. You were the one that got away."

Gods, much more of this and Si was gonna end up a happy puddle on the floor. He pulled himself together. "We're gonna take your stuff back home, and go to bed, and in the morning, we'll make a plan to deal with all this. Together. *And* involving the proper authorities." He shook his head. "You ain't on your own no more. Not now; not ever."

Chapter Forty-Nine
Zig

Walking back home—*home*—with Si felt unreal. Zig had been so certain he'd never come this way again. Never see the witchy window display of Esme's shop, dark now but ready to be lit up come morning. Never again climb these stairs, weariness in every limb.

Si made him go first, like maybe he was worried Zig might bolt again given half a chance. Zig couldn't blame him for that. He was wrong, though. Leaving once, although it'd seemed the only way to keep Si safe, had been hard enough. Zig wasn't gonna even think about leaving again. Not now he had hope.

And friends, maybe? "Are they really gonna do it?" Zig couldn't help asking, as Si opened the door to the flat.

"Who's doing what?"

"Your mates. Are they really gonna stand up to Dad and Trent? They don't have to. It ain't their fight." Zig hesitated on the doormat.

Si pulled him inside and put both arms around him. "Course they are. And course it is. We're mates, ain't we?"

Zig sank into that warm embrace, wondering how he'd ever thought he could do without it. "Don't think I've ever had that kind of mates. And yours don't like me."

"You're growing on 'em." Si chuckled. "Sasha wouldn't have nicked your shoes if she didn't want you hanging around, would she?" His voice softened. "And hey, did you miss the bit where Adam was defending you to me?"

"Still can't believe he did that. I mean, why would he wanna? It's not like I ever did anything for him."

"What, he can't count you making his best mate the happiest he's ever been?"

"Really?" Zig looked up at Si's face, desperate to find the truth in it.

"Really," Si confirmed. Then he frowned. "Course, not gonna lie, I was pretty bloody ecstatic the day I got me Harley—" He broke off laughing. "Your face!"

"Git. Dunno why I love you." And that was the biggest lie yet in a lifetime of fucking whoppers.

Si grinned. "Want a refresher course?"

Without waiting for an answer, he swung Zig up into his arms, bridal-carry style.

Zig burst out laughing. "You bastard!"

"Your bastard," Si said with a knowing look. "Now, the doorways are a bit narrow, so mind your head. Keep your arms and legs inside the vehicle at all times." He carried Zig swiftly into the bedroom, thankfully without any collisions.

"Gonna throw me on the bed and make me yours?" Zig asked.

"Well, only if you want me to," Si said politely.

Zig was gonna laugh again, but somehow his eyes were prickling. "I want. I've always wanted you."

Si smiled fondly. "That's all right, then. You got me."

He didn't throw Zig on the bed; he laid him down gently. And that was the fucking word of the day: *gentle*. His hands were tender as they stripped Zig of his clothes, and soft as they caressed him. His lips didn't take; they gave, but then that was Si all over, wasn't it? Zig had to tell him *Get on top of me*, because he needed that solid weight on him, grounding him. Even then, Si was careful, and it drove Zig wild with love and desire and fucking *thankfulness* he hadn't thrown all this away. It spurred him on to turn the tables and take control; to make sure Si felt every bit as loved as Zig did right now.

Si was the best man he'd ever known, and Zig planned to spend the rest of his life making sure he knew it too.

God alone knew how long it was before they were lying under the duvet, cuddled up together, coming down from a high so bloody stratospheric it had to be a danger to satellites.

"I'm never getting out of your bed." Zig sighed happily.

"*Our* bed," Si insisted. Then his stomach gave a loud rumble. "And while the spirit's willing, the flesh is bloody famished. Gonna see what I can rustle up."

He stood, and Zig took a moment to admire the solid bulk of him as he pulled on a pair of jogging bottoms, before jumping up himself and grabbing his jeans. "I'll give you a hand."

"You don't have to. Stay there if you want."

Zig smiled. "What, without you? Fuck that. The bed's dead to me now."

Despite Zig's complete failure to keep his hands off him, Si made short work of cooking up a quick veggie chili, and opened a bottle of red wine.

Yeah, Zig felt like celebrating too.

"You know your mum wants us round for Christmas dinner?" he remembered to say as they carried their plates into the living room.

"What?" Si asked.

"Bumped into her on the street when I was having a wobbly about it all. She thought I was hungover." Zig paused. "She said she thought I made you happy?" Despite everything, he couldn't stop it coming out like a question.

Si looked at him askance. "Course you bloody do, you muppet. Didn't I tell you? Now sit down, eat your chili, and stop asking daft questions."

Chapter Fifty
Zig

Dad called a couple of days later. The day of the solstice. Zig's birthday, and he'd be willing to bet the old bastard had planned it that way. *Happy fucking birthday.*

It'd started so well too. Like Si had promised, they'd gone up the tor to see in the dawn, and it'd been magical. A crowd of hundreds had felt their way up the path in the dim before-dawn light, and gathered around St. Michael's Tower. Some were in ceremonial robes but most were wrapped up in warm winter coats.

Zig was one of them. Si hadn't waited for Christmas to buy him a coat. It was a gorgeous thing in soft, warm wool that reached nearly to his ankles, in a navy so dark it was almost black. It was probably a bit swish for Glastonbury Tor—army surplus looked to be more on trend there right now, although as usual with Glastonbury, anything seemed to go—but Zig fucking loved it.

They stood together, arms around each other, as the officiants gave thanks for the return of the light, and a fire was lit. A beat sounded out from more bodhráns than you could shake a drumstick at, and everyone knelt to touch the earth. At the end, there was singing. It reminded Zig of a church service his gran had taken him to when he was little, only happier.

The musicians he'd seen before were there, and so was Kai, so Zig went over to say hi, and to introduce the bloody awesome bloke he was with. It turned out Si already knew Kai, which maybe Zig should have guessed: Glastonbury was a small town, after all.

Zig walked down the hill with Si afterwards feeling not only in love, but also connected, somehow, to the community that was here, even if he didn't actually know many people yet.

Then in the evening, when he was on his way to his shift at the pub, the phone rang, and when he saw the caller ID was *Arsehole Cunting Fuckface*, Zig nearly threw up in the street.

He pulled himself together and answered the call. "Yeah? I ain't got long. I'm due at the pub in ten minutes." Okay, so it was twenty. Zig liked to get there early.

"You'll make time for your old man if you know what's good for you. We need to meet."

"Right. Yeah." They'd expected this; they'd *planned* for this, so why was Zig's heart beating like it wanted to break a record and probably his rib cage while it was at it? "Tomorrow? Cos, like I said, I got work right now."

"You think you're the only one who's got things to do?" Dad's tone was belligerent. "You'll call in sick if you know what's good for you. And that boyfriend of yours."

Shit. Zig had thought he'd have time to prepare. Time to make sure Si and the others were available to back him up. "When?" he asked harshly.

"Now. Somewhere we ain't gonna be overheard. We got a job to plan."

"You can't come to the flat," Zig said quickly, his heart pounding and his thoughts racing. "Si's home. How about the tor, in half an hour?"

"The bloody tor?"

"Perfect, innit?" Zig crossed his fingers. "No one's gonna be up there this time of day. Just follow the path up to the tower." *And if you can manage it, trip and break your bloody neck in the dark, and save us all a load of trouble.* "See you there in half an hour."

He ended the call, hands shaking. Then he dialled Ange's number. "Ange? I'm really sorry. I can't make it in tonight. Something's come up. Family emergency," he added bitterly.

There was a brief silence, then a sigh. "A little more notice might have been nice, but I suppose it can't be helped. I'll see if one of the others can cover, so be prepared to owe them a favour."

"You too, Ange. Thanks. You're the best."

Next, he called Si. "It's happening," he said, nausea rising.

Half an hour later, Zig stood alone by St. Michael's Tower, shivering in the icy wind that whipped up from the levels. It was brighter than he'd expected, a full moon shining down on him like a pale, cold spotlight. No chance of anyone missing the path tonight.

Despite this, his heart skipped a beat when he spotted the two bulky figures walking towards him, closer than he'd expected. *No escape now.*

Dad stopped walking when he was a couple of yards away and stood there, his face stony. Next to him . . .

Trent.

He was dressed as sharply as ever, in a dark peacoat that made his shoulders look a million miles wide. He looked meaner than Zig remembered, his features coarser and thicker, somehow ghoulish in the pale moonlight. His hair was, as ever, spiked up with gel, untroubled by the strong wind up here.

Zig swallowed and concentrated on not shitting himself.

"S'pose you think this is funny, dragging us up here?" Dad sneered.

He was breathing hard from the climb. Zig tried to focus on that and not the threat in his voice. "It's a good place to meet, innit? Out of the way."

Trent spat on the ground. "I don't know why the fuck he bothered to come out here to hippie-land for you."

There was no sign of exertion in his voice.

No sign of weakness at all.

Zig smiled faintly. "Guess blood really is thicker than water."

Dad stepped forward. "Want to test that theory? Time to get down to business. Or you and your little fairy boyfriend are going to be finding out just how thick blood is."

"Not that little," Si said mildly, stepping out from behind the tower.

Zig's heart raced. It hadn't been part of the plan, Si showing himself so early. Or maybe it had, seeing as Si's main contribution to the plan had been *"If he threatens you, all bets are off."*

Dad lifted his chin. "Bigger they come, the harder they fall. Ain't that right, Trent?"

Feeling like he was about to throw up, Zig ignored his dad and turned to Trent. "Ain't it time you found someone better to work for? Instead of an aging petty criminal who talks like a movie and thinks he's the bloody godfather?" He didn't know where the courage to say all this was coming from.

Yeah, he did, and it was standing right beside him in a wicked leather jacket.

"We're partners," Trent snapped.

Hah. Touched a nerve.

"Oh, is that right?" Si piped up. "Congratulations. Hope you'll be very happy together."

"You fucking—" Trent broke off as Dad put a hand on his arm.

"Easy, now," Dad said. "Just blowing hot air, ain't they? We all know who's got the upper hand here. Now, *son*, you're going to listen while I tell you what you're going to be doing for me, and you're going to keep your pet ape under control, or it'll go badly for both of you."

"No." Zig's voice came out in a croak, but the meaning was clear.

Dad's face darkened. "No? Have you forgotten who you're dealing with?"

Zig gathered his courage. "I ain't forgotten, but I ain't dealing with you, neither. This is it. The end. You go back home, you and Trent, and you don't bother me and mine no more. Neither of you."

The gold tooth glinted in the moonlight as Dad sneered. "Gonna make me, are you? You and whose army?"

"That'd be mine," Rob the copper said brightly, stepping into view. Adam and Corin flanked him, grim-faced, like a pair of movie henchmen, and behind them were a couple of lads from the locksmith's. "Although we don't like to think of ourselves as military, of course. Sergeant Knight, Avon and Somerset Constabulary. Off duty right now, and I'm sure you wouldn't want me to have to break into my time off to deal with any parole violations anyone in the vicinity might be committing. I'd hate to have to arrest anyone for, say, threatening behaviour. Although I'm personally quite keen to stamp down on insulting language and hate speech, mind."

Funny how Dad's face could turn white so quick. He didn't seem so scary anymore. As he dropped his fists and took a step back, he looked old, and tired.

"So, Dad," Zig said. "You and Trent go back to London and never come back, and the sergeant won't have to do any of that."

Dad gave him a long look. "Fine. You got me. Guess there's nothing to do but head home." He turned to Trent, who was glowering at Rob the copper like he was imagining his head on a pike. "Come on then, *partner*. Better leave them to it. Forgive and forget."

Zig stared, lighted-headed with relief and triumph. He'd done it. No, *they'd* done it.

Trent gave him one more filthy look, then turned away.

Dad patted Trent on the shoulder as they began to walk off. "That's it." He raised his voice. "After all, who cares about all them years in jail, just cos sonny-boy here got cold feet and called the cops?"

Zig's heart stopped.

So did Trent. "What?" He spun to face Zig once more.

"Oh, didn't I tell you?" Dad's tone was light. Conversational. "It was him what set off that alarm. Told me he done it, in so many words."

Fuck, fuck, fu—

Trent was a blur as he hurtled towards Zig, fists clenched.

Another blur came out of nowhere, as Zig was bodily yanked to one side, out of range.

His head reeling, Zig became aware he was tightly clutched in Si's embrace, while Trent was on the ground, Corin on top of him, holding him in some kind of arm lock.

"Sorry, Sergeant Knight," Corin was saying. "Didn't mean to overstep but, ah . . ." He gestured towards Zig.

"No worries." Rob's tone was cheerful but firm. "I think we'll take it from here, though. Constable Walton?"

Huh. The female copper had turned up too. And she was in uniform. And had handcuffs. As she made excellent use of them on Trent, Zig saw, with a touch of unreality, that Sasha had come up to join them as well.

Overwhelmed, he sagged into Si's arms. Fuck knew why, but he was *this* close to bursting into tears. It was stupid. They'd won, hadn't they? All of them: him, Si, and Si's mates.

Maybe Zig's mates too, now? "Shit," he muttered weakly, and hid his face against Si's shoulder.

Big arms held him tight. "Didn't I tell you it'd all be okay?" Si whispered, and he stroked Zig's hair. "Course, I'm gonna give my Harley a good going-over next time I ride her. Just in case."

"Good," Zig mumbled into slightly damp leather.

Chapter Fifty-One
Zig

Adam's house, it turned out, wasn't far from the tor, so that was where they all ended up afterwards. Well, Zig, Si, Adam, Corin, and Sasha. The lads from the locksmith's had stayed on the tor to provide moral support to Rob the Copper and Constable Walton as they waited for some backup to escort Dad and Trent to the police station.

"Whisky? Or tea?" Adam asked as he showed them into an old-fashioned living room in shades of brown. There was a painting on the wall of a Scottish scene, with a stag, and rich purple heather. "Or tea with whisky?"

"That one," Si said fervently, and Zig nodded, not feeling much like talking.

Corin went into the kitchen with Adam to give him a hand or a snog, whatever, which left Zig and Si perched awkwardly on the brown sofa and Sasha directly opposite them on an equally drab armchair.

There was a silence.

"I'll see if Adam's got any snacks," Sasha volunteered, springing out of the chair.

The throw cushions matched the purple of the heather in the painting. They looked a lot newer than the furniture.

"Adam grew up in this house," Si said. "I came here after school once or twice. Mostly he came to mine."

It sounded like there was a story in that, and Zig made a mental note to ask about it. Sometime when he was feeling up to taking in an answer. "Nice cushions," he said vaguely.

Si laughed. "You gotta tell Adam that. Never seen a bloke so bloody excited over a shade of purple."

"Oi, are you dissing my interior decorating?" Adam had returned, mugs in both hands.

"Nah, Zig was saying he likes it."

Adam looked suspicious, but he still handed over a steaming mug each. Zig sniffed his and felt better already at the strong scent of alcohol. He took a cautious sip. Yep, plenty of whisky in that. "Cheers, mate," he said automatically, then darted a glance at Adam, cos calling him *mate* might've been a step too far.

If Adam was pissed off about it, he was a master at hiding the fact. Zig relaxed as Corin came in with another couple of mugs.

"Sash done a runner?" Si asked.

"Nope, I was just bunging stuff in the oven," the woman herself replied, appearing in the doorway. "Dunno about you lot, but I'm starving. It's the violence. Always gives me an appetite."

Si grinned. "Sasha my love, you're an angel. Gotta say, I got no clue how come you're still single."

"It's because I've got standards," she said with a fake-sweet smile.

Zig flinched and then wanted to sink into the browny-beige swirl carpet.

Si squeezed him tight. Sasha rolled her eyes. "It's not all about you, skinny-boy," she teased. "I liked you from the start."

"No, you didn't." Zig was touched, though.

"Okay, I didn't, cos you hurt my mate here, but I could see why Scra— why Si liked you." She smiled and took a sip of her whisky tea. "Oh, and happy birthday, by the way."

"Cheers." Zig took a hefty gulp from his mug. Yep, definitely feeling better now. "What's gonna happen to Dad and Trent? Do I have to, like press charges?" He caught himself. "Uh, is that actually a thing?"

Si chuckled. "Call yourself a bloody criminal?"

Zig winced. "Not if I have a choice in it, no. *Ex*-criminal, maybe."

"Sorry." Si squeezed him. "And it weren't your fault, that stuff you did when you were younger. You weren't brought up to know any better."

"You did the right thing when it really counted," Adam put in, which felt all kinds of weird, him saying nice stuff about Zig.

Must be the whisky tea.

"Rob looked 'em both up," Si said, his arm still a comforting warmth around Zig's waist. "Your Dad and that Trent. They're out on licence, he said, so after what happened tonight, they're gonna get recalled to prison. Twenty-eight days, then they get a review by the Parole Board."

Zig could feel his face scrunching up. "Fuck. Why the fuck do I feel guilty? They threatened you. But—"

"But it's your dad, and someone you were mates with once," Si insisted. "I get it. But you ain't gotta feel bad about it. They brought it on themselves."

"Me and Trent weren't mates," Zig mumbled into Si's neck. "Used to wanna be him, mind. Dad always liked him better than me."

Adam stood abruptly, startling Zig. "Christ. I'm gonna see how the food's doing."

Zig stared after him.

"It ain't my story to tell," Si murmured. "But Adam's parents weren't perfect, either."

Corin got up more slowly and went to join his lover in the kitchen.

Sasha shrugged. "What? My mum and dad did okay. Course, I was adopted, so."

"Wish I'd been," Zig muttered. Did he, though? If he'd been adopted, he'd never have known Gran and her bloke. God knew what his life would've been like.

Fuck it. It didn't happen; move on. "Thanks," he said, looking Sasha in the eye.

"What, for stealing your shoes?"

"Yeah," he said, with a smile that was dredged up but for all that, genuine. "That."

Chapter Fifty-Two
Si

It was late when they got back home. Si shut the door behind them both with a heartfelt sigh of relief. "Bed? Or cocoa and *Doctor Who*?"

"Think I need to drink something nonalcoholic before bed. That tea was bloody strong."

Si grinned. "Nobody held your nose and forced you to drink it. Or the second mug, neither."

"Was I complaining?" Zig smiled, weak but real. "Think it's hit me all at once, though."

Not only the alcohol, Si reckoned. "You sit yourself down, and I'll make the drinks."

"Right." Zig stumbled to the sofa and more-or-less fell on it. "Talk to me, though? So I know you're there?"

"I could sing, if you want?" Si dropped his leather jacket over the back of the sofa.

Zig gave a startled laugh. "Mate, nobody wants that."

Si grinned and headed to the kitchen. "You dissing my singing? I'll have you know my manly baritone's brought strong men to tears, and not in a bad way, neither. Least, that's what they said, and I didn't even have to bribe 'em."

As he spoke, he put the kettle on to boil, grabbed a couple of mugs, and spooned in the instant hot chocolate, adding an extra spoonful for luck. "I'll have to see if I can find a karaoke night to take you to, so you can experience me vocal talents for yourself." He poured in the water and stirred vigorously, slopping a bit over the counter, so he grabbed some kitchen roll to clean it up. "We could do a duet together. One of them classics, like 'Babe, I've Got You.'" When he lifted the bin lid to chuck the kitchen roll, there was a crumpled bit of paper inside. Something made him pick it out and open it up.

It was a note in Zig's handwriting. *Sorry, you're better off without me. I love you.*

Si stared at it for a long moment, blinking. He carefully tore off the last three words and put them in his pocket before chucking the rest back in the bin where they belonged. "You have got me, you know," he said quietly, his voice cracking. Then he picked up both mugs and carried them into the living room.

Zig was asleep, his face on Si's leather jacket, which had somehow slid down the sofa to be with him. Si put one mug down on the floor, then sat down, careful not to wake him, and put an arm gently around his shoulders.

Chapter Fifty-Three
Zig

Zig must have slept for a good ten hours and woke up the next morning to Si kissing him goodbye before heading off to work. He only vaguely remembered Si getting him to bed sometime during the night, and his head was thick from last night's alcohol. A stiff cup of coffee helped put that right, though. He got dressed and started wondering what to do with the day. Hit the library, maybe. He still needed to read up on those gay gods.

It felt weird knowing he didn't have to worry about Dad and Trent anymore. A huge weight off his mind, but somehow almost scary too. Like, he could live his life the way he wanted to now. If only he could figure out what that was. With Si, of course, that was a given, but did he really want to do bar work for the rest of his life? He didn't mind the job, but having most of his time off while Si was at work sucked.

Course, the less Si sees of you, the longer it'll take him to get fed up with you . . . Zig shut down that line of thought sharpish. That was Dad's voice telling him he was worthless. Zig didn't have to listen to that anymore. Si loved him.

A steady warmth settled in Zig's chest as he jogged down the stairs.

As he got to the bottom, he heard Esme calling him. "Zigmund? A word, please?"

Zig stuck his head into the shop and grinned. "You *know* it's just Zig."

"Are you sure? Because I can have the name badge made up with either."

"Uh . . . What would I want one of those for?"

She shrugged. "It's not compulsory, but some of the customers seem to appreciate having a name for the person who's serving them. I'll leave it up to you. Now, I can be flexible on the hours, but I assume you'd prefer to work weekdays? To give you more time with Si, now you two have finally sorted things out."

Zig stared at her, not quite sure he was hearing right. "You were serious about offering me a job?"

"Why not? You did very well minding the shop for me while I was out. And while I enjoy meeting customers, I need more time to focus on my creativity."

Zig swallowed. "I've been in prison. Thieving. Still want me to work here?"

Esme shrugged, like she genuinely didn't care. And wasn't surprised, for that matter. "Nobody's perfect. My late husband didn't always manage to stay on the right side of the law, I'm afraid, but he always dealt honestly with me."

"You hardly know me," Zig said in confusion. "Why would you wanna trust me?"

"I know your Mr. Greczik. And I trust his judgement. If he thinks you're worthy of a second chance, then so do I."

"Okay, then." Zig wasn't gonna give this particular gift horse any more dental examinations. It might bolt, and then he'd feel a right tit.

"I'll need to know your legal name, of course. For the payroll. I'm assuming your last name isn't Freud."

"You're gonna be disappointed. It's Jones. David Jones."

"No!" Her eyes widened. She didn't look disappointed in the least. "Like . . ." She sketched a lightning bolt in the air. "And with the eyes as well!"

He smiled wryly. "Yep. Getting nicknamed Ziggy was a total no-brainer."

"Who gave you that moniker, or is that lost in the mists of time?"

"It was me gran. Big Bowie fan, she was."

"Aren't we all?" Esme smiled. "Now, I was thinking you could start in the New Year."

Zig nodded. "That'd be great." He meant it.
New year; new job.
New life, with Si.
Yeah, things were definitely looking up.

Explore more of the *Glastonbury Tales* series at:
riptidepublishing.com/collections/series-glastonbury-
tales

GLASTONBURY
TALES

Face Blind

JL MERROW

Dear Reader,

Thank you for reading JL Merrow's *Fool Me Twice*!

We know your time is precious and you have many, many entertainment options, so it means a lot that you've chosen to spend your time reading. We really hope you enjoyed it.

We'd be honored if you'd consider posting a review—good or bad—on sites like **Amazon, Barnes & Noble, Kobo, Goodreads, Twitter, Facebook, Tumblr,** and your blog or website. We'd also be honored if you told your friends and family about this book. Word of mouth is a book's lifeblood!

For more information on upcoming releases, author interviews, blog tours, contests, giveaways, and more, please sign up for our weekly, spam-free newsletter and visit us around the web:

Newsletter: riptidepublishing.com/newsletter
Twitter: twitter.com/RiptideBooks
Facebook: facebook.com/RiptidePublishing
Goodreads: tinyurl.com/RiptideOnGoodreads
Tumblr: riptidepublishing.tumblr.com

Thank you so much for Reading the Rainbow!

RiptidePublishing.com

Acknowledgements

Many thanks to Larissa and Kristin Matherly for their valuable feedback.

Also by

J.L. Merrow

About the Author

JL Merrow is that rare beast, an English person who refuses to drink tea. She read natural sciences at Cambridge, where she learned many things, chief amongst which was that she never wanted to see the inside of a lab ever again. Her one regret is that she never mastered the ability of punting one-handed whilst holding a glass of champagne.

She writes across genres, with a preference for contemporary gay romance and mysteries, and is frequently accused of humour. Her novel *Slam!* won the 2013 Rainbow Award for Best LGBT Romantic Comedy, and her novella *Muscling Through* and novel *Relief Valve* were both EPIC Awards finalists. Recently she has collaborated with Sue Brown and Ripley Hayes on the DI Leon Peterson mysteries under the penname of Alex Henry.

JL Merrow is a member of the Crime Writers Association, International Thriller Writers, and Verulam Writers.

Find JL Merrow on BlueSky as @jlmerrow.bsky.social, and on Facebook at facebook.com/jl.merrow

For a full list of books available, see: jlmerrow.com or JL Merrow's Amazon author page: viewauthor.at/JLMerrow

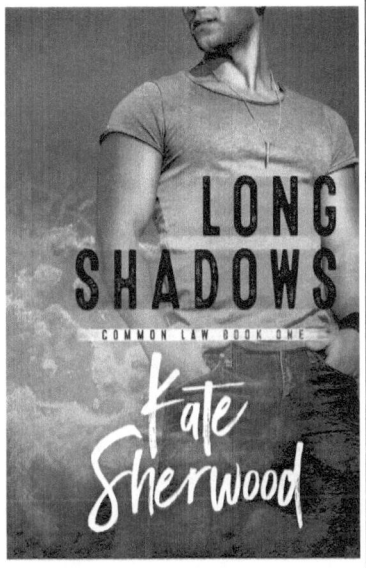

www.ingramcontent.com/pod-product-compliance
Lightning Source LLC
Chambersburg PA
CBHW031342020726
47499CB00005B/1368